PRAISE

BESIDE

This book is a keep
I was transported into
sive storytelling and viv
ache and joy of the characters as if they were real people. So
compelling.

—Robin Jones Gunn, author of the Christy Miller series

With *Beside Still Waters*, the talented Tricia Goyer adds a new flavor to the popular Amish genre. Journey with Marianna from the plains of Indiana to the mountains of Montana as they join a new group. But the journey is about much more than a physical move as Marianna learns an important truth about herself. A story that will stay with you long after the last page is read. Another winning read from one of my favorite authors.

—Cara Putman, author of *Stars in the Night*

Only a gifted writer like Tricia Goyer could present such a captivating story about a group of Amish forging a new community in Montana. Tricia writes in such a way that the reader can't wait to turn the page and learn more about main character Marianna's experience. Tricia's talent for connecting our heart to Marianna's plight also connects us to our need for one another. *Beside Still Waters* draws you in with its genuine characters, and it holds you there with its enduring bonds of love and family.

—Suzanne Woods Fisher, best-selling author of the
Lancaster County Series

Beside Still Waters is heart wrenching and meticulously researched by Tricia Goyer. You feel as though you are truly experiencing the Amish lifestyle and the struggles the main character faces. It is a beautiful, thought-provoking work.

—Alexa Schnee, author of *Shakespeare's Lady*

The inspired pen of talented author Tricia Goyer has done it again—brought to life characters and events that tug at our hearts and transport us to faraway places and times.

From the tragic accident that snags us at the book's opening in the otherwise peaceful Amish setting of Indiana to the wild big-sky country of Montana, we travel with Marianna as she searches for love and acceptance in much the same way we all do. And in the midst of it, we are reminded that sometimes we find what we didn't even realize we were searching for.

—Kathi Macias, award-winning author of more than thirty books, including the popular Extreme Devotion series

I've discovered a new favorite author of Amish fiction—Tricia Goyer! *Beside Still Waters* is a moving and gentle story that touched my heart and stirred my soul. I'm recommending *Beside Still Waters* to all my friends who enjoy Amish fiction.

—Marlo Schalesky, author of Christy-award winning *Beyond the Night* and *Shades of Morning*

Tricia Goyer brings her considerable writing talent to the Amish genre. *Beside Still Waters* is a sweet, tender tale that's sure to please readers. Amish fiction fans will be wanting more from Ms. Goyer!

—Kathleen Fuller, author of *A Summer Secret, A Hand to Hold*, and *The Secrets Beneath*

BESIDE
STILL
WATERS

TRICIA GOYER

BESIDE
STILL
WATERS

PUBLISHING GROUP
Nashville, Tennessee

ISBN: 978-1-4336-6868-5

Published by B&H Publishing Group
Nashville, Tennessee

Dewey Decimal Classification: F
Subject Heading: AMISH—FICTION \ FAMILY LIFE—
FICTION \ SPIRITUAL LIFE—FICTION

Published in association with the Books & Such Literary
Agency, Janet Kobobel Grant, 52 Mission Circle, Suite 122,
PMB 170, Santa Rosa, CA 95409-5370, www.booksandsuch.biz.

Scripture references are taken from the
New International Version, copyright © 1973, 1978,
1984 by International Bible Society.

Scripture references marked KJV were taken from
the King James Version of the Bible.

1 2 3 4 5 6 7 8 • 15 14 13 12 11

"Be not conformed to this world: but be ye trans-formed by the renewing of your mind, that ye may prove what is that good, and acceptable, and perfect, will of God." (Romans 12:2 KJV)

DEDICATION

To Ora Jay and Irene and your daughters in heaven.

Thank you for sharing your story. Thank you for sharing your life and your faith. May many be as touched by glimpses of your story as I have been.

ACKNOWLEDGMENTS

I am thankful for my friends who have welcomed me into their home and who've shared the Amish lifestyle with me:

Ora Jay and Irene Esh
Dennis and Viola Bontrager
Ida Miller
Betty Yoder
Marilyn Miller
Linda Keim
Irene Beachy

This book also wouldn't be possible without my dear friend Martha Artyomenko. Martha was my guide through Amish country, my research buddy, and my first reader. Growing up among the West Kootenai Amish, she provided valuable influence. Also thank you to Amy Lathrop and Cara Putman for reading through my story and giving your input, too.

I also appreciate the B&H team, especially Karen Ball and Julie Gwinn. Thank you for loving this story as much as I do and believing in me!

I'm also thankful for my agent, Janet Grant. You always encourage, always believe!

And I'm thankful for my family: John, Cory and Katie, Leslie, Nathan and baby Alyssa. I couldn't write about a loving family unless I experienced one myself.

Finally, to my best friend Jesus Christ. None of this would be possible without You. Thank You for meeting me beside still waters.

PROLOGUE

The memory of laughter mixed with the sound of the horse's hooves on the asphalt lulled him into a half-sleep. They still had thirty minutes until they reached home. Thankfully, the horse knew the way.

His wife nestled at his side with their son Levi, three years old, on her lap—well, as much on her lap as the little one could fit. Their next son or daughter would be joining the family in a matter of months, and the thought of it brought a smile to his face. He'd always wanted a big family, a good wife, a small piece of land to call his own. Yes, for a time he'd considered not joining the church, but it was the thought of a family and nights like this that had helped him decide to join. He cracked his eyes open, gazing up to the stars with a heart of thankfulness. And checking the road ahead.

Only one part of the ride home required he stay awake. It was a stretch of highway that split their country road in two. Sometimes, especially during the daytime, he had to wait minutes and minutes to cross because the traffic flowed so fast and heavy. Yet on nights like this he didn't expect a problem. He glanced at the highway ahead. *Almost there.* Once across, he could close his eyes and let the horse finish the trek.

His wife's breathing fell soft beside him, as did the sweet breaths of his two girls. They lay on the back platform of the buggy, snuggled in heavy blankets like a warm cocoon.

Many of his friends had wished for sons first, to carry on the family name and to help with chores—but he was overjoyed with his daughters. His love for them grew by the day, expanding from the moment he first held Marilyn's tiny hand in his. Expanding when he brushed Joanna's blonde curls. Or showed them how to make a necklace of dandelions. They were six and four years old now, impossible to believe. It seemed yesterday his eldest was born, and now two others followed. *Soon to be four.* He glanced at his wife's hard, round stomach.

His own stomach felt full of too much ice cream, and the buggy's gentle sway lulled him once more. The snores of his daughters brought a smile, and he looked to the stop sign up ahead, a gray shadow under the night sky. He leaned over to rest his head on the back of the seat. His eyes fluttered closed.

It was the blare of the horn that startled him first. Loud, deep, close. The horn of a big truck. Then bright, white light. *Headlights.* The jolting of the horse. An overwhelming screech of brakes.

A terrified child's cry pierced the air. The semitruck hit the back wheels. The buggy crumbled into pieces. His body propelled forward. Pain filled him. Fear stabbed. *My wife. My children!*

He heard his son's cries. Listened to his wife's moans. *The baby . . .*

He slammed against the hard, jagged gravel with bone-crushing force, but adrenaline pushed him up from the ground.

Standing, his eyes darted from side to side as he tried to make sense of what had happened. The sight of the truck shuddering to a stop filled his vision. The scent of burning rubber from the truck's tires overpowered him. Up ahead the horse raced down the road. The buggy lay around him in pieces.

Staggering toward his wife's cries and the cries of his son, he sunk onto the ground next to them and embraced them, thankful they were safe. His whole body trembled. He looked back over his shoulders to his daughters—

His daughters.

Red and blue lights swirled in the peaceful night sky, and Abe told himself to turn and walk away. There was nothing he could do for his daughters now. He reached down and took his daughter, Joanna's, tiny hand in his. It was cold. Limp.

Footsteps sounded on the gravel. A cold air picked up, and Abe thought he smelled rain.

"Sir, can I ask you a few questions?"

Abe swallowed hard and lowered his head. *"Ja.* I—" The words grew in his throat and he pushed them out. "I fell asleep."

He could hear the Englisch officer writing something in his small notepad.

"It is the Lord's will . . ." A guttural cry escaped Abe's lips. It didn't sound like his own voice.

"Abe!" Ruth's cry carried through the night. His wife called his name again. *"Abe!"*

He rose, hurried toward the ambulance. When the paramedics had arrived, they checked Levi and Ruth first. Seeing Ruth's pregnancy, they forced her to lie down in the back of the vehicle. Abe thought for certain she'd protest, but with a hand on her stomach she nodded.

Now her pale face reflected horror, disbelief, heartbreak. Abe looked away.

"We should take you to the hospital for observation." The paramedic's voice was gentle.

"No." Ruth shook her head. "No."

She wouldn't leave. Not yet. A mother doesn't leave her daughters behind.

Now Abe looked to his wife, frail, pale, tucked under a white sheet. Levi stood beside her, eyes wide. He was dirty but only had a few scratches. Levi had insisted on putting his hat back on even though the rim was crushed. It sat on his head crooked.

Two paramedics tended to Ruth now, and there wasn't room for him inside. Abe stretched his hand for his wife. Tears streaked her cheeks and her neck was flush.

"Did you see them?" The words came out in a moan.

"Our girls stand before their Creator now." It was the only assurance he could give her. He'd told her the same thing fifteen minutes ago, before the ambulance arrived. She'd been curled in a crumbled heap on the ground, rocking Levi, and he'd told her they were gone. Ruth hadn't wanted to believe him then, and from the look on her face she still wouldn't do so.

Her lips pressed tight and the smallest moan escaped. Her hands clenched her abdomen and he realized these tears weren't only for their daughters, but for the child to come.

"The baby comes now, Abe." Her hazel eyes, the color of a backlit storm cloud, widened.

"No," he whispered. "It is too soon."

The paramedic's large hand touched Abe's arm. "We have to get her to a hospital now, sir."

"There is not time, Abe. Tell them there is not time! The baby comes." Ruth panted the words.

The pain of losing his daughters magnified—they would lose another this night. *Two months yet.* Ruth birthed small babies anyhow. This one . . . how could it make it so soon?

Abe looked to her face. Ruth's jaw clenched.

One of the paramedics jumped down from the vehicle, preparing to shut the doors.

Abe stretched out a hand, stopping him. "There is no time."

He watched his wife draw back her legs and only then did the workers understand. Abe reached inside the ambulance and pulled Levi into his arms, hurrying to the side of the vehicle.

He leaned against the cold steel frame of the ambulance. His shoulders trembled. His fingers twitched as he clenched Levi to his chest. His knees softened like butter melting in the sun. A pain clenched his side as more fire trucks and police cars arrived. A clomping of horse hooves filled the air too. Their Amish neighbors were beginning to gather. And then came Ruth's cries—a sound that chilled his soul. She never cried when birthing her babies. Few Amish women did. Perhaps her moans came from the knowledge of another child to be lost.

Dear Lord, isn't our pain great enough? Save this child. Please, Lord.

His wife's cries quieted, and Levi's hands clutched around his neck. Abe nestled his cheek against his son's ear, and the boy pulled back from the scratchiness of his father's beard. Abe knew he should do something, anything. He should pray. He should seek strength from his neighbors. He should be by Ruth's side to carry the burden. Instead, his heart crumbled like freshly tilled soil. His legs rooted, unmoving.

"Dat?" Levi's hand wiped his face, and the sensation of tears on his cheeks made its way through the fog of Abe's brain.

And then he heard it. Over the blaring siren of yet another vehicle approaching.

A baby's cry.

He expected it to be weak, but the cry grew louder. Abe hurried to the back of the ambulance. Ruth held the tiny bundle to her chest. The baby's red body wiggled. The paramedic's surprised laughter met Abe's ears.

"A boy?" Abe looked to the paramedic.

"A girl. Small but healthy."

My daughters.

Abe looked behind him where police officers were carrying away two bundles in sheets.

Marilyn. Joanna.

He looked back to his wife. Instead of looking at the baby, her eyes stared into the dark night. The baby cried again.

My daughter.

"Marianna. We will name her, Marianna." He climbed in the back of the ambulance, clambering to get to his wife's side. "We will name her after our gir—our girls."

His wife nodded, but she did not respond. Then she looked to him, and her gaze said it all . . .

How could one ever take the place of two?

Dear June-Sevenies,

Can you keep a secret yet? One I haven't told my mom or even my best friend, Rebecca? Aaron Zook has asked me on a date. Yes, the Aaron I always talk about. The one who cleans my fish for me at the river and who sat next to me at the last youth gathering. He wants to wait until fall, I'm not sure why. Have you ever heard of having to wait four months for someone to take you for a buggy ride and a picnic? His eyes were bright as he asked me. As clear of blue as any bright, spring morning sky. Listen to me. I sound like a woman in love. Not quite, but I could see it happening. When I look to the rows of corn stalks low and green in the fields, I think of them tall, golden, and swaying in the wind as I ride in Aaron's buggy.

If the truth be known, I couldn't have dreamed of anything better. Dat always tells me I have my head in the clouds when I'm working around the house. What would he think if he knew all my daydreams centered on having a house of my own with a special man? With the very same special man who confessed he thinks I'm special, too. That dream is only followed by imaginings of our children, ach, what pretty little tykes they'll be.

I'm glad I can tell all of you and know it won't get back to Mem. I've told my older brother Levi, too. He's the only one. He hasn't spoke to Dat in months. Hasn't even shown his face round the farm. A few of you have met my father and you might wonder what Levi fears. I don't think my brother fears my father's words or his wrath. I think it's the disappointment in Dat's gaze, and knowing the hurt he's caused. Some people carry their heart around in pieces. A bit in this pocket, a few pieces in that satchel. Even during their happiest days my folks protect their fragile load.

Lena, congratulations on the new member of your family! Do your sisters number five now? Finally, more than the boys!

The evening light is fading, I best be going yet. This will be a short letter, but I want to get the envelope moving along. Oh, one more thing, Clara, you can be sure I'll find a ride to your wedding in September. I have no plans except tending to my siblings and the neighbor's children. And waiting for that promised date, of course.

Marianna

CHAPTER ONE

*H*er future hung as warm breath on the chilled spring air that carried her parents' words. They spoke in low tones as they rode along the country road, the horse's hooves clomping on the damp pavement. Marianna Sommer snuggled her three-year-old sister tight to her chest. She lowered her head and breathed in the scent of her sister's hair peeking out from under the dark blue kapp, brushed her lips against the softness of her forehead. Marianna's eyes fluttered closed and she wondered if little Ellie could sense the racing of her heart, the tightening of her chest. The trembling of her embrace.

Dat cast a sideways glance at her mother, his thick beard falling to the second button on his shirt. "How long do you think it would take to pack up?" He spoke in English, as he always did when he didn't want the younger ones to understand.

"Everything?" Mem's eyes furrowed as she looked to Dat.

"Not everything. Just enough to get us by for a month or so. Ike said he knows a man who has a semi-truck and often moves the Amish.

Marianna tried to pretend they were talking about someone else. Some other family interested in adventure, bent on leaving a place where everyone knew of your loss and every gaze held a mix of pity and judgment.

"I suppose a few weeks yet is all it would take to get affairs in order. The boys are nearly finished with school for the season, but there is Mari's job to consider. Mrs. Ropp needs her." Mem answered his questions but there was no excitement, no joy. Marianna wished Mem would be stronger. To make it clear leaving wasn't an option.

No one asked Marianna her opinion, spoke to her about matters. Though nearly twenty, they treated her the same as when she was fourteen and had just finished school. She spent the days no different now than then—caring for children, working at the neighbors', spoken to, watched over. Didn't they realize more than anything she wanted to stop caring for someone else's children and start a family of her own?

Sometimes she'd pretend. She'd rock Mrs. Ropp's baby and imagine that was her home and her husband out in the fields, providing. She'd straighten up, arranging things how she'd like them. And when she imagined her husband walking through the door, there was only one face she thought of. Only one smile.

But now, with this talk of leaving . . . her parents could ruin everything.

She turned her attention away from the talk of change, and her mind filled with thankfulness over the familiar. After all, they hadn't left Indiana yet. Maybe it was just talk. She focused on the three school-aged brothers pressed around her, lulled into a half-sleep by the motion of the buggy. The sight of the sun stretching pink rays into the morning sky. And the comfort of soon seeing their neighbors and friends unified in purposeful work.

A random lightning strike a week ago had cost the Yoders

a barn. A community of church members, who believed what affects one affects all, would see to it another barn—newer, better—would rise today.

Three-year-old Ellie's eyes opened, perhaps because she sensed the horses slowing as they turned onto the road leading to the Yoders' place. If only, like her younger sister, Marianna didn't understand her parents' words. She attempted to hide her scowl, telling herself it was just talk. She needed something to distract her. Marianna opened her mouth and forced a soft song from her lips to entertain Ellie.

"In der Stillen Einsamkeit, Findest du mein lob bereit." She sang the traditional children's song in Pennsylvania Dutch, blocking out her father's words. *"Grosser Gott Erhöe mich, denn mein Herze suche dich."*

In the still isolation, Thou findest my praise ready, greatest God answer me. For my heart is seeking Thee . . .

The second verse carried through her mind, and though Ellie looked to her in expectation, the words caught in Marianna's throat as their buggy passed the school she'd attended for eight years. Where David, Charlie, and Josiah now went. As the buggy rolled past, she pictured the rows of small wooden desks. She imagined Ellie in her blue dress and white kapp joining them in a few years. Learning English. She thought of her sister Marilynn who'd attended the school a year before the accident.

"Remember how smart Marilyn was? Readin' by age four," she'd overheard her mother say to her father once. Sometimes, when they didn't think they were being heard, they talked about her sisters. But Marianna had heard enough . . .

"That Joanna, a voice like a songbird."

"Marilyn had a way in the garden, never saw a youngster 'cept her know how to coax a wilting flower back to life."

"I remember their care for others most. The way they'd tend to Levi like two mother hens . . ."

Yes, Marianna had heard plenty. And from her earliest years, she'd known. Known the painful truth.

She could never take their place.

Compared to her two sisters, her life paled like a thin shadow following two bright stars.

"Such pretty little girls," her grandmother always commented at the anniversary of their deaths. If only Marianna could have seen them. If only, this one time, her parents had foregone the Amish way and taken pictures. But no. There were no, nor would there ever be, pictures in their home.

More than that, she wished she could celebrate her birthday without a heavy gloom filling the day.

Marianna tucked a strand of flyaway hair behind her ear— she didn't get her bun tight enough again. She let out a low sigh imagining her mother's reprimand: *"Can't you take five extra minutes to see to it yer put together proper like?"*

Her father cleared his voice, bringing her attention back to his words.

"Ike knows of a cabin that's available now." His voice reflected excitement she hadn't heard in a while. "The family who owns it moved away, closer to be to their newly married son."

"But Montana? Of all places?" Her mother tucked a strand of brown hair up in her kapp. "Why not move someplace closer, more civilized?"

"What if I don't want to go?" The words tumbled from Marianna's lips like hail from a darkened sky. She adjusted Ellie on her lap and leaned closer to the front, poking her face in the space between her parents. "I like it here. I don't want to move. And Aaron Zook. He asked me on a date."

Her father nodded but wasn't listening. He didn't turn, just fixed his gaze on the road ahead and on the Yoder's two-story house in the distance.

"If Aaron cares, as you believe, a year won't matter. I waited two for your mother." Dat stroked his beard like he always did when he didn't quite believe what he was saying, but still hoped to convince her.

"Only because she was too young to get married. This is different. I—"

Her mother winced as if she'd been slapped, then jerked her head around to look at Marianna. "Do you hear yourself?" Mem's eyes narrowed and voice lowered. Then she faced the front again, adjusting her black bonnet over her white kapp. "We've never heard you speak in such a way."

Marianna leaned back in the seat, pressure tightening her gut. Mem was right. She never talked this way to him. But how could she just let them continue without hearing her opinion? How could they not ask?

If Marilyn or Joanna were here, they'd listen to them. If Levi hadn't left . . . they'd care what he thought.

She swallowed her breath, willing herself not to cry.

Up ahead the Yoder farm came into view. Though it wasn't yet 7:30 a.m., dozens of buggies were already parked, lining the edge of the paved road.

Forget about their words, their plans, she pleaded with her heart. Today was a day to enjoy without the worry. Her hand reached for the seat back in front of her, ready to climb from the buggy as soon as it stopped. She'd spend time with her friends. She'd watch Aaron from afar. Marianna closed her eyes, picturing his oval blue eyes, his long face, fine nose, and strong jawline. Her breathing resumed, steady and even.

She felt a pinch on her cheek, followed by Ellie's laughter. Marianna opened her eyes as if surprised. Ellie giggled and squirmed with delight, kicking her small feet.

"Ouch!" Eight-year-old Charlie rubbed his arm. "Ellie kicked me," he complained in Pennsylvania Dutch.

"Stop *rushing* around, Ellie. You'll get all wrinkled," Mem chided.

Seeing the line of buggies, Marianna's excitement trumped her despair. She knew what the day held, just like she knew the song of the tree swallow and the scent of rain. She'd attended many barn risings. The mixing of concrete. The hoisting of beams thicker than her body, with the help of pulleys and ropes. Numerous neighbors, including her father, had already spent time at the Yoders' place over the previous days, cutting beams to length, laying them out, gathering supplies.

"*Gukamalldoe!*" David sat up in his seat, rubbing his eyes. "Look at that!" A line of buggies rolled toward the farm from the opposite direction, reminding Marianna of an oversized line of ants.

Her Dat was parking when Marianna saw a flash of a blue shirt, straw hat, and wide smile approaching. The tension in her stomach from the ride loosened as she noticed Aaron's quickened pace. Seeing him, the muscles in her stomach bunched again. But this time, she didn't mind.

He tipped his hat. "Do you need help there? I can carry your basket, Mrs. Sommer."

"Aaron Zook. How nice of you."

As the buggy rolled to a complete stop, Aaron reached his hand inside and took the large picnic basket off the floorboard. "Is there anything else I can do?" He glanced at Marianna and then back to Mem's gaze.

"Well, if you have an extra hand, my husband has some tools in back . . ." Gone was the sharpness in Mem's voice from a moment before, replaced by a singsong lilt that rose and fell with her words.

Before Mem even finished talking, Aaron hurried around the buggy. Marianna watched him out of the corner of her eye and couldn't help but notice that his blond hair, peeking out from under his hat, was already lightening, as it did every summer.

With a smile, he took up a tool box in his free hand. "Beautiful day, isn't it? I'll take these for you." He held up the basket and the red metal tool box. Aaron took steps and then paused and looked back.

"Everything all right, Marianna?"

"Yes, fine." She rubbed her eye. "Think it must be an eyelash . . ."

"Good to know. See you at lunch." He moved to the Yoders' house with quickened steps. He looked taller today than she remembered. Tight muscles across his shoulders were evident under his plain, blue shirt.

Her father climbed down, then leaned into the back seat, taking Ellie from Marianna's lap. She was surprised to see Dat's brows furrowed. He looked to her, then to Aaron's retreat, shaking his head.

"Aaron Zook is a nice boy." Her mother climbed down from the buggy, holding on to the side, ignoring her husband's look.

Marianna's brothers tumbled over the side with the same enthusiasm and zeal as the puppies on the back porch when she'd fed them this morning.

"I hear he's building a small house on his father's property," her mother continued. "Aunt Betty said she spotted it nigh a week back when she was visiting some friends."

"Is he also building a buggy that can carry him to the moon?" David smirked.

"Has he taught a cow how to lay eggs yet?" Charlie chuckled, tossing his head.

Mem placed hands on hips. "David, Charlie, that is unkind. One mustn't say a word behind another's back that he wouldn't say to his face."

David jutted out his chin. "I'd say it to his face."

Mem blew out an exacerbated sigh and then turned to Dat, in expectation of his reprimand.

Her father set Ellie on the ground, then turned to the boys offering a wink instead.

"He's almost too perfect an Amish youth if you ask me." Dat shrugged. "And likes having folks take note of it."

"And there's a problem with following the rules, living by the Ordnung?" Mem straightened her kapp and walked to his side.

He stroked his beard and looked to Marianna, even though he was answering his wife. "It's just that a person who gets all wrapped up in himself makes a mighty small package."

"How can you say that?" Marianna folded her arms over her chest, then turned away from the gathering, focusing instead on the Yoders' field and the small, green stalks of corn about a foot high.

"If he wasn't kind and helpful"—she attempted to keep her

voice steady—"you'd accuse him of being slothful and rude." It was the second time she'd confronted her father in the last thirty minutes. The weight she carried earlier returned.

Footsteps crunched through the gravel as her father approached, and she felt his presence behind her.

"It's just that no man, in my opinion, will ever be good enough for my girl. I'm sorry there. You're right, Aaron is a nice boy."

Marianna felt the smallest smile tug on her lips, and she turned to him, noticing the morning light reflect in his gray eyes—eyes everyone said she'd inherited. "He's more than a nice boy. Aaron's a good man. Far good enough. And this fall . . ." She stopped her words when she noticed her father's eyes narrow.

"No talk of this fall, at least not anything that has to do with Indiana. We won't be here, no matter what you think. No matter what your mother thinks. There's a time when a man needs to do right by his family. Trust what he feels inside."

"But how could moving to the wilderness, away from everything and everyone, be good for us? I don't understand." Tears filled her eyes and her arms trembled. She looked to him and waited. She wanted to hear his explanation. She wished he would hug her, hold her like he did when she was a little girl, and tell her everything would be okay. Mem waved the boys forward, and they raced off in a single line, oldest to youngest toward the gathering crowd. Her mother looked as if she wished to say something, but instead she took Ellie's hand and followed them.

"Dat, you haven't decided, have you?" A gathering of geese honked as they flew overhead, heading north. Marianna lifted her head, watching them for a moment before continuing. "There would be so much we'd be leaving. So many." Marianna didn't mention her older brother, Levi, but he and Aaron were in the forefront of her mind.

"I know what I need to do and that is all I'm saying. But for now keep it to yourself, all our plans. One word of us moving today and I'll be getting messages from my cousins in Ontario by sundown. Sometimes I think the geese carry our news with them, either that or the wind for the way it spreads." He offered a light chuckle, and his eyes begged her to laugh or at least agree.

Marianna pressed her lips into a tight line.

"Promise me?" Her father's tone was firmer. As she studied him, she realized he'd aged over the last few months. He looked tired, and his shoulders slumped as if the weight of the world rested upon his broad back.

She nodded and then turned toward the gathering of men in dark pants and shirts and women in blue dresses, like a garden of larkspurs that had come to life.

Not only did her parents object about her voicing her complaints, now she was forced to keep the news inside. How could she look into Aaron's face and not burst into tears, realizing their date may never happen? How could she not watch Aaron work among the other men and wonder if she'd soon be losing what she wanted most? A life here. With him.

CHAPTER TWO

*A*aron Zook placed Mr. Sommer's red tool box next to a line of others and then moved toward the long tables, picnic basket in hand.

"Did yer wife make you a lunch?" Jed King ran his hand over his new beard that was still coming in in patches. Married just a few months, the beard wasn't the only thing noticeable about his new status. The twinkle in his friend's eyes and his stomach that was already starting to round due to Lilia's good cooking were also evident.

Aaron looked to the basket in his hand. "No wife yet." He shrugged. "But it smells good." Aaron took in a deep breath, appreciating the scent of moist summer grass after the rain, cut logs, and his ma's cinnamon rolls carrying on the wind from the nearest table.

"Did ye hear John Stoltzfus say they're hiring o'er the factory? Good wages. I'm thinking of applying."

Aaron's chest felt tight, as if one of those thick ropes they were using to heave beams was cinched around it. He hoped he hadn't looked too eager, running up to the Sommers's buggy like that. It was the best way he could think of to dismiss himself from talking to Mr. Stotlzfus and the other guys gathering at the worksite. He'd witnessed his father's work at the factory. The pay wasn't good, considering the long hours and the slow buggy ride there and back. Then there were the chores around the farm every night. Animals to feed, crops to tend to, fences to mend. Aaron had done his part around the farm, but he knew once one started working in the factory it was hard to leave. Besides, he had his own place he was homesteading in preparation of a wife and family. He just hoped the rumors he was hearing about Marianna's folks wanting to move out of their community weren't true.

Nearing the long tables Aaron placed the Sommers's basket among the others, then he glanced over to where Marianna was approaching with her parents. From the time she was eleven and complimented him on a picture he'd drawn of a meadow-lark during recess, he'd known she was the woman he wanted to marry. Not only because she liked his artwork, but mostly because she was as serious about their Amish lifestyle as he was. Many, like her friend Rebecca, had gone out to explore the world. But not Marianna. She lived her life as if she'd already made a commitment to the church.

He liked that.

He looked up and watched as she approached. Instead of looking toward their neighbors gathering, she stared at the ground in front of her as she walked. Her shoulders slumped more than usual. Her steps were slow.

His mother said that even when Marianna was a child she had sad eyes. Aaron had to agree. Everyone knew about the accident. It was a story told often, or at least referred to. "Don't be falling asleep on the trip down to Jed's," his mother had mentioned to him more than once. "You know what happened . . ."

In a strange way Aaron liked that about Marianna too. Well, not that she was sad, or that that sadness framed her life. Rather, that on some days—most days when they were together—he could make her smile. It gave him a sense of accomplishment. Made him think that if he could achieve that, well, the rest of his dreams were in reach, too.

Marianna took a deep breath and the pounding of the hammers on the barn's frame matched the rhythm to the words thumping in her skull: *Montana. Montana. Montana.* She wiped her brow and turned her attention to the small gathering of toddlers playing in a large sandbox. Small bare feet wiggled in sand still damp from the morning rain.

She sat on the grass by the sandbox, making sure everyone played together nicely while their mothers prepared lunch and their fathers worked. Already the shell of the barn was up, and she had no doubt that by tonight a metal roof would grace the top, reflecting the evening light.

"Do not pour sand on your brother's head," she said to two-year-old Helen Ropp. Helen was one of the neighbor children she watched every afternoon. Helen's lip quivered as it always did when she was reprimanded, even though Marianna had used a gentle tone.

As the second oldest of five children—not counting her sisters gone from them—tending to the little ones was a task

Marianna did well. She couldn't remember a time when she wasn't diapering, comforting, scolding.

"Tell me again why you can't say what's bothering you?" Aaron hunkered down next to her, removed his straw hat, and wiped his brow with a red handkerchief he pulled from his pocket. He stretched his arms to his little cousin, and Elijah scurried into his embrace.

More than anything Marianna wanted to turn, to glance over her shoulder to see if anyone was watching. It was bold for Aaron to approach with so many neighbors around. No doubt seeing him next to her would start all types of rumors.

"Who said anything was wrong?" She plucked a blade of green grass and twirled it between her fingers, trying to act natural. Trying not to let any onlookers witness how much Aaron's nearness unnerved her.

"I saw it when I went to your buggy. You'd been crying. Either that or you were about to start."

He knelt next to her, tossing a yellow ball back into the sand box, much to Elijah's delight. Light-haired Elijah squirmed from Aaron's arms, chasing the ball.

"Just a disagreement with Dat. He—" She dared to glance to Aaron out of the corner of her eye. "He has a strong will and when his mind is set on something, no one can change it."

"Does it have to do with moving? You're not leaving are you, Marianna?"

Her head jerked his direction, and her eyes studied his. She opened her mouth and then closed it. What could she say? If she answered truthfully she'd be disobeying her father. And she couldn't lie.

"Don't answer that. I can see it *is* the problem."

"But how did you know?"

"Yer Uncle Ike gave me a ride to town the other day. He was talking about Montana as if God placed a bit of heaven on earth." Aaron glanced behind him, eyeing the men lining up for lunch. "There are some folks around here that don't like that talk."

Marianna looked around and noticed many eyes on them. Aaron's behavior—the fact that he'd approached her and was spending time with her—was no doubt noted by many.

"Yes, speaking of talking, I don't think that's why yer here. Don't the Yoders have a barn that needs to rise?" She forced a laugh. "You don't want to neglect your duties, do you? Go get yerself a plate. Maybe we can talk on Sunday night yet. You'll be at the singing, won't you?" It was Tuesday, and her mind made a mental countdown of the days until then.

"*Ja*, and I'll be at church, too. Suppose I'll see you both places." He offered a quick wave to the children, then moved a few steps to the lunch line. It was only as he paused and turned back that Marianna realized she'd been watching him go. He noticed, too.

"Oh, and Marianna?"

"*Ja*?" She placed a hand to her warming cheek.

"Your secret is safe with me. Although if I have any say, you'll be staying right where you are."

"By this sandbox?" She stood and straightened her skirt, running her hands down the thick fabric.

He laughed, and her heartbeat doubled at the sound of it. The sun brightened, the day warmed.

"No, you don't have to stay there." Aaron pointed to the ground beneath her lace-up black leather shoes. Then he swept his hands, motioning to the land, the sky, the community of people beyond them, and the men lining up for food. "You have to stay *here*. Don't you dare go anywhere, *ja*?"

She laughed as he hurried forward. The men always went first, eating quickly before they went back to work. The women and children would be next. Filling their plates and then sitting in collective groups on picnic blankets, spreading out across the yard. The voices of women talking and children playing rose in volume as the men neared, as if the groups were trying to outdo each other.

The men strode toward the food line with smiles and laughter, happy the work had gone well. The small ones noted the gathering of men, assembled and quieting for prayer. And the children, too, bowed their heads.

"*Vella Still Halta*," the bishop said loud enough for all to hear. *Let's be still for prayer.* Marianna bowed her head and prayed a silent prayer for the meal, as was tradition.

When an appropriate amount of time passed, Marianna turned to the children. "Helen, Ellie." She called each one by name. "Brush yourself off. We're going to be eating soon, are you hungry?"

"*Ja!*" Ellie clapped her hands and then brushed them together to wipe off the sand. Helen did the same, and the other little ones got the idea that play was over.

Their voices chimed together like little birds squawking. "Eat?"

Just as the adults had worked hard, the children too had been busy—hard at work with their play. Creating fields in the sandbox, using sticks as teams of horses making rows. Some of the little girls had also made flower gardens, plucking dandelions from the grass and standing the yellow flowers up in their own little plot of sand.

Watching them, Marianna was reminded of when she was their age and her favorite thing to play had been horse and buggy. She and Levi had done so often. Sometimes they used rocks and sticks. Other times they were the horses. And once . . . Marianna bit her lip. She'd been the buggy and her brother had been the semi truck.

At the time she'd thought it was her scream, as Levi tackled her to the ground, that had upset her mother. But as she'd grown older, she realized it was the game itself that had caused so much pain. Or rather, it had resurrected a pain that had been there for quite some time. That was the last time she'd played horse and buggy. Her mother's sobs had not calmed the rest of that day, and Marianna never wanted to risk that again.

"Good children. Are you hungry? Would you like some bread and peanut butter? Maybe some cookies, too?"

Small heads bobbled and smiles brightened faces.

Marianna lined up the toddlers, preparing to take them to their mothers, when she spotted Mem serving up large pieces of pie. Her mother's smile lit her face as she handed a plate to Aaron. His smile mirrored Mem's, and then he turned, both of their gazes fixing on Marianna. She waved, not knowing what else to do, and then looked away. She again focused on the small ones, making sure they still followed. And as the bright sun warmed her kapp, a new hope sprang up in her heart. Her mother wouldn't allow them to leave when Aaron's interest was so evident. The goal of every Amish mother was to find a good husband for her daughters. Mem wouldn't risk leaving now, would she? Marianna glanced back again and noticed Mrs. Zook talking to her mother.

Marianna quickened her pace, urging the little ones to follow, knowing the only proper thing to do was find a way to talk to the older woman before the day's end. Marianna didn't know Mrs. Zook well. They'd exchanged small talk at church and socials, but perhaps she should make an attempt to get to know Aaron's family better.

Ten minutes later the children were under the care of their mothers, and she held Ellie's hand as she joined the women who were lining up for lunch. The grass was soft under her footsteps as she neared Mrs. Zook. Marianna approached from behind. Mrs. Zook was huddled with a few other older women, and their eyes were fixed at a long table where the men were sitting.

"Do you wonder why he's returned?" The gray-haired woman from a neighboring community studied the women around her. "Some say he's been spending too much time with the Englisch and they're corrupting his ways."

Others joined in. "My husband says they saw him reading an English Bible in his buggy. Is he trying to be smart or something? Thinking he knows more than the bishop?"

"Maybe Ike has come for a wife, but I don't think it's likely."

Marianna's hand covered her mouth—they were talking about her uncle! She took a step back, preparing to walk away, but not before she heard Mrs. Zook's response.

"There is not a pot so crooked that there isn't a lid to fit it. There has to be a woman desperate enough."

Laughter followed the woman's comment, and Marianna no longer felt like eating. Ellie looked up at her, her little brow creased, and she pointed to the long wooden tables laden with hot dishes, salads, the fruit tapioca Mem had brought, and loaves of homemade bread. Ellie's question was clear: When were they going to eat?

Marianna had heard talk like this before. Sometimes at the small Amish store or other times in their sewing circles. But during those times the ladies had been talking about other people. Now they spoke of someone she didn't know well but felt she ought to defend.

It was as if a dozen sewing needles pierced her heart as she heard the woman's laughter again and realized it was at her uncle's expense. She made a small plate of food for Ellie and sat her next to Mrs. Ropp and Helen.

"Is it okay if Ellie eats next to you?"

Mrs. Ropp burped her baby at her shoulder. "Yes, of course. Find yourself something to eat and take a break from the young ones for a spell."

"*Denke.*" But despite her word of thanks, Marianna didn't feel like eating. She lowered her head and hurried in the direction of the sandbox, where the children would be returning after lunch. Sometimes the children disagreed, not wanting to share or to play nicely. Sometimes they called each other names, but they hadn't yet learned to pierce each other with carefully calculated words. Children were learning, adults should know better.

She wove through the bodies of men rising to get back to work and women cleaning off the tables, refolding picnic blankets, gathering plates. The sun grew warmer, and she fanned her face.

"There you are."

Marianna felt a hand on her arm and turned to find Aaron standing there. It was the second time he'd snuck up on her.

"I've been looking for you." He ran a hand down his cheek and it was then she noticed the slightest amount of blond hair on his jaw line. Her mouth dropped open, and her eyes widened. Aaron must have noticed her recognition, and he pressed his lips into a tight smile. Amish men didn't wear a beard until they were married, and yet some young men started "practicing" before— growing out a shadow of facial hair as they got closer to the transition in their lives.

"You've been looking for me? Do you, uh, need me for something?" She placed a hand to her neck and was surprised to feel the beating of her heart under her fingertips.

"I've been thinking about it, and maybe waiting until fall to go on a date is too long. I was thinking I could drive you home this Sunday. After the youth sing, if you don't mind."

"No, I mean yes. Yes, you can drive me home, and no I don't mind." Marianna felt a tug on her skirt and looked down to see Ellie clinging to her leg.

"*Essen mit mir?*"

Marianna should have known the little girl wouldn't be happy unless she were sitting with her while she ate.

"*Ja, ja.*" Marianna took her sister's hand.

"So, I'll see you Sunday then, if not sooner." Aaron straightened his shoulders and then hurried toward the other men heading back to work. She couldn't help but notice an extra skip in his step.

"Sunday, then." She whispered after him, then gave in to the tugging of her hand and moved back to the lunch table. A new hope bubbled up inside her with each step. Maybe news of this would fix everything. After all, who would take their daughter away from such a promising future? Such a perfect Amish young man.

Dear Journal,

I had to start a new notebook today because the other one is full. In between the journal pages are also my letters I've pulled out from the June-Sevenies circle letters. Sometime I'll have to go back and read through them, seeings how so much as changed in the years my friends and I have been writing. We've moved on from talking about our first quilts and how the boys at school were so bothersome, to marrying some of those same boys and setting up house.

In my last circle letter I spilled the news that Aaron has asked me out on a date. I should be getting the envelope around again. I'm always eager to read what everyone else said, but sometimes it's insightful to read what I wrote the previous month. Things tend to change quickly around here.

I can't sleep tonight because I'm thinking about Sunday. Trying to figure out what in the world I could talk to Aaron about on the drive home. We haven't talked much—been doing mostly lookin' at each other. I could ask about the herd he's building, but that might make him feel as if I'm questioning if he's a good provider or not. I could ask about the house he's building, but maybe if I did he'd think I'm already hanging my curtains in his window. Maybe we can just talk about his art. I haven't heard much about it lately. When we were kids, not a day went by when he wasn't sketching some creature when he should've been doing math equations.

I also can't sleep thinking about this move. I hope Dat's words are more clouds than rain.

CHAPTER THREE

*M*arianna opened her eyes, then scanned her room. The only glimmer of light was a beam of moon penetrating through a sliver of curtain that she hadn't fully closed. She'd tried to fall asleep for hours, and nothing worked. She'd hummed to herself, tried to count back from one hundred, she'd even written in her journal, which usually helped her mind wind down. But not tonight. Maybe it was the light that bothered her—or at least that was a good excuse.

Marianna sat up in bed and reached for the window curtain, tugging it closed all the way. As in all Amish houses, the curtains were white, but at age ten she'd convinced her father to install two hooks to hold up an extra blanket over the window. She'd lied to him, telling him that the light from the moon had kept her awake. But the truth was that when she was small, her mother had said her sisters looked down on them from above. That might have been comforting for her mother, but Marianna hadn't liked it one bit. What would they think of her sleeping in their bedroom. In their bed?

Her first dresses had belonged to her sisters. Her dolls too. It was only later she realized that might have been the reason her mother had looked away when Marianna tried on her "new" dresses. Had refused to play dolls with her. Had made excuses when Marianna wanted to be tucked in at night.

"I want this time to be for just me and my girl," Dat had said as he unfolded the quilt and laid it over her. Yet she could see the truth in his gaze. He hadn't fought for this time. He'd accepted it as his. And she tried not to let it bother her as she could hear Mem in the other room, reading to the boys.

But that was long ago . . . Marianna turned to her side. Dat hadn't tucked her in for five years at least, and now it was only occasionally she heard Men reading to the other kids. Marianna tucked the pillow under her chin. That didn't mean the empty void she felt inside had filled. She'd enjoyed her siblings, worked hard at her job, enjoyed writing her friends, dreamed about Aaron . . . but nothing could fill the hole the size of her mother's handprint, centered on her gut.

Outside she heard the sound of a breeze rustling tree branches—and something else. A car perhaps?

She rose, her toes curling against the cold floor, and went to the window to lift the curtain. She could see taillights in the distance. Could it be? Was it Levi?

She didn't want to think about that now—about him leaving. She didn't want to think about her sisters, especially since she still lived in their room, slept in their bed. Instead, she thought of the day, and the conversation with Aaron.

The barn raising had resulted in a large barn, filling the horizon, but even larger loomed Marianna's questions. Did Aaron like her as much as she liked him? Would she be around long enough to find out?

She let the curtain drop and grabbed the battery-powered

flashlight she kept on her dresser, then she walked to the trunk where she'd tucked away the quilt she'd worked on during the winter. It was white with an intricate pattern. She'd started hand stitching the pattern in brightly colored thread.

Spring planting, caring for new baby animals, and her work at the Ropps and in their own garden hadn't allowed time for her quilt. The months to come wouldn't either, but it made her feel better to see she was farther along than she remembered. It had always been her dream to make a special quilt to give to her husband some day. Imagining Aaron accepting it as a gift—sometime in the future—made her smile.

Her room and bed had never been her own. Her parents couldn't look at her life without remembering two deaths, but it wouldn't always be like that. Someday she'd have her own family. She'd care for a home and work hard to see her husband smile. She'd sleep under a quilt she made with her hands. And wake up to a curtain letting in morning rays from the sun.

Marianna was returning the quilt to her chest when she heard a knock on her bedroom door. She rose and hurried to it, shining the flashlight beam out as she opened it. Twelve-year-old David stood there rubbing his eyes and brushing his blond bangs from his face.

"Marianna, did you hear that?" He sounded half asleep.

"Hear what, David?" Listening, she heard the wind pick up. "I think that's only the breeze in the trees."

"No, it was a car. Someone was parked outside. It mighta been Levi." David's eyes widened, and the hope in his face caused Marianna's heart to ache. The oldest of the little boys, David had been Levi's shadow. They'd tended to the cows and sheep together. They both enjoyed playing checkers on cold winter nights.

"I don't think Levi would come by this late."

"But last time I saw him in town, he said he'd come by and show me his car."

"David . . . not this late." Not with Dat home. She tried to redirect his attention. "It was maybe just a tourist who'd taken a wrong turn."

David's shoulders slumped and he lowered his head, staring at his bare toes.

"Tell you what"—she placed a hand on his shoulder— "tomorrow we can each write Levi a letter and then mail them. It'll be a nice surprise."

David nodded, but instead of lifting his face to hers, he turned and plodded to the room he shared with the other two boys. Marianna sighed. It wasn't much to offer, but at least—unlike their sisters—their brother wasn't dead. Although sometimes knowing Levi left to live among the Englisch seemed worse. The girls had no choice in their leaving. He, on the other hand . . .

Marianna closed her door and moved to the table she'd fixed into a desk. She pulled out paper and pen, deciding to start her letter now. But what could she say?

Levi, I never thought Mother and Father's hearts could break any further. I was wrong.

Levi, the little boys "play" Englisch when they think no one is looking. They've always tried to be just like their big brother.

Levi, how could you leave me with all the chores? Didn't you think I had enough to do on my own?

Although all of those were true, Marianna decided to start by writing what was heaviest on her heart.

Levi, I miss you, and if Dat has his way, I'll be missing you from afar.

Chapter Four

The afternoon sun cast a long shadow down the unpaved, country road. Marianna walked with slower steps than usual, hoping to catch a glimpse of Aaron who often passed by on his way home from work at a nearby dairy. Still in his *rumspringa*, Aaron could drive an automobile like most of their friends, but he didn't. He'd yet to join the church, so there was much he could experiment with—drinking, smoking, Englisch dress—yet he hadn't done that either. Like her, the things of the world seemed more hassle than they were worth—or least that's what he told her. Also like her, he was one of the oldest children in his family and he knew the best thing he could do for his parents before moving out to live on his own was to provide a good example for his brothers and sisters.

She neared her family's two-story farmhouse with a gray door and white curtains in the windows, like every other Amish home in the area. A large oak shaded the front porch and two blue jays danced from branch to roof to branch. Watching this, a strange peace came over her. On the buggy ride home yesterday her parents hadn't spoken about the move, and she hoped that being around their community of friends had changed Dat's mind.

A smile filled her face at the sight of her mother taking down sheets from the clothesline. Everything appeared like it always was until the older woman turned. Marianna saw a look of sadness mixed with anger peering out of her mother's hazel-eyed gaze. The air smelled of wildflowers, mixed with the scent of soap from the sheets and the rich soil of her father's fields and something else. Was it her imagination or could she smell automobile exhaust drifting on the wind?

"It's about time you found your way home. Did ya lose your way?" Mem's tongue was sharp. "I thought you'd gotten lost. It's nearly supper. I need yer help."

"Sorry. Mrs. Ropp needed me to entertain her older kids while she bathed the baby. We picked wild flowers." Marianna swung the small bucket filled with foxgloves, black-eyed Susans, and—her favorite—larkspur, brushing it against her apron, hoping her mother would notice them. "And before that I was making pies with Rebecca. We have six apple ones cooling in her window sill for church."

"*Ja*, well, you should help at home first. I haven't had a break all day, and now my head aches." Her mother folded a bright white sheet, plopping it in the wicker laundry basket, not taking her normal care.

Marianna looked to the porch and noticed Ellie humming as she sat on the green, wooden front porch swing, kicking her legs and rocking. Everything looked content. What had gotten her mother so riled?

From her mother's countenance, and the smell of car exhaust, Marianna was certain her older brother Levi had stopped by. David might have been right about him lingering around last night, too. *Maybe he's missing us . . .*

Marianna couldn't imagine how it pierced her mother's heart seeing her oldest son driving his Englisch car down the dirt road in full sight of all the neighbors. Part boy, part man, her brother came around when he needed money or to fill his belly. He lived with friends in a mobile trailer near town and supposedly had a job, but Marianna had never heard him talk about work. Most nights she prayed Levi would leave his corrupt ways, return to his Amish roots, join the church, and be baptized. Other times she wished he'd move away.

Instead, Levi lived just far enough away to keep their mother up at nights with worried thoughts and close enough to bring their father shame.

Since Levi refused to join the church, her father had told her to treat her brother as if he were dead to them, but every time he said that, pain tightened her mother's face and darkened her gaze. To Marianna, death meant the shin-high gravestones protected by a crooked rusting metal gate on her grandfather's land. It also meant the two trees her mother had planted south of the house after her sisters' deaths. Levi was still very much alive.

The oldest, he was twenty-one—the age when most young men joined the church—and although Marianna was only two years younger, she worked hard to let her parents know her path was already set. As soon as scents of autumn filled the air, she'd start meeting with the ministers in preparation for baptism into the church. Her decision was without question. It's something she'd always known she'd do. It was the right thing.

It was what Marilyn and Joanna would have done, she was sure of it.

The sound of a chair leg scraping on the floor inside carried through the open window and pulled her attention back to the house. Her other brothers most likely played down by the creek making mud cookies. Twelve-year-old David probably frolicked in the corn crib or the hayloft with the new kittens, if Mem was lucky. On more rebellious days he tried to walk the roofline or parachute from his bedroom window. And Marianna doubted her father would be home. He was never home this early in the day.

Marianna looked at her mother. "Is someone inside?"

"Naomi came by." Mem's proffered explanation was simple. "She's in the house kneading the bread dough. Told her she needn't help, but she insisted. Said she missed being around our family."

Marianna took a step toward the house, then paused. There was something in her mother's gaze. Mem wanted to say more but didn't.

Naomi had been a fixture at their home as long as she could remember. Well, at least until Levi left. Once he was on his own, Naomi's visits dwindled considerably. And when she did come, the pain in her eyes matched Mem's.

Naomi's family was their closest neighbors, and they'd all played together as children. They'd fished together, swam together, played hide and seek around the farm. As Levi and Naomi entered youth it was obvious they'd grown to be more than friends. Everyone knew they'd be married some day. Or at least they thought so until Levi's attention wandered to the trappings of the outside world. If anything would have committed Levi to joining the church, it should have been Naomi. How her heart must break that even her love wasn't enough to distract him from the temptations of the Englisch world.

Levi's attraction to the things of the world wasn't unusual. Many youth were drawn to the same, including Marianna's friend

Rebecca. Even as they'd made pies this morning, Rebecca had talked about a recent movie she'd seen at the theater and about the party she'd be going to next Saturday night. Of course, she also talked about quilting and asked how Marianna's quilt was coming along. It seemed her friend was torn between two worlds. Marianna just hoped that, unlike Levi, Rebecca would stay at home and realize the narrow path was indeed the better way.

Overhead a robin chirped in a high tree branch, but the lovely sound didn't bring a smile to her mother's face. In the distance the gray silo and tall silver windmill peeked over the red barn's sloping roof. Her mother turned to her, placing hands on her hips.

"Hope you were *only* making pies with Rebecca, not getting into any trouble." She smoothed her hand across the taunt clothes line, as if feeling the warmth of the sheet before she unpinned it. The breeze ruffled the sheet and tussled the strings of her mother's kapp. As if also wanting to join the dance, a strand of her mother's brown hair escaped its hold and fluttered on the wind.

"Yes, we made pies. That is all." Marianna sighed as she hurried up the front steps. Then she turned again. "Rebecca's father said he saw Aaron this morning," she said, hoping to bring brightness back to her mother's gaze.

"That Aaron is such a nice boy. Is he still a hired hand at the Stoll's dairy farm?"

Marianna's fingers tightened around the handle of the pail. "*Ja*, and I heard he purchased a few head of cattle for his own." Heat rose to her cheeks, remembering their conversation yesterday.

Her mother's eyes brightened, and the storm cloud that had swept over her countenance blew away.

"*Ja*, good, good. He always was a hardworking lad. He'll make you a fine husband some day. The perfect Amish boy." Wistfulness laced her mother's voice, and Marianna could almost finish her thought: *Unlike Levi.*

Marianna heard the jingle of the tack and traces on her father's buggy and, without turning, she knew he crested the hill behind her. She also knew he neared from the way her mother straightened her kapp and tucked the stray strand of hair behind her ear. It was moments like these when she witnessed her parents' love. Outward expressions weren't seen often—it wasn't the Amish way—so Marianna appreciated every hint of affection she saw between them. Would she have the same eager glint in her eye when she saw Aaron?

"I thought about making a berry pie, for after dinner. There's still some filling in the pantry—" Marianna noticed her mother's smile fade and her jaw tighten. She turned, already guessing who she'd see riding by her father's side. There was only one person other than Levi that caused her mother such grief.

"I'll finish this, Mem." Marianna set the pail of flowers on the ground, near the back porch steps, and took the basket of clothespins from her mother's grasp.

But Mem didn't move, didn't speak. Instead, she stared at the two men as they parked the buggy in front of the barn. Uncle Ike was the first to jump down. His laughter boomed, overwhelming the sound of the birds. His eyes twinkled. His face wore a wide smile, and to Marianna the laughter was the booming of thunder just before a storm.

Chapter Five

aomi's back was to Marianna as she entered, and Marianna paused in the kitchen doorway. A few strands of Naomi's red hair could be seen at the base of her neck under her kapp. Her shoulders were slumped, her head down. Two large ceramic bowls sat on the kitchen table, covered by white, clean cloths. The bread was rising. Her work was done. And still Naomi didn't leave.

Marianna took a step forward on the bare, wooden floor. Her footfall hit a loose board and squeaked. Naomi turned, eyes wide. Marianna expected tears, but instead noted Naomi's red-tinged cheeks and eyes bright. The excited look made the pail of flowers in Marianna's hand look drab.

"Mari, I didn't see you." Naomi rose, tucking what appeared to be a letter into her pocket. She bit her lip, lifted her chin, and tried to relax her features, but it did little good. Then she glanced behind Marianna, as if expecting others to follow. Marianna shook her head.

"You look so happy." Marianna frowned. Why did Naomi look so . . . joyful? Levi had turned his back on Naomi. He'd walked away.

Unless . . .

Unless there was news in that letter stating he'd changed his mind. That he was coming back. Coming back to Naomi. To his family. To the community. To join the church.

"Levi was here, wasn't he?" Marianna walked around the kitchen table and approached the sink. She set the pail of wild-flowers on the counter and then reached into the open cupboard and took out a large jelly jar filled with berry pie filling.

Naomi lifted the towel and peeked in at the rising dough, looking away from Marianna's gaze. She turned her attention back to the sink. Clear water from the faucet bubbled and splashed in the jar and hopefulness did the same in Marianna's heart.

If Levi decided to return to the way of their ancestors, not only would her brother once again be in right standing with God, perhaps her parents wouldn't want to leave. Loss over the deaths of their sisters had caused them to withdraw from the community— or at least that's what her grandmother had said. It had been hard for them to bury two daughters and see everyone else's children growing, changing, joyfully interacting in the community. All the while knowing their girls would never do any of it.

Things were different concerning Levi.

The adventure of the mountains might be calling her father, but the rumors of her brother's actions were no doubt giving her father a big push out the door. Being farther away, they wouldn't see Levi so often, wouldn't hear about the many ways he was becoming more Englisch. Wouldn't see the downward spiral. She wished she could talk to her brother, make him understand. His choices didn't just affect him.

Not even close.

Naomi rose and grabbed a wooden cutting board from where

it hung on the wall on a single nail, then she placed it on the table in front of her, sprinkling it with flour, sitting once more on the bench. "Levi *was* here, not too long ago. How did you know?"

Marianna turned off the water and then arranged the wildflowers in the jar, mixing up the brown-eyed Susans between the Indian grass and the pink foxgloves. "Two clues. Your reaction and Mem's. She's not happy."

"No, it wasn't a nice visit." Naomi poked the dough, but seeing it still needed more time to rise, she returned the dishtowel and pushed the floured cutting board to the side. "Levi picked up some clean laundry. I'm sure your father doesn't know your mem is still washing Levi's clothes. He took some food, too. Your mother was kind but didn't say much. Maybe she would have said more if I hadn't been here."

"That doesn't sound bad. I thought you were going to say they got into an argument."

"It's worse. The little kids climbed into his locked car through an open window. The boys were honking the horn over and over. Your mother said she was sure the neighbors could hear the ruckus in the next county. She spanked all three boys and told them to head to the creek and sit there until she went for them. And even worse, Ellie clung to Levi's leg, not wanting him to leave." Naomi sighed, as if remembering one good part of his visit. Then she pressed her hand against her pocket. Marianna wished she could read the letter. If it had been Rebecca here instead of Naomi, Marianna would have heard every word of it. Twice.

"I'm sure Mem was horrified by the horn, but it wasn't that loud. I was at the Ropp's house just down the lane and I didn't hear."

"That's good." Naomi laughed. Her face reddened, making her freckles blend in with the color on her cheeks. "Try to convince your mother of that."

Marianna approached the table covered by a pale yellow tablecloth, placing the jar of flowers in the center. Then she moved to the sack of potatoes on the counter. Her mother had told her this morning she was planning potato soup for supper. Might as well get that started. She placed the sack of potatoes and two knives on the table, inviting Naomi to sit and talk.

Naomi picked up a potato and a knife and began peeling. "I knew he was coming." She peeled slow, wearing a half smile. "He told my cousin to tell me. They share a house, you know."

"I heard it's a small trailer."

Naomi shrugged. "Yes, well, you know what I mean."

"So why did he come?" Marianna turned over the potato in her hand, sliding the knife over the peel. She tried to keep her voice steady, even. She didn't want to prod Naomi too much that she'd stop talking. Yet Marianna also wanted her to get the words out before Mem or the guys came inside. She secretly hoped chores would take longer than usual.

"He came to bring me a letter and," Naomi looked down at her hands, "tell me a few other things."

Marianna cocked an eyebrow. "The letter seems to have made you happy."

"It did. It confirmed what I'd been hoping. There are many things Levi left, but not me." Naomi paused her peeling as if caught up in a memory. Her lips puckered as if remembering a kiss.

"*Ja*, he's told me many times how he cares for you." Marianna placed one peeled potato on the table and picked up a second. "And from that smile does that letter say what I'm hoping it does?"

"I'm not sure what you mean." Naomi resumed peeling again, and her eyes darted to the door and then to Marianna.

Marianna was almost afraid to ask, but the joy on Naomi's face was clear. Marianna knew the only thing that could make Naomi that happy was news that Levi was returning. "Are you going to be together soon?"

Naomi's eyes widened and she leaned forward. "Yes. How did you know?" Her smile reminded Marianna of the look Ellie gave when she'd gotten in the cookie jar. Marianna expected Naomi to stop talking, to try to be evasive, but just as Ellie always confessed to eating the cookies, Naomi continued. "I didn't think anyone would figure it out." Naomi glanced up from under pale lashes.

"We went to school together most of our growing years. You don't hide your feelings. If you're sad, everyone knows. And if you're happy," Marianna shrugged, "it's easy to see."

Naomi placed the knife on the table and touched her fingertips to her face. "I need to do better about that, or everyone will know for sure, and Levi won't like it."

"He doesn't want everyone to know?"

Naomi scoffed. "Of course not. Not yet. Not until it happens."

"But why doesn't he come today? Why does he have to wait?"

Naomi shook her head. "Needs more time. To make more money yet, to support us."

"Money isn't everything." Marianna noticed through the window that her father and Uncle Ike were talking in the yard, just beyond the porch. They were looking at the house, as if sizing it up. She hoped they would stay there a bit. She needed to get the rest of the story.

"I understand why he wants to wait. He told me in the letter that everything costs so much. A house, food. When I leave, I'll need new clothes."

"When you leave?" Marianna's eyes lifted, but the knife continued down the potato. "I thought Levi was returning?" Before she could take in Naomi's words, pain burned her hand, and she glanced down to see that the knife had sliced into her palm.

"Oh no. Oh, ouch!" The potato and the knife clattered to the table. Marianna rose and ran to the sink. Pain throbbed in her palm to the beating of her pained heart. She focused on the ache, on the blood dripping over her hand. She didn't want to think about Naomi's plan. A plan that would slice through the community and sting deep.

Naomi's words called after her. "Did you cut yourself?"

Marianna reached the sink, she turned on the cold water, placing her hand underneath. The cool water flowed clear over her hand, but then turned pink as it splashed into the sink.

"Do you need me to bandage it?" Naomi approached and rested a hand on Marianna's arm.

She nodded and swallowed down the tears. This couldn't be happening. She squeezed her eyes closed. The pain in her hand stung, but it wasn't noticeable compared to the anger that bubbled up inside.

For too long she'd tried to sympathize with Levi. He was alone. He was hungry. He was confused. But how *dare* he talk Naomi into following. She wasn't strong like he was. She was close to her sisters. She had a dozen nieces and nephews she adored. Didn't he understand what he was asking Naomi to do? Turn her back on that. To walk away. To be looked upon differently. To be talked about, especially if she was leaving to live with him. Even if she someday returned, knowledge of her actions would always trail her. Draped around her shoulders as a cloak of shame.

The anger tightened her shoulders, pinched her gut.

Marianna opened her eyes again and focused on the soft, wispy red curls that framed Naomi's face. She didn't dare look into Naomi's eyes, lest her friend think the anger was directed at her.

"Where are the bandages?" Naomi asked again. Her voice quivered as if she just realized what she'd shared wasn't what Marianna expected or approved of.

"In the cupboard behind the bathroom door. Second shelf." Marianna dared to look at her hand again, seeing it was a deeper wound than she thought, but not deep enough to distract her from the pain piercing her heart.

Naomi hurried to the bathroom. A moment later she returned with a strip of binding material Mem used for tending wounds. In her other hand was a cotton square. Naomi placed the cotton on the wound, adding pressure, and then wound the strip of cloth around Marianna's hand three times, tucking the end within a fold. She didn't speak. Instead she tilted her head to the right and ved her eyebrows, as if asking *Are you all right?*

Marianna looked away and curled her bandaged hand to her chest, covering it with her other one. She pulled it tight against her, wishing she could keep pulling, folding the pain inside until it was hidden away deep. Her knees softened, and she looked to the bench at the table, wanting to sit. But her feet were heavy. So heavy she expected them to sink through the floor to the root cellar. She sucked in a shuttering breath, and a small whimper emerged from her lips, surprising her.

"Do you think you need stitches? I can get your dad."

"No, that's not it." Marianna wiped at her eyes with the back of her bandaged hand, feeling the pressure of the world winding around her. What could she say for Naomi to reconsider? Marianna leaned with one hand against the counter and braced herself. It was the same motion she'd seen her mother do in labor pains, but the pain wasn't in her stomach. Her heart hurt. She again covered it with her bandaged hand.

Naomi placed an arm around Marianna's shoulders. "Don't be sad. We won't be far. Levi is finding us a house in town. We'll see you often, and with Levi's new job we'll have a good life. We will."

"What about everyone else?" The words fell from her lips and plopped onto the countertop with a wayward tear. "What will your family think? How will they feel?"

"I'm not the only one. My oldest sister left five years ago. I've had a few cousins—"

"Yes. So you know. You've seen the pain, which makes it all the worse. And you've no doubt heard their cries. Doesn't your aunt still wear black after your cousin's leaving? And didn't you see my mother today?" Marianna lifted her head and met Naomi's gaze. "How did she react when Levi came? Was she smiling? Full of joy?" Marianna stepped back, letting Naomi's hand fall back to her side. "What you choose affects so many. We're a fabric and when one thread unravels—"

"You sound like the bishop." Naomi's sad smile made the tightness in Marianna's chest even worse. No, it wasn't sadness but pity. Naomi stepped back and crossed her arms over her chest, not in defiance, but aloofness.

She still wore the long dress with cape. A white prayer kapp rested snugly on her head, but her face reflected the truth. She'd already left them. A strand of red hair curled against Naomi's cheek, but she paid it no mind.

Naomi jutted out her chin. "We each have a choice. That's what *rumspringa* is all about, correct? A time that allows us to experience life outside the community before deciding. Yet, in truth, there can only be one decision. I can see it in your face that you hate me already. I shouldn't have told you. You enjoy living here. You'll never understand."

"You're not leaving for anything other than my brother. You know if he came back you'd stay."

"Of course. But to me that is enough. He is enough." Naomi's eyebrows pointed down, into a red arrow and her nose scrunched up. "But think about it, Mari. Is my choice any worse than yours to stay—acting the part of a pure and perfect girl because of a man? I saw you and Aaron Zook talking the other day. I know your plans."

"I have no plans other than to serve God and family." Marianna looked to her hand again. Disturbing thoughts filled her mind. *What if Aaron wanted to leave?* She wouldn't go, but it would hurt, and she would question her life in ways she never had before.

She shook her head as if chasing away those thoughts. Aaron wasn't leaving. She didn't have to consider that.

Marianna saw movement through the window. Her brothers ran toward the house with a line of three fish dangling between them.

"I know the way." She jutted out her chin as she spoke, but inside a coolness filled her chest, pushing out the words—words she knew she had to speak. "And I don't need to wander. I've tried to be understanding of my brother, tried to allow him the space he desired to make his decision, but I'm sad for you. Sad you don't see how the life Levi's living is drawing him away from everything good. Sad to think you'd find anything in the world that can come close to replacing all you'll lose." Marianna cocked her chin, feeling much, much older than her nineteen years . . .

When had that happened?

The front door swung open, and though Marianna could see that Naomi wanted to respond, she pressed her lips into a thin line and glanced over her shoulder at the boys, offering a forced smile. Mem and Ellie followed right behind.

"Naomi, you staying for dinner?" Mem strode up and checked the bread dough. "Almost done rising, I'm sure the kids would love your help rolling the dinner rolls."

"I can help." Marianna went to Ellie, extending her arms to her little sister, thankful for the distraction. "Let's get you washed up."

"Mari, what happened?" Her mother grabbed her bandaged hand. The faintest tinge of red was seeping through the bandage. "Did you cut yourself?"

"It's nothing, my knife slipped while I was peeling potatoes."

"You need to be more careful, but maybe that goes to show you you should start spending more time in the kitchen and less tending to babies and animals. A good husband is to expect good food."

Naomi cleared her throat, and Marianna looked to her out of the corner of her eyes. Naomi was frozen in place and her eyes sent a silent plea.

"Yes, Mem." Marianna lowered her hands. "You're right. I'll finish the potatoes and then help the kids with the rolls. But first

I'll walk Naomi to the door. The sun is already beginning to set, and we'd hate to have her walking home in the dark."

They walked to the door and Naomi paused on the porch.

"I won't say anything," Marianna whispered, "but only because I hope you'll reconsider."

Naomi nodded and moved to the steps. "Yes, of course."

Yet even as she strode away Marianna knew it was just words. Naomi's mind was set. The community was on the verge of yet another heartbreak.

CHAPTER SIX

The slightest breeze blew through the open kitchen window, ruffling the pages of the scenic calendar hanging on the wall. Her mother stirred the potato soup on the stovetop, and then sat down on the table bench with a heavy sigh. She looked tired tonight. Dark circles ringed her eyes. Levi's visit had taken its toll.

"Just break off a little piece of dough and roll it in the palms of your hands like this," Marianna explained to Ellie and Josiah, trying to keep her tone light. Trying to brighten the mood of her siblings. Charlie and David had set up checkers in the living room, which was connected to the kitchen, but they sat silently, not starting the game.

All the younger ones loved Levi, missed him. Twelve-year-old David understood the rules of the church and knew what Levi's leaving meant. But at eight and five, Charlie and Josiah hadn't fully grasped their brother's actions, and Ellie no doubt wondered what all the fuss was about.

"Like dis?" Ellie rolled the dough with her chubby hand.

"Yes, then we're going to line them up all in a row." Marianna placed a lump of warm dough on the cookie sheet. With a wide grin, Ellie plopped her dough next to Marianna's.

Ellie's navy blue kapp contrasted with her bright blonde hair, and her looks and coloring couldn't be more different from five-year-old Josiah's dark complexion, more like their dat. Marianna wondered again who Marilynn and Joanna looked like most. Her chest clenched when she realized Joanna hadn't been much older than Ellie was now when she died.

Marianna sighed as she looked at her sister. If only she could stay that innocent and sweet forever. If only she didn't have to hear the story of the night Marianna was born. To grow up and discover that, even though they lived a simple life, there was nothing simple about their losses. If only she could escape the pain that lingered like the May chill creeping in with the sunset, not allowing spring to occupy the night.

Her brother and sister lined up more misshapen lumps next to hers.

"Great job." She, of course, could make rolls better and faster, but her siblings had to learn—just as she'd learned from her mother. Even though she'd rather be rocking a baby or bottle feeding one of the new lambs, she did fine in the kitchen, despite her mother's admonitions.

The soup simmered on the stovetop, filling the room with an aroma that made Marianna's stomach growl. The steam from the pot also brought a moistness to the air, fogging the kitchen window and making it harder to see her father outside. He and Uncle Ike had been talking a good hour. A conversation that long could only mean their discussion was serious in nature. Dat never stood around, wasting time chatting unless there was a purpose.

Working full time in the factory in town and caring for a family and a farm saw to that.

Her mother flipped through the stack of mail. Marianna liked nothing better than enjoying a quiet evening at home with her siblings. But there was no joy tonight. The truth of Naomi's plan seized her, chilled her. The secret like ice expanding from within.

"You received a letter from the Junes." Her mother set a small stack of letters on the table, then rose and checked the cook stove, readying it for the rolls.

Marianna turned to Josiah. "Can you finish these up?" He nodded, his dark bangs swishing against his forehead.

"Me too!" Ellie chimed in.

Marianna hurried to the stack of mail. She needed something to distract her. Something to get her mind off her heavy heart.

Levi and Naomi wouldn't be the first couple to leave. Though it wasn't common, Marianna had seen this type of thing through her growing up years. First one would leave, then the other would follow. Sometimes they came back after years of hardship. Life in the Englisch world wasn't easy. Some Amish didn't have birth certificates or Social Security cards. Even harder was their lack of education, and work was hard to find. Some got jobs and were paid under the table, a fraction of what other workers received. In the Englisch world they had to find new clothes and learn to talk different. Sometimes they were taken advantage of, and many times they had no choice but to take advantage of others, living with them, eating food and wearing clothes that they couldn't afford.

There were those couples who came back and lived within the community. Often just one would return, choosing God's way over the world.

"King me," David called from the checker game. He looked most like Marianna, with light brown hair and hazel eyes. In a couple more years, he'd no doubt be her height.

Marianna didn't need to look at the address label to know which envelope was hers. She pulled the large yellow envelope from the bottom of the stack and carefully opened the flap, turning it upside down. A stack of ten letters slid out along with a dirty penny, a pressed violet, and eight other small trinkets. Marianna didn't know who came up with the idea of sending small things with their letters, but she was glad they did. It added extra fun, even though the letters were entertaining in their own right.

"Read one letter, and then I need you to get those rolls in the oven."

"Yes, Mem." Marianna glanced to her siblings, who were making more of a mess than anything, then she focused on the loopy writing on the page.

Their circle letter started as a school project, writing to other girls who shared two things: the same birthday and the fact that they lived in an Amish Community in Indiana. They'd started with seventeen participants, but over time ten, including her, remained faithful—all of them born on June 7.

Marianna began reading the first page, which was always a letter from Beverly. Somehow in the midst of their chain letter writing, someone had decided to stack them in alphabetical order. Over time this became as closely observed as the trinkets in the envelope and the manner that the letters were sent around—each girl receiving the package, reading the letters from the others, pulling out her old letter, and adding in a new one before sending it off again.

Dear June-Sevenies, May 4 (1 month, 3 days)

I love that spring has come to Indiana. The flowers and grass popping up. Not the tourist popping up. I will never get used to them. Yesterday I was in the store and the clerk was telling me about her husband's experience. He is a police officer and he received a call about problems with an Amish man.

You know that our area (yours too) is often advertised as the place to see Amish. Well, this lady was quite upset because she wanted to take a photo of an Amish man while he was plowing. She wanted him to stand next to her husband with his horses, but he refused, stating he had work to do. Not to mention the problem of taking a photograph. The clerk said this woman went to the police station to report it! She wanted the police to fire him or to have him arrested. She thought the Amish man was working for the state of Indiana and that his job included entertaining the tourists. I suppose she thought he was an actor playing a part. Would you believe that?

Dat entered the room with quick steps and placed his flat-brimmed straw hat on a nail near the back door, distracting Marianna from her reading.

"*Dat!*" Josiah and Ellie called in unison, dropping their dough balls and running toward their father, reaching out with sticky, dough-covered hands and flour-sprinkled clothes. Marianna knew that most fathers in their community would have scolded their children for not washing up first, but Dat patted David and Charlie on the shoulder, where they sat at their game, and then squatted down to scoop the younger two up in a hug.

"Mem, I've found two more bags of seed. Do you know how these got in the house?" Dat tossed Josiah and Ellie over his shoulders and held them by their legs, their heads dangling down his back.

"Weez not seed bags," three-year-old Ellie countered, snapping her father's suspenders with her small hands.

"Yer, not? Good thing you said so, I almost put you out in the barn with the cows." He set the two down and ruffled their heads, before moving into the kitchen, sidling up to his bride. Knowing their game was over, the youngsters returned to their dough at the table. Marianna slid the letters and the objects back into the envelope, placing it with the other mail. After talking to Naomi, the letters seemed frivolous. And then there was the look on her father's face. Even as he joked, there was a seriousness in his gaze.

Without a word Marianna rose and moved to the table, sitting in the chair beside Ellie. She again pulled a piece of dough from the dwindling ball and rolled it in her hands.

"Ike's not coming in for supper, is he?" Mem's voice was curt.

"No. He's heading down to the Stoll's place. They invited him to eat with them."

"Hope Ike doesn't go telling his stories again. It's prideful, you know, talking so much about a place." Mem took down eight bowls from the open cupboard, by habit, before returning one.

"It's my brother you don't care fer, not the idea." Dat placed a hand on Mem's shoulder. "You have to admit seeing something new, taking an adventure with our children, doesn't sound like a bad idea."

"Some Amish man you are, speaking of adventure. You never were content just being a farmer, were you?" Her mother pouted. "Maybe that's why my dat never approved much of you. Then again." Mem's voice quieted and she peered over her shoulder to where Marianna sat. "So you really think it's a good idea?"

Dat lowered his voice. Marianna strained to hear, though she kept her gaze on her hands as she worked another piece of dough between her palms.

"Just for a year. That Zook boy is still working to build his herd, establishing his home. One year won't make much of a difference. Marianna's not planning a wedding yet."

They talked about her as if she wasn't in the room. As if she couldn't hear.

"Can you tell me again of the community? Are the people nice?" Mem angled her knife and sliced a cucumber into ovals.

Marianna rose and placed the first tray of rolls into the oven, yet even though they were her favorite recipe she'd lost her appetite. She returned to her envelope, fingering it. Dat was just talking. He had talked about moving for six months off and on. Perhaps another six months would go by and they'd still be talking.

"Ike says the people are friendly, and the mountains are nothing like you've ever seen. And the community is smaller and life's slower paced. Ike's friend offered me a spot at a log furniture workshop. Without the farm I'll only have one job, and we can spend more time together. Montana seems like my type of place. I'll call and check on train ticket prices."

Train tickets? The envelope slipped from Marianna's fingers, spilling the contents on the floor. The penny rolled, spinning under the kitchen table. Her body grew hot, then cold, and the conversation continued in slow motion. Even Josiah's gleeful shout as he jumped down from the bench and chased the coin sounded flat to her ears.

Pain pierced her forehead right above her temples, and she knelt to retrieve the items. Her hand reached for the pressed flower and she noticed fresh blood seeping through the bandage. The pain was nothing compared to her heart. She imagined it split open and bleeding within.

They couldn't do this. They couldn't take her from Aaron. If they ever loved her, surely they'd let her stay.

Dear Journal,

I wish my brother were here. I have a thing or two to say to him. Haven't our parents been through enough? Does he wish to shame them even more by causing Naomi to stray?

That's only the beginning. I've been thinking about so many things. If he came back and joined the flock, I doubt Dat would want to leave. But even more important, what about God? I wonder if Levi realizes that walking away from God's way is sure to bring wrath upon him? We are to be set apart. We were the ones chosen to do God's work. Levi should embrace the fact he was chosen—not run away from it. Even the tourists that visit can see God's hand upon us. They are drawn to us because they see something different.

What I hate even more is to think how much

*God is displeased by my brother's actions. I've
heard of what has happened to people who've left the
faith . . . and I don't want anything to happen. I'm
scared for this and for so many things. I wish things
were the way they used to be. I was used to Mem's
sad gaze as she looked to Marilyn and Joanna's
trees. But losing a brother, and possibly a home, is
something I'll never get used to.*

A chill travelled up Aaron's arms as he sat on the front porch of
his small house. Or at least what would be the front porch soon.
All it was now was a few concrete blocks with boards set on top.
His feet rested on the mud, that hadn't quite dried up from the
last rain. He knew his mom would most likely get on him for
muddying up his boots, but that couldn't be helped. A construc-
tion project wasn't the neatest place.

Beside him a lantern's glow sent a halo of light into the night.
On his lap was his sketch book. He opened it, glancing over the
sketches he'd drawn of his cabin. It was nothing fancy. A living
area with kitchen, a large bedroom, and a small bathroom. It
would be enough to get started.

He flipped past that, turning over blank pages. Near the
back was his sketches. Yesterday he'd finished a landscape of
his favorite fishing spot. Looking at it, he could almost feel the
tug of the pole in his hand. Could almost hear the lapping of
the water against the rocky bank. On the next page was one of
their barn cat's new litter of kittens. He turned to the next page,
and that was the one he paused on. It was a sketch of Marianna.

He'd captured her in his mind sitting on the grass near the sandbox at the Yoder's farm. Her eyes were bright, surprised like they'd been when he'd looked back and noted her watching him. Her lips were lifted in a soft smile, and it warmed his heart just seeing them in the sketch. Aaron lifted his pencil and worked on her hand holding a piece of plucked grass. He could almost smell the scent of spring as he drew.

His smile faded as the sound of footsteps in the gravel on the side of the house took him by surprise. He dropped his pencil and quickly flipped back to the sketches of his house plans.

"Don't have a heart attack. It's only me." His friend Joseph walked around the side of the building. "It's not yer pa."

"You could have said something . . . when you were getting closer."

"And miss the look of panic on yer face?" Joseph folded his arms across his chest. "Although I don't see what yer so worried of . . ."

Aaron leaned down and picked up his pencil, wiping off the mud on his jeans.

"You know how my father is. There's work and there's sleep, and not much time for anything else."

"Too bad. You have a real talent."

Aaron cleared his throat. "And where will that lead? You think I'm gonna have a gallery showing like the Englisch? Have my name on a sign out front so everyone in the community can whisper on how prideful I am?"

Joseph kicked his boot against the gravel. "Maybe not, but God did birth you with that talent."

"Since when did you believe in God?" Aaron glanced at his friend. Though Joseph still dressed like a good Amish boy, and drove a buggy, his heart didn't reflect the beliefs that Aaron cherished. The beer under his bed and videos hidden in his closet proved that.

"So why'd you come by anyway? Jest to harass me?"

"Just wondering if you wanted to go over to the Yoders? Some of us are meeting in the new barn."

"Sounds like you'll be up to no good."

"What did I say?" Joseph scoffed.

"Nothing." Aaron closed his sketchbook. "You said nothing, but I know you too well." He stood. "No thanks."

"Marianna doesn't have to know."

Aaron lifted his gaze. "But *I* would." He motioned to his house. "Building this I almost think of us as married."

Joseph removed his brimmed hat and ran a hand through his hair. "Does she know that? Sounds pretty serious."

Aaron stroked his chin. What would it be like telling her how he truly felt? Showing her this place? Sharing what it meant?

"Nah, but maybe I'll tell her soon," he finally said. "Should be seeing her tomorrow. Not once but twice."

"I wouldn't wait too long." Joseph turned and moved back toward the road. "You might not get the chance if you wait . . . from what I hear and all."

CHAPTER SEVEN

unday dawned with a sweet scent drifting through Marianna's bedroom window, but before she could enjoy it, the throbbing of her hand reminded her of Naomi, of their conversation.

Marianna thought about staying at home, sleeping in, giving herself a day to mope and question if her father was serious about moving to Montana, but thoughts of Aaron Zook pulled her out of her slothfulness. She rose and opened her bedroom window wide, letting in more of the scent of green, new leaves and the slightest hint of rain.

In the next hour she dressed, fed her siblings, and they headed for church—in a hurry, like always. Wasn't Sunday supposed to be a day of rest and peace? Not for her. Not for as long as she could remember.

This day seemed like any other Sunday, but soon thick raindrops fell, plunking on the top of their buggy as they neared the Hershberger farm, where her friend Rebecca lived, and she realized that soon everything could be different.

"I imagine those pies you and Rebecca made will be quite a treat." Dat looked back over his shoulder. "I bet Aaron Zook will ask you to save a special piece for him."

Marianna bit her lip. It wasn't like her father was interested in Aaron. If he was, then he'd give up his plans immediately. He just wanted to try to cheer her up before they got to church—to make her smile and look like the good Amish family they were supposed to be.

She thought of a cutting response but held it inside. Daughters and sons were taught to always show their fathers respect, and she had to show him double to make up for her sisters.

"*Ja*, I suppose he will." She clasped her hands on her lap as their buggy turned into the Hershberger place. When the buggy stopped at the front door, Mem climbed down first, and then Marianna who scooped up Ellie, settling her on her hip. Mem held her stomach as she walked, and her face looked more pale than usual. Marianna could tell that even if her mother went along with her father's plan she wasn't happy about it.

They hurried toward the door, attempting to dodge the fat raindrops. Marianna didn't have to watch to know that her father would park the buggy next to the others, unhitch the horse and talk with the married men while the younger, unmarried men talked behind the barn and the children played.

Marianna pictured Aaron standing with the other older youth, talking about the same things the married men talked about—crops, animals, the weather—while also fidgeting from side to side, knowing they'd soon be seeing the girls.

Inside she removed her shawl and hung it on a hook inside the door, remembering the first time Aaron had talked to her in a caring way. She'd been eleven and he was the same age. He'd told her he'd liked her *Fonna-zu ruck*—her new dress that buttoned in the front. The *Hinna-zu ruck*, the dresses of little girls, buttoned in the back, so Marianna had felt like a grown woman as she wore the dress for the first time. Aaron's comment had added to her joy that day, and she'd liked him more than the other boys. And it was obvious the he liked her, too.

Inside the Hershberger house, the portable walls between the living room and dining room had been taken down, opening up the space. A group of men now worked, lining the room with long wooden benches without backs. Propane lanterns lit the space. A few women had already taken their seats, occupying the dining room area. Soon the men would fill the living room, filing in and sitting according to age.

Ellie rested her cheek on Marianna's shoulder, and even though the toddler was heavy, Marianna wasn't ready to find her seat yet.

She glanced around but didn't see Rebecca anywhere. Ever since she'd turned sixteen, her best friend Rebecca had missed more days of church than she'd attended, yet Marianna thought it would be different since this week's meeting was in her aunt's house, not twenty feet from Rebecca's home.

A glance at a long bench she saw Mem was already deep in whispered conversation with the woman sitting next to her. Marianna looked at the clock and noticed they still had twenty minutes before church started. She could run over and check on Rebecca and still be back in time for the beginning of the service.

"Go to the bench. Mem wants you." Marianna placed her sister on the floor. With a slight pout Ellie made her way to where her mother sat.

Marianna walked through the kitchen, slipped out the back door, and strode across the damp grass to Rebecca's house. Opening the door Marianna slipped inside and made her way up the stairs toward Rebecca's room. She wasn't sure if her friend was even there. There were many nights Rebecca stayed in town with Englisch friends, but Marianna hoped she was home. If she wasn't able to talk to someone, she was afraid her words would burst from her—like the fat drops falling from the clouds outside.

She knocked on the door, but there was no response. Marianna pressed her ear tighter against the unpainted, wooden panel and thought she heard the sound of music. She turned the knob and pushed the door open. Rebecca sat in the window sill, smoking a cigarette and listening to the radio. The battery-powered radio was turned down so low it sounded like a jumble of noise. But Marianna knew that Rebecca's reason for even bringing a battery-powered radio into the house, playing Englisch music, wasn't because she liked rock music, but because she could—no one would stop her. It hurt Marianna's heart to see. As Dat would say, it was the sign of a hardened heart when one turned one's back to the ways of their ancestors.

Rebecca's eyes widened in horror at the opening of the door. Then they narrowed again to their half-opened state when she saw who it was.

Marianna nodded to her friend, entered, then closed the door behind her. "Good morning. Yer braver that I, smoking in the window in that outfit in full view of the boys."

With tentative steps Marianna approached the window and peered down into the yard behind the barn. It was there the unmarried men hung around, close enough under the barn's eves not to get wet, but far enough into the yard to get a view of Rebecca wearing a night dress.

"Yes, well, I know for a fact, that a few friends of ours went on dates with those very boys, sleeping over at their houses last night, so don't try to make me feel ashamed. My father does a good enough job of that." As if emphasizing her point, Rebecca took a long drag from her cigarette and then tossed it to the ground two stories below.

Heat rose to Marianna's cheeks, but she didn't say a word. Her parents used to talk about their dates—including the sleepovers or "bed courtship" as it was called—and to Marianna it seemed natural, pure. Maybe it had been innocent back when her parents were young, but if Rebecca's wild stories were true, that was no longer the case.

Rebecca moved from the window and sunk down in her bed, pulling a colorful quilt over her thin frame. "So I hear your parents are moving?" The words were so blunt it surprised Marianna. She felt her throat tightening and tried to swallow down the emotion.

"They're talking like that, but I didn't know it was common knowledge." She moved to the bed and smoothed the wrinkled quilt, remembering many a night when they'd slept side by side under it, singing silly songs and making up stories about talking deer that lived in the woods beyond their farms.

"Are you going with them?" Rebecca sat on the side of the bed, brushing her mass of dark curls back from her face.

"I'd have to. What did you think, I'm going to live here alone?" Even as Marianna said the words the room around her darkened in shades of gray. She'd had yet to spend a night alone. She couldn't imagine her father not turning out the lanterns, wishing everyone a good night. Couldn't imagine her mother not waking her with her humming as she started the laundry as soon as the morning light filtered through the window.

"Why not? Your house is going to be empty, right? You're almost twenty, a grown woman, and there's a pretty good looking guy outside who I'm sure would be interested in a few dates, if not more."

Marianna's stomach tightened as if Rebecca's words wound up a crank. Part of her knew Rebecca was right. She had to admit she wondered if things would move quickly with Aaron. Some of her friends had started dating at eighteen and were married within a year, others even sooner. She also liked the idea of staying in the house. It was familiar. It was all she knew. It was home.

"I suppose I could talk to Dat and see what he says. Maybe I can care for the animals and gardens." Marianna moved closer to the window and got the briefest glance of Aaron before he hurried to the house with the other unmarried men—which meant church would be starting soon, and she wasn't in her seat. Heat rose to her cheeks at the thought of hurrying inside late, in full view of everyone.

"I have to go, but if I don't see you this afternoon, I'll try to stop by tomorrow."

Rebecca nodded, and she leaned her head against the white wall, empty of all decorations. She waved, but it was half-hearted. She wasn't the same as she used to be. It was as if Marianna's friend had died and someone different, distant, had taken her place. There'd been no funeral, no burial, just a numbing that happened over time.

CHAPTER EIGHT

hurch service was the same as always. The singing of
slow weis songs, without the accompaniment of instruments. Preaching and Bible reading in German, and
prayer time—lots of time down on one's knees, with heads bowed.
Time in which one could think.

And Marianna had plenty to think about.

They rose again for another song, and even though Marianna
had sung it a hundred times or more, she couldn't understand
the words. Each word was sung slowly, drawn out. Every syllable
received equal attention, until one couldn't tell where one word
ended and another began. She squirmed in her seat, her rear
growing tired of sitting on the hard wooden bench. Her mind
growing weary of trying to pay attention to the service when
there were so many other things wrestling for her attention.

After the song they sat again and the bishop stood, quiet for
a moment, scanning the crowd.

"I would like everyone to remain seated."

He shuffled his feet, shifting his weight from side to side until
his gaze fell upon a young woman one row in front of Marianna.
People around the room squirmed in their seats, uneasy. Everyone,

like her, was following the bishop's gaze, wondering what this was about.

"I've asked you to remain seated because a member of our congregation has a confession to make."

The girl, Viola, stood and walked to the front of the room, and Marianna's eyes widened. What on earth the girl done?

Whether someone confessed to a deacon, or their sin was found out and confronted, confession in front of the church was the only way to get guilt off of one's chest. Her uncle, Ike, had confessed once for stealing a lighter and cigarettes from the county store not long after he joined the church as a young man. He'd told her he was glad he'd gone before the church and confessed. He'd said it felt good to go on with a clear conscience.

"This is Viola Mast." The bishop rolled back on his heels and scanned the congregation. "She came to a deacon just this week and told him she'd been listening to records at the house of the woman she cleans for."

Viola's head was lowered, and Marianna noticed the woman's hands trembling. Knowing how things worked, Viola walked to the front door and exited. A deacon with an umbrella walked with her, and the door was closed behind them.

When Viola Mast was gone, the bishop led the men in a discussion of what her punishment should be. When it was decided, the bishop went to the door and invited them back in.

Head still lowered, Viola stood before the bishop, waiting to hear her punishment, waiting to know what she must do for her misdeed to be pardoned. The bishop spoke only loud enough for Viola to hear. When he finished, Viola nodded and turned to face the crowd. Her sleeves and hem were damp where the umbrella hadn't covered her, but she didn't seem to notice. With sincerity on her face, she knelt before the congregation.

Uneasiness filled Marianna. To have to do such a thing! She lowered her head, queasiness coming over her from the woman's forced humility. Marianna imagined herself kneeling in such a way, and prickles covered her arms as if a thousand invisible ants climbed them.

Her chest tightened as if someone had put a harness around it and pulled. The slightest headache beat along with her heartbeat in her temple. If she learned anything growing up, it was that others were watching, God was watching. And even though others in the congregation didn't know what was going on inside, God could read her thoughts.

"I confess today that I am sorry for sinning in this way, and I promise not to do it again." Following Viola's words, came the release of a deep breath.

"You are forgiven." The bishop motioned her back to her seat. As the woman returned, Marianna noticed the hint of a smile, and she knew the woman no doubt felt better not carrying her transgressions on her shoulders any more.

Seeing the woman's clear relief, Marianna couldn't help but wonder if *she* had anything to confess. She couldn't think of anything worthy of going in front of the church—not that she'd have to confess if she did think of something. She was still in her *rumspringa* and had yet to join the church. Only official members who'd been baptized into the congregation had to go through such steps. Of course, she would be an official member soon. Her plan was to start meeting with the deacons, to prepare for joining this fall with the rest of the like-minded young people.

Yet at this point she didn't even know if she'd be here in Indiana, and the last thing she wanted was to go through such an important event in a different place, far from everything she knew. Which meant she'd have to wait another year. Her life would be put on hold for her father's desire for adventure. Marianna clenched the palm of her bandaged hand, and her nails dug into the cloth. And as the others began to rise around her, she wondered if having angry thoughts for one's father and brother was a sin according to the Ordnung? Those were becoming a regular occurrence.

After the church service came time for lunch. Marianna helped in the kitchen as the men added legs to the sitting benches, transforming them into narrow tables that ran the length of the room in rows. Once the tables were up, she joined the other women in draping long tablecloths over them. Then she worked at setting out lunch: peanut butter, jam, sweet pickles, and pickled beets. It was the same every week. Next came the large loaves of bread. She took three loaves at a time and set slices along the tables for the men who sat and ate.

"How are you doing today?"

The voice came from behind her, and Marianna's heart felt warm and full, as if it had doubled in her chest. She knew Aaron's voice without turning.

She rearranged the bread on the plate, almost afraid to look at him. Finally Marianna took a deep breath and glanced over her shoulder. Aaron was taking the seat beside where she stood, sitting down next to his younger brother who was just a toddler.

"I'm fine, and you?"

"Good, good. Just helping my brother get some lunch. Your mother said you made some of those pies."

She turned her body toward him and met his gaze.

"Yes, the apple ones. I can cut you a piece if you'd like."

Aaron looked up at her from where he sat. His eyes were light. Almost as light as the sky after a rainstorm, and they sparkled as if they were filled with a thousand raindrops. His hair was the color of golden wheat and had a halo around it from where his hat had sat. He looked part boy and part man. Mostly man.

"I would love a piece, Marianna. *Denke.*"

Her heartbeat quickened and even though the words were simple she sensed emotion behind them.

She left the bread on the table and hurried to the kitchen. And even though they didn't serve pie until after everyone had finished their sandwiches, none of the women said a word as she cut a large slice of apple pie, slid it onto a plate, and then took it to Aaron, setting it before him.

"*Denke.* It looks delicious." His hand brushed against hers as he reached for the plate, and tingles raced up her arm.

Marianna looked away, noticing the women in the kitchen were still watching, and she felt as if her soul was bare before them. It wasn't a comfortable feeling.

She walked away without saying another word, and then felt bad for doing so. She should have asked Aaron about his work. Or if he still planned on attending the youth singing tonight. Instead, she returned to the loaves of bread and continued to place them out on the tables. As she moved, she had a feeling that a hundred eyes watched her. She didn't care about all the other eyes. She just hoped Aaron liked what he saw.

The ride home from church in the buggy was solemn. The rain had stopped and the sun had come out, but it did nothing for her parents' mood.

Marianna tried not to let their sour faces bother her. She thought instead of Aaron Zook and wondered what it would be like to be his wife. She didn't seem ready, not really, then again many girls married at her age.

"Did you hear Ollie Smucker yet? What he had to say about our talk of a move to Montana?" Mem straightened the bonnet on her head as if even thinking about his words was pushing her out of shape. "He says if we move it's because we want to lead a more liberal lifestyle. Without an ordained minister in the area, they are certain we're going to move into a house with electricity, get our own car, and maybe even a television." Mem spat the last word and turned to look out the side of the buggy, staring off into the fields sprouting with new life. Marianna again wondered if Mem were thinking of her oldest son and all he was experiencing.

"*Ja*, but not everyone was so negative. I noticed from the interested expressions in more than one man's eyes that they wished they could go themselves." Dat leaned back in the seat, his fingers loosely holding the reins.

"Well, all their unvoiced thoughts can't make up for your mother's response." Mem's jaw tightened. "She says we are tempting Marianna to run off and live *Englisch* ways by forcing her to leave behind her home and her beau. She didn't listen as I insisted our daughter is not getting married tomorrow. It's not like we're canceling her baptism and wedding."

Marianna's shoulders tightened as she listened to them.

While her brothers played rock, paper, scissors beside her, Marianna adjusted her little sister in her arms. She snuggled Ellie close to her, breathing in the scent of her freshly washed hair. What would it be like to hold her own child some day? It was a nice thought. Maybe she should mention to her mother what she'd been thinking about during church. The idea, that, in fact, had grown on her.

"Actually, I have a plan for that . . . for the move." Marianna leaned forward from the back seat, leaning toward her mother and father. "Rebecca suggested I stay here and take care of the house. I can keep the garden, care for all the fruit trees and vegetables. The animals, too."

"Rebecca's the last one you need to be seeking advice from."

Marianna knew from the tone of her mother's voice that inputting more of Rebecca's advice would take the conversation in the wrong direction.

Marianna straightened her shoulders, readjusting Ellie on her lap. "What I meant to say was that I'm considering staying home, caring for the farm, spending time in the community before my baptism."

Her father reached back over his shoulder, and patted Marianna's hand that was resting on the seat back. "Daughter, while we can't make you go with us, we wish you would consider coming. It seems there are too many influential people in this community who can sway your heart, Levi and Rebecca being two. But more than that, I was just talking with that Moser lad this afternoon. William's looking to take up a bride in a few months—Martha Sutter from next county over. I told them they could live in our house for the first year of marriage. You can stay in the area, but I'm afraid our home will be unavailable."

Marianna felt her mouth drop open, and she tugged on her hand, pulling it out of her father's grip.

"You can live with Levi," David commented. Marianna hadn't realized her twelve-year-old brother also had been listening. David's eyes were bluish gray—the same color as the cloud-filled sky above the buggy. Though David would start his eighth grade year in the fall, which would mean the end of his schooling, he was small in size and it made it easy to lump him with the younger kids.

"Levi?" Marianna looked at David. "Why would I want to do that? He lives with Englisch friends."

"*Ja*, but he said they have a television and a car and they can go to bed and sleep anytime they want. Levi said I can move in with him as soon as I'm sixteen. He's going to show me the ropes." David jutted out his chin, and for the first time Marianna noticed how much his personality reminded her of Levi.

And, as she looked to the front of the buggy, she wasn't surprised to see her mother's fingers pressed to her lips, trying to hold in the emotions that her brother's wanderings and careless words stirred. Marianna also noticed her father's fixed jaw and the click of the reins that forced the horse to pick up speed. Her father's mind was set. He was determined. This—no doubt—was the very thing they were trying to avoid.

They'd be moving to Montana. She was sure of it. All of them.

"Can I speak with you for a moment, Marianna?" It was her dat's voice following her, carrying on the damp air. She turned and paused her steps. He stood by the buggy and watched as the others moved toward the house.

"Of course." She looked down at her sister, who was asleep in her arms, and then looked up at him.

He approached her, and his face looked tired. He looked sad too, as if regretting the words he had to say. "I know this isn't how you planned your life. I know you have dreams of your own." He lifted his hand and touched Ellie's hand that was curled against her neck. He let out a low sigh. "I wouldn't ask you if I didn't think I had to do this—for my family. Your brother David, he sees Levi and wants to follow. I'm worried for him. I know it's a few years yet, but those thoughts settle in one's mind and grow like weeds, choking out the good lessons he ought to be learning. And then there's the job. Trying to tend to the farm and work in town is hard. I don't have enough time with the boys. Can't help your mem."

"I'm doing the best I can. Maybe I should tell Mrs. Ropp that I can't help at her place anymore." Even as Marianna spoke the words, a twinge of sadness pinged against her heart. She counted on that job to get extra money to pay for fabric for her quilts.

"That's not enough, I'm afraid. Your mother, well, I thought she would have told you by now, but she's with child."

Marianna thought back to the numerous signs, her mother's paleness. The way she was just holding her stomach today, as if she thought she was going to be ill.

"But that's a reason to stay. She shouldn't travel—shouldn't have to try to set up a home if she's with child."

"The midwife thinks differently. Thinks it will help your mother to get away. There is a good midwife in Montana she knows and recommends. She believes your mother needs to get fresh mountain air and—"

"And not be around Levi."

"It breaks her heart." He lowered his head. "And now to hear David . . ."

She wanted to argue. She wanted to pout, but the look on her father's face was one of pure love. He had no selfish motives. It no doubt was hard leaving his farm—the place he took pride in for so many years.

"And after the baby?" She lifted her eyebrows.

"Then you can return. If six months comes and you're still not settled, I'll pay for your ticket. Aunt Ada already volunteered her room—for you to stay with her." He lowered his head and she could see how hard it was to ask this of her.

Ellie stirred in Marianna's arms, and a horse tugged on her lead and whinnied, as if wondering what they were doing standing there, instead of taking her to the warm barn and her feed. The bark of the neighbor's dog could be heard from down near the creek and the songs of birds in a distant tree.

Marianna looked away from his face to the land around them. Sometimes she liked to walk through her father's fields and imagine what it would have been like when her great-grandfather had first settled the land. When two thin lines of wagon trails had led him to this place. She heard from the lady at the grocery store that from the sky the fields looked like a quilt. She thought of that every time she worked on her own hand stitching. They were one small quilt square sewn together amongst so many others. It gave her comfort knowing that they were part of a larger pattern. That they were stitched to others. That there was a good design that God somehow knew.

She closed her eyes and imagined her seam ripper, unfastening the threads and yanking them out. She looked to her father's gaze and again realized he knew what he was asking. And for him to ask meant he was desperate for her help. Needed her support to make it.

"*Ja*. I'll do that. I'll go for a time. I'll help." She meant it. She'd move. Help her mother. And return. She focused on his eyes and nodded, making sure he understood she *would* return.

He looked away, staring into the fields he'd planted but wouldn't see harvested. "Six months then for you. Tomorrow we pack our things."

CHAPTER NINE

Twenty of Marianna's friends had gathered for the youth sing at the Zook's house, but Marianna was only interested in one. For the last hour they'd been sitting around a small fire, boys on one side and girls on the other. They sang the same type of hymns they did at church. The same songs that their parents had sung as youth, their grandparents too, and before them many generations of Amish. Marianna thought little about the words lifting from her lips. She repeated as mindless as a young child reciting his ABCs. Her mind was on Aaron, and she hoped he was thinking of her. Would he keep caring after she was gone?

The odor of burning wood and smoke mixed with the fresh scents of spring. In the distance the setting of the sun turned the sky a soft pink. She hadn't realized how beautiful it was.

A few times during the gathering, her eyes had met Aaron's across the campfire, but most of the time she kept her eyes focused on the blades of green grass under her feet, her shoes, even her hands on her lap. Other guys and girls were more obvious with their flirtations—mostly those who'd already begun dating.

After an hour passed, Mrs. Zook exited the house with a platter of sandwiches, placing them on the picnic table. The singing stopped, and excited conversation and laughter filled the air. Marianna rose and followed the others, noting how awkward it was without Rebecca or Naomi. She was friends with the other girls, but she'd always been closest to those two. She patted the back of her kapp, making sure every hair was in place and then stood to the side of the table, not hungry.

Her nerves were balled up, like pea pods under her skin from being this close to Aaron for the last hour. Add that to the fact this was her last youth sing for many months. It was strange to know that all her friends would still be here, gathering to sing and in the summer to play games and visit by the river, but she wouldn't be with them. Would they miss her? Would they even notice?

A hand touched her arm. A small bolt of lightning jolted up her arm and zipped her heart, but when she glanced over it was Mrs. Zook, not Aaron, who stood there.

"Aren't you hungry? I've made plenty. Don't want you returning home telling your mother I didn't feed ya."

"Oh no, I'd never say that, ma'am. Just waiting till everyone got theirs first." She stepped forward and took a bread and cheese sandwich from the stack and then stepped back to Mrs. Zook's side. She smiled and then took a big bite, forcing herself to chew and swallow.

"So, I hear you're going to be moving soon?" The older woman with graying hair tried to make her tone light, but Marianna noted concern in her gaze.

"Yes, my father wants us to go west for a year. Montana."

"Oh, I see." The woman cocked one eyebrow, and Marianna could read from her face what she was thinking. It wasn't an

I-am-worried-about-my-son's-care-for-you type of look. Instead her eyes said *I-am-worried-you're-leaving-so-you-can-do-as-you-wish-without-the-church-knowing* type of look.

A cry sounded from the house. Mrs. Zook looked over her shoulder to see one of her children standing in the doorway, holding a hand to her head, chin tilted up, crying.

"Will you excuse me? That's Hilly, she could fall and get hurt in a room full of goose feathers. We'll have to talk again, dear, before you leave."

"*Ja*, of course."

She hadn't gotten five steps away when Aaron approached, taking his mother's place.

Aaron crossed his arms over his chest, shifting his weight from side to side. "Can we talk?"

Marianna glanced up at him, but the pleasant look he had during the sing was gone.

"Sure."

They walked to the side of the barn, still in view of the others who were finishing their sandwiches and once again gathering around the fire. Marianna leaned her back against the wall. Her knees were soft and she used the support of the barn to hold her up.

"You're leaving? Did I hear my mother right, Marianna? I thought it was just a rumor." He removed his hat, turning it in his hands. A ring was left on his blond hair where his hat had sat, and she even found that appealing.

"Yes, Dat has made the plans. I . . . it wasn't my idea."

"But the cabin. I've been working on it for six months."

"You speak of a cabin, but you've yet to even ask me out for one drive, Aaron Zook."

"Nonsense." He ran his fingers through his hair, focusing his eyes on hers. "You've always known how I've felt about you. There hasn't been another girl I've paid attention to since the last year of school when we used to walk home on the same path."

"We were just children. That was four years ago. How was I to know?" Even as she said the words, Marianna felt heat rising to her neck. Aaron was right, she'd always known.

"Do you think I walked one mile out of my way if I didn't care?" He pointed toward the woods behind their house, toward a house she knew he was building back there. "Do you think I'd invest everything I have in a house . . . a home?"

Another song started and the others around the fire sung with gusto. Marianna felt a stirring in her gut. They shouldn't be gone too long. It wouldn't look right.

"Aaron, listen, even if I have known, there's nothing I can do about it. But my father and I have made a deal. He talked to me after church. If I don't like it after six months, I can return and live with my aunt."

"That old maid who always has her nose in everyone's business?" He slapped his hat against his leg. "I won't be able to come around without everyone from Ontario to Kentucky knowing about it. She'll write up all our comings and goings in that *Budget* column she prides herself in."

"It's better than me being a thousand miles away, isn't it?"

Aaron scrunched his face, as if he wasn't quite sure about that, and Marianna punched his shoulder with a soft fist. It was the first time she touched him—well, at least in the last ten years, and not counting that time she'd joined the softball game and he'd tagged her arm with his mitt as she approached third base. Marianna felt warmth spread through her.

"But Mari—" He focused his eyes on hers. She could read questions there. Fears. "What if you find another guy? Maybe there's someone out West who's already ready for a wife?"

Laughter burst from Marianna's lips. "You can't be serious. They're all mountain men from what I hear, and that's not interesting to me at all."

Aaron lifted one eyebrow, as if unsure he believed her. Then returned his hat to his head. "*Ja*, well, it would make me feel better if I could see you at Christmas. I can come to Montana. I suppose I'll be busy building our—my place until then."

He looked to the fire, where the others were gathered, and then back to her again. The pain in his eyes was clear. "I'm worried about you, out in the Englisch world. There are people that will take advantage of your kindness. Men who will see your beauty."

Her stomach flipped as he said his last word, and she pressed her hands down her apron, as if trying to smooth an invisible wrinkle. "You're talking nonsense. We're going to another community. I'm sure it will be very much like here, only smaller. All Amish live the same types of lives. I bet there will be no real difference at all."

"Not from the way your uncle was talking. The people there don't pay as much attention to the *Ordnung*. I heard their women are allowed to work in woodshops along with the men, not just as school teachers and store keepers. My mom said she heard women were allowed to take communion even if their cape is sewn instead of pinned. And . . ."

"And what?" Marianna shook her head, Aaron should know better. She'd never sew her cape.

"And they hire drivers every week to take them to town. That seems like a lot of interaction with the Englisch if you ask me.

They let Englisch worship with them, too. Ike said some even attend Englisch prayer meetings. I told my father and . . ." Aaron paused and looked at her. Then he lifted his hand and stroked her cheek.

His hand was warm and strong from work. He took a step near her and a million needles pierced her skin, moving from her neck down through her arms. She felt the rising and fall of her chest, and she told herself to breathe. Aaron's breath was warm on her forehead and she knew if he dipped his head just a bit more their lips would touch. The tip of her tongue licked her lips and her knees quivered. He ran his hand from her temple, down her cheek, stopping just at the corner of her lips. A burst of laughter carried from the other young folks who were still at the fire but they no longer concerned her. Nothing concerned her beyond Aaron's touch. She'd never felt more joy, like hot flames in her chest, than to see the way he looked at her. Then, just when she was sure he would kiss her, Aaron took a step back.

"My father said he's worried about you. About your reputation."

The emotion that had been building in her throat tightened into a knot. She cleared it away, her forehead folding, her eyebrows lowering. "Excuse me?"

"Who knows what type of community is there. What if they are wild? What are you going to do, Mari, stand up to all of them?"

Anger replaced the joy of a moment before, heating her. She balled her fists, feeling her nails dig into the almost healed cut on her palm. "Your father said that, did he? And how did you respond? Did you agree with him, Aaron?"

Aaron looked away, gazing up at the dimming sky as if it held the right words there. But Marianna didn't know if there were any right words. She turned her back to him, crossing her arms in front of her, pulling them tight. Then she stepped away a half-dozen steps. Away from the singing, the fire. Away from him.

"I know how things work, Aaron. I was six years old when I realized that eyes were on me every moment. It was my first week of school and I felt so independent. It was just Levi and me walking to the schoolhouse, and I ran and shouted down the lane, just because I could. Just because my mother wasn't around to tell me to act like a little lady.

"One day that first week, I was trying to knock a birdhouse out of a tree when one of the rocks cracked a window on an Englisch house down the road. By the time I reached home my mother knew. My father's discipline was firm. I—" Tears pooled in her eyes and the fields that stretched beyond the barn blurred. She felt his presence behind her, nearing, but she didn't turn. She couldn't turn. She was sure if she looked in his face she wouldn't be brave enough to say the words she needed to.

"My whole life, our whole lives, everything we do, say, wear is under the scrutiny of others. We must be sure we are proper and kind. We dress like the others and work together. But just because you can't see me, does that mean that I won't obey? My parents are there, Aaron. God can see me, too. Unless you believe they are incapable of their job. God is incapable."

"It wasn't me, it was my father. You know how he is."

"He's an elder. His job is to help watch over the flock, yes, I know. It's not like I'm becoming Englisch. It's just a new place, an adventure."

Even as she said the words, Marianna wondered where they came from. She hadn't liked the idea of moving until Aaron said that his father—and no doubt others in the community—worried they would stray. Worried about their eternal souls. Well, he hadn't said that last part. No one had said that, but it is what they meant. And Marianna understood. She'd thought the same about others when they'd decided to move out of the community. *I wonder what they're running from? I wonder what they want to hide?*

She turned to him, ashamed of herself—of her past judgments—just as much as she was angry with him. She would have the same questions and concerns if the roles were reversed.

"So maybe it would be best if you rode home tonight with the Lapps. They're heading right by your house." There was more to his words than he was saying. By taking back his offer for a ride, he was also pulling back the reins on the idea that their friendship would grow into something more in the near future.

Marianna felt tears rim her lower rids, and for the briefest moment reconsidered the conversation she had with her father. Maybe she could stay with her aunt now. Maybe . . .

But she could see from the firm set in Aaron's jaw, his mind was made up. Even if she stayed, there was a rift between them that would take a while to mend. And she was sure his father would have his own opinion of his son's involvement with a girl from a family whose crazy uncle was leading them astray.

"*Ja*, fine. I'll ask the Lapps." She cupped her hands together and then blew into them, for the first time realizing how cold she was. How tired. "I think I'll return to the fire."

"Can I sit by you?" Aaron's voice held a hint of apology.

She shrugged. "If you'd like. If you think your father would approve." She said the last words with a tone sharper than she meant and from the corner of her eye recognized a pained look on Aaron's face. Marianna opened her mouth to apologize, but before she could he turned and headed toward the fire.

She cleared her throat again, lowered her hand, and pressed her fingers to her eyes, telling herself not to cry. A new burden settled on her chest, adding to the bricks of worry that were already there. She was angry at her parents for making her leave, and now the anger had seeped out, contaminating her relationship with the one person she wanted to stay most for.

If she could just talk to Levi. On many nights when they couldn't sleep, she and her older brother would slip out of the house, finding themselves in front of the raspberry bush, eating the ripe fruit under the light of the moon as they talked about their friends, their future, their parents. It was during those nights her brother had told her about a time when their home had been filled with laughter and fun. Even though he was just three at the time of their sisters' deaths, he could remember Marilyn and Joanna. He could also remember the night of their deaths, the same night Marianna was born.

She'd always wondered if her birth had ever eased the pain of her sisters' deaths. One daughter to replace two. She could never replace them, of course. But that didn't mean she didn't long for a home filled with laughter and joy like Levi spoke about with fondness. Of course, that was the old Levi. He'd changed. He no longer cared for home and family as he used to.

One by one those she'd been closest to were being led away. Why? What was so wrong with staying? With belonging?

She rubbed her arms, and with slow steps headed back toward the fire, realizing that maybe it was better to go to Montana after all. Maybe this would be the very thing to bring back the joy in her family that Levi had told her about. It was worth a try. Her parents deserved to feel happy, settled. And when she returned to Indiana, she'd do so knowing she'd honored her family. Then she could start again with Aaron and, hopefully, he would have forgotten her harsh words.

Dear June-Sevenies,

Next time you receive a letter from me, it will be from the new address I've enclosed. My family is moving to Montana, and I have no choice but to go. For as long as we've been doing this chain letter, I figured that change was to come sometime. Clara was the first to get engaged. Wynne was the first to travel to a foreign country—even if it was Canada. I suppose I'm the first to move far way. I'll try to write from the train, although it may not be legible. It's a mighty long ride. I'm not sure what to expect in Montana. Dat says there is a dozen families, and I picture twelve little shacks clinging to the side of a mountain, sort of like in the book Heidi. *I suppose I'll soon find out.*

You may wonder what's going to happen with Aaron. I wonder that too. Last night I dreamt I was in Montana and Dat told me I could return to Indiana. I left the house on the way to the train station, and I somehow got lost in the woods. I was wandering around in the dark trees. It was a very scary dream! Then, in the distance I could see water—like a pond—down the hill, and someone calling to me. I woke up thinking of Aaron, wondering if he'd come for me in Montana and then chiding myself for that notion.

Rachel, that's exciting about your cousins visiting from Pennsylvania, although I'm not sure how your house could hold so many people. And, Beverly, to answer your question I'm still working on my quilt. I have the panels sewn together, but I have a lot of hand stitching work to do. I'm taking the quilt with me. Hand-stitching takes forever when I'm up and down with the kids. Still, I'm determined to finish it by the time I return to Indiana in six months.

Have to go. I hear Ellie and Josiah rustling about. I imagine they'll need some breakfast and then need help packing. Much to do today.

With care,
Marianna

CHAPTER TEN

She was a stranger in her own bedroom.

The bed was made with an old sheet set. The closet was empty, her clothes and bedding now in one of two boxes. Her books had been boxed up and were stacked on top of the cedar chest her grandmother had given her the year she turned fifteen. Inside the chest her grandmother had included a set of kitchen towels and a cookbook of recipes. Marianna had added to that over the years—sheets, towels, dishes—things she'd need for her own house some day. All of it would remain except the cookbook. She'd packed that with her clothes. Maybe her mother was right. Maybe she did need to spend more time in the kitchen, honing her skills in preparation for caring for a home. Or rather, a husband.

She placed her hands on her hips and turned, scanning the room, checking to see if there was anything she'd missed. Not that she had more room for anything else. They were allowed two boxes each, and one of hers was taken up with her half-finished quilt. She assumed she'd have plenty of time to work on it seeing as she wouldn't know anyone. That would mean no social gatherings to attend. She pictured many lonely nights sitting and sewing under the light of Dat's lantern.

The sound of sniffling carried from her open door and Marianna turned to find five-year-old Josiah with red, puffy eyes and a dripping nose. He wore a hand-me-down nightshirt that hid his arms in his sleeves. His dark hair stuck up in the back and his bare toes peeked out from under the hem of the long shirt.

"What's the matter with you? Are the bed bugs biting?" Though she joked with him, she opened her arms and allowed him to scamper into her embrace.

"Mem says we can't bring Fred." He pushed up his sleeve and wiped his runny nose with the back of his hand.

Marianna led him to the water basin on her side table.

"Well, no, that would be too confusing. He's an Indiana rooster. I've heard there are big mountains in Montana. The sunlight comes over them, but the sun doesn't peek over till hours later. Do you know how confusing that would be?"

Josiah allowed her to wash and dry his hands, and then she led him back to the doorway. "Now, scamper back to bed because Fred still has a few mornings left to wake you, and I can imagine he's going to do a good job tomorrow. Bright and early."

Josiah nodded, but just as he turned what sounded like hail hitting her window filled the air. Marianna's heart leapt, and she turned in time to see a bit of gravel fly through the open window, hit the floor, and skitter under her bed.

Josiah rushed back into her room, eyes wide. "What's that?"

Marianna knew what it was, but *who* was beckoning from below? Maybe Aaron coming to talk. To apologize for not giving her a ride. Or maybe Rebecca—not in her right mind. Or . . .

She looked to Josiah again. "Oh, it's just some bugs wanting in. They must see the light. Now hurry to bed." With his eyes still filled with sadness, he did as he was told, and Marianna shut the door and then scurried to the window. It was dark out. A narrow wedge of moon hung in the sky, and she could make out a man's form. He wasn't wearing the typical Amish hat and clothes, which gave him away.

Levi stood in the yard near the cottonwood tree. Close enough for her to make him out, but far enough that he couldn't be seen from the house unless someone knew where to look. She waved to him and then tightened the belt on her bathrobe. She turned off her bedroom light and made her way downstairs with slow, soft steps. With bare feet, she exited the door and crossed the cold porch and then hurried over the moist grass toward the tree.

"What are you doing? You scared me. Josiah was in the room, and he heard the noise of the gravel hitting the window."

She had to look up to him. Her brother was tall, like her father, and the top of her head barely reached his shoulders. But the look on his face reminded her of Josiah just a few minutes before—tired, scared, afraid—even though he tried to hide all three.

Levi shrugged. "I had to talk to you." He didn't say anything about Josiah, but peered over her shoulder to the house as if watching for an unwanted visitor.

"So you're moving? All of you?" He kicked his white tennis shoe against a clump of dirt. His shoe laces were undone and the hems of his pants were ragged and torn near the heels. Even though it wasn't the first time, it seemed strange to see him in non-Amish clothes. Marianna thought about all the things she'd wanted to tell him. All the harsh words she'd poured out in her journal, but seeing him here . . . sadness replaced anger.

Marianna nodded. "Yes. To Montana."

He pushed up the sleeves on a gray sweatshirt that looked two sizes too big and then sank his hands into jean pockets. Even stranger was his haircut. Buzzed short on the sides and spiked up on top.

"That seems like something Dat would do, leaving, but I'm surprised Mem is going. I'm surprised you're going."

"It's hard, Mem being here." Marianna moved her gaze in the direction of the two trees, planted in memory of her sisters. She didn't mention that his life choices were just as hard as their deaths had been. She didn't have to. She could see in his gaze he understood.

"It's wrong, you know. The decisions you are making talking Naomi into—"

"I didn't talk her into anything," he growled, "and you can save that conversation till it happens."

"What did you expect me to say? You came here after all." She touched her head, adjusting her thick, starched sleeping kerchief, holding in a yawn, and also pushing down her annoyance that he'd come to her like this. That he'd make her defend a move she didn't believe in.

He shrugged. "Guess I expected to hear as much, considering yer feelings for Aaron, still I wanted to tell you I'm surprised you're leaving, that's all."

"We wouldn't have to go, you know, if things changed."

"You mean if Aaron Zook proposed tomorrow?"

She blinked. "No, I'm afraid that wouldn't stop them. There are other things our parents are running from. Heartbreaks."

"You might as well say it. They're leaving because of me."

"Mostly." She reached for his arm, but then pulled back when she realized touching him was like touching a stranger. It wasn't Levi . . . more like a shadow of him. Even in the moonlight his gaze seemed empty. His voice flat.

"I'm not coming back into the community. Don't you see? I didn't come this far just to return."

"This *far*? You make it sound like a good thing. Like you've accomplished a lot. What do you mean by that?" Her toes curled on the grass.

"Do you know how hard it's been? How hard I've worked? I have an eighth grade education. I've been building houses making half as much as the other guys. And I'm lucky to have the job."

"So why don't you just return? You can work on the farm while Dat is at the mill—"

"Return? Return to what? I've never fit in, Marianna."

"How can you say that?" She shook her head.

"I've always done a good job playing the part, but I never felt like I was supposed to be Amish. It just didn't seem right."

"So leaving feels right?" She rubbed her forehead, realizing how tired she was. Wondering why she was even bothering to talk with him. It was obvious his mind was set. "I've never understood why you left. I thought at first it was just *rumspringa*—"

"No, that's not it. I've known since I was twelve that I was going to leave." He rubbed the back of his neck and sighed.

"What do you mean?" David was twelve, and her father's fears for him doubled in her own mind.

"Do you remember? Maybe you don't—you were only nine, but there was a neighbor down the road. And he decided to go on his way. He left the Amish, but he didn't leave and just get a job. No, he stayed around and got into trouble. He caught a few Amish barns on fire. He ended up in jail. His name was Henry."

She rubbed her chin. "I don't remember, but I've heard something about the barn fires before. So what does this have to do with you?"

"It was during that time—just a few weeks after they caught him and jailed him—when I was supposed to be tending to some sheep out in the pasture. Instead, I went fishing with a friend. We caught a few, but then got hot and decided to jump in. That's when Dat found me."

Marianna covered her mouth with her hand, imagining her father's anger. She eyed Levi, wondering still what this had to do with his leaving. A whipping couldn't have done that. "I bet he got a big switch from the willow tree for that."

"No. It was worse."

She spoke in a loud whisper. "What could be worse than meeting him out by the woodshed?"

Levi was silent.

"What? You have to tell me now." Overhead in the tree an owl hooted and the sounds of frogs croaking came from the creek as if urging him on too.

Levi shrugged. "He just looked at me. You know that look. I was standing there dripping wet, and he asked if I wanted to change my name to Henry. Then he stalked off."

"Levi, that's horrible. He compared you with him? With that?"

He shrugged. "I felt like my fate was sealed. I thought from that moment this is the way things were going to turn out. That I would leave and cause trouble in my leaving."

"But they don't have to turn out this way. You're making a choice here. Those words long ago—Dat didn't mean them. I'm sure he doesn't remember."

Levi didn't argue, but she could tell he wasn't giving her words any mind either. She followed his gaze up to the sky, taking in the view of the stars and wondering if he too was remembering when they were little kids and lay out on nights like this and made their own dot-to-dot pictures with the pins of light.

"Maybe I should have died that night too." He leaned against the trunk of the tree as if no longer able to hold up his weight. "Then they wouldn't have to leave."

"Are you talking about the accident?" Even as she said the words she knew he was. She stared at him and shook her head. "It would kill Mem to hear you talk like that."

"Yes, well, consider what the Amish believe. I've attended many a child's funeral. They believe death saves them from the world of sin. Maybe I could have been saved."

"Levi, you need to get some sleep and not go on like this. Does it have to be this way? Can't you just come back? Is our life so horrible?"

He stood there for a while, silent. Finally he shrugged. "Dat's running from it, too. Just in a different way."

She wanted to tell him it wasn't this life, this place, their father was running from; it was loss. And it was fear of more loss—of the other children following—that quickened his steps, but she didn't. Levi knew that, just as she knew.

"I'll write you." She didn't know what else to say. "And I'll tell you about what it's like to live in the mountains with the bears."

He nodded and fixed his eyes on hers, but it wasn't the defiant Levi who was looking at her. It was eight-year-old Levi who got scared of a thunderstorm and came to her room even though he was the older brother.

"And who knows. Maybe Naomi and I will come for a visit. I've always wanted to go to a western rodeo."

Marianna nodded, but both of them knew that wouldn't happen. They were all running, and he was going the opposite direction. Away from family. Away from the way of life he knew. He was caught up in a wandering that had straddled him between two worlds, leaving him hanging in a void and uncertain about what to do about it.

And more and more . . . Marianna knew exactly how he felt.

Chapter Eleven

en women sat around Marianna's living room, like they did every last Thursday of the month. Today there were no quilts stretched onto frames. There was no lively chatter fluttering between them as their fingers worked. There were no colorful strips of fabric spread on their laps, spilling onto the floor. Marianna didn't like that she wouldn't see the finished quilts she'd been watching progress. Just as they wouldn't see hers. She knew that once they left, life would go on around here, people would congregate, laugh, cry together at times—all without her. Quilts would be finished and spread onto beds, their beauty transformed into comfortable warmth.

"Whatever you do, don't let the children leave the train, even to stretch their legs during a stop," Eleanor Ropp said, refolding Josiah's and Ellie's clothes that filled a box, as if not knowing what else to do with her hands. "My cousin's son did that and they didn't realize the boy was gone until they reached Detroit. Thankfully another Amish family had gotten off at that stop and had taken care of him until his parents returned the next day, or who knows *what* would have happened."

"Marianna is always good with the kids." Mem took a sip of her lemonade, wiping the drops of water that beaded on the side with her thumb. Weariness wrinkled her face, and though her lips were tipped up in a tight smile, Marianna knew Mem wished for a nap, and longed for a few moments of peace to process the fact she'd be leaving her home.

"Abe will be there, too," Mem continued. "Without our farm to tend or his job to head off to, I'm sure the boys will stick to their dat's side, not believin' they have him all to themselves."

The looks on the women's faces were somber, and Marianna knew her family's absence would be felt. Her parents had lived in this house since before she was born, and her grandparents owned it before that. She couldn't imagine someone else living here. Another woman cooking at the stove. Another man sitting in the large chair by the woodstove like her father always did on Saturday nights as he read the Amish paper—*The Budget*—cover to cover. Tears rimmed her eyes, and she didn't care to wipe them away. She thought again about staying in Indiana, but it would be impossible. She'd have to get a job and still she'd be living in someone else's home. Then there was the new baby to think about.

Her mother wouldn't say anything until her pregnancy was obvious—it was always the case. Even though she had no problem carrying children—unlike others in the community—it took her mother time to grow excited. Perhaps losing Marilyn and Joanna had something to do with that.

Marianna had only talked to her father once about her sisters, but he'd confessed how much her mother had loved them. How much time she'd spent with them, caring for them. She'd been full of joy and laughter, he said. Marianna loved her mother, but ever since that conversation she'd been a little hurt too. Didn't

Mem love the others as much? Her mother wasn't hurtful or mean. She was always kind and caring, but Marianna was jealous of what her sisters' experienced—what she'd never had.

Maybe Montana would help. A new life, a new baby. Marianna dared to hope she'd get a glimpse of her mom happy and content. Maybe someday she'd witness her mother's unhindered laughter and broad smile. Things everyone spoke of, but she'd never seen.

"Do you want to pack the food—the canning—in your cupboard and take it with you?" Mrs. Ropp asked her mother.

"No." She sighed. "There isn't room. Leave some for Williams and you can take the rest I suppose."

"Are you sure? You'll need food there."

"Yes, I very well know we'll need food, but I need clothes and bedding for my children even more. And I need my sewing machine to make more. Besides . . ." She gave a tired smile. "My husband talks as if it's the Promised Land. Maybe the food will grow and can itself."

Forced laughter spilled from the women's lips, but no joke could lighten Marianna's heart. She turned back to her boxes, taped them up and hoisted one, carrying it to the porch. As she attempted to look over the top of it to find the porch stairs, she heard the sound of footsteps hurrying toward her. And then arms wrapped around the box, taking the load, lifting it.

"I'll get that for you." It was Aaron's voice. "Any place special you'd like me to put this?"

"Just inside the barn door. There's supposed to be a truck coming tomorrow to load it all up."

"Is there room, do you think, for one more person to ride with your family to the train station?" He placed the box on the porch and turned to her.

"You?"

Aaron nodded. "If you don't mind."

She smiled. It was the first smile she'd allowed herself in days. "I don't mind at all. *Denke*."

He smiled at her thanks. "I was hoping for a chance to talk to you before you left." Aaron ran a hand down his face. "I suppose this is as good a time as any." He glanced in the window, and she followed his gaze. The women still worked inside, cleaning things that didn't need to be cleaned. Repacking items that were fine as they were.

Mrs. Ropp looked to the window, catching Marianna's eye, and then looked away. Another woman did the same. Not being shy at all, her Aunt Ida walked to the front side of the house where they stood and began to wash the interior of the windows with ammonia and ripped pages from an old *Budget* newspaper. While Marianna didn't enjoy the prying eyes, she knew that if she and Aaron went somewhere where they couldn't be seen, it would be inappropriate and lead to all types of questions. She straightened her shoulders and focused on Aaron.

"What do you want to talk about?"

He cleared his throat. "I wanted to ask you something."

"What is it, then?"

"That you wouldn't go. I talked to my mom and maybe it wouldn't be so bad for you to stay with your aunt—I mean, if it meant you could stay." His eyes were wide, and he looked younger than his twenty years.

"I can't. There are important things for me to do. I need to help my mom, but maybe after—" Marianna stopped midsentence. She was going to say after the baby was born and her mother was settled, but that was her mother's news to share.

"I'm working on the house. And I was thinkin' maybe you'd want to come see it. Maybe that'll change your mind. I could take you later . . ."

"Tonight?" She glanced over to the sun that was halfway down the horizon. "But by the time we get there, it would be supper. I don't think so."

He went on as if not hearing her refusal. "It has a large kitchen and two bedrooms. The larger room is connected to the bathroom. And the view of the sunset . . ." He shrugged. "It's something to see."

She turned her attention from their audience in the window back to him, noticing how his cheeks were reddening. He was imagining them living together. Did he think about those things just as she did?

She bit her lip and tried to picture the place he was describing. The day brightened around them, and she smiled. To think he'd done that for her.

Marianna felt her neck grow warm. She tried to imagine the front porch. Wondered about the view from the kitchen window. Was there a nearby tree for shade? A garden spot?

She studied his face. How could someone care so much about her that he'd do such a thing? She had never felt so loved. Aaron's eyes held hers and she could tell his arms wanted to hold her, too.

But then she looked away. Lowered her gaze. To see the house would make her want to stay. And if she lost him, then she'd always think about what she could have had. It had to be better, not knowing. Not regretting. Pain tightened her gut. She had to say *nay*.

The joy that had flooded her a moment before crashed and shattered into a million pieces like a glass vase hitting the floor. Reality told her to sweep up the pieces and move on.

"I would love to see it, but I don't think I'll have time today. We're leaving in the morning before dawn."

"Is that it?" His voice held a note of sharpness.

She glanced up at him and noticed pain mixed with anger in his gaze.

"Is what it, Aaron?"

"That's your excuse? I've been putting a lot of work into it, Marianna. Maybe you should act as if you care, even a little."

"I do care. I mean it's a nice gesture, but Aaron before this moment I truly didn't know your intentions. I mean, we haven't even had one date. I didn't want to presume—"

"That I was building it for you? Of *course* I am." His gaze narrowed. "And I can't believe you're going knowing that." He stepped forward. "I shouldn't be so bold. My dat always says patience is a virtue, but I can't help but picturing you going to Montana and meeting some other guy. My cousin told me there are many bachelors."

"I'm not interested in anyone else, Aaron—"

"Then stay."

She turned away from him and walked to the porch rail, leaning against it. She knew the women inside watched and were coming to their own conclusions as to what this conversation was about, but their opinions no longer mattered. Marianna's heart felt as if Aaron had pushed an invisible hand into her chest and squeezed. Didn't he realize that her whole life she'd waited to hear words like this? Didn't he realize that if she had any choice she would stay?

Her eyes focused on the two trees in the distance. For as long as she could remember she felt their boding. Her mother had lost two daughters and she'd been the replacement. She couldn't just leave Mem like this. Couldn't disappoint her and Dat.

"My mother needs me. I have to help her. She can't do it all on her own."

"Being the perfect daughter won't make up for the accident." His voice was low, yet the breeze that rattled the leaves on the trees swept his words to her.

She turned back to him, her hand still gripping the top rail. "Excuse me?"

"Don't you think everyone in the community can see it? You try so hard to be the perfect daughter. They talk. They all talk, you know."

Heat filled her cheeks again. A moment ago it had been pleasure at Aaron's attention. Now anger filled her. Shame. The community must think her a fool. Trying so hard and failing. She thought about Mrs. Zook's comments about Uncle Ike. Did they talk about her like that too? Did they laugh at her futile efforts to make up for the loss of her sisters? She swallowed down the emotion, but it stuck like a large cherry pit blocking her wind pipe. "I . . . I've never told anyone that I'm trying to be the perfect daughter."

"You don't need to tell them." He reached his hand, as if wanting to take hers, and then paused and pulled it back. "I'm just telling you because I care. I really do, Marianna."

She bit her lip, no longer feeling cared about in the slightest. "How dare you be so presumptuous? First, just because you've decided you've gone fancy on me you think I should get excited about this cabin. Maybe if you'd put the same effort into wooing me that you put into the cabin, I would stay. And second . . ." She lowered her voice and unclenched her fists. "Second, maybe it'll be good for me to get out of this community. Maybe other people, at another place, will stay out of their neighbors' business." She turned to him. "Have you ever thought that maybe I changed my mind. That maybe I *want* to go?" Marianna squared her shoulders. "Maybe I want to go some place where everyone doesn't already know the story of what happened the night I was born. Maybe I want to be seen for *me*. Maybe I've changed my mind about just settling down and getting married without seeing a little of the country first."

"Have you?" He looked at her—not at her eyes, but her soul.

She didn't answer, because to answer would be the first thread of a lie she'd have to continue to weave. She knew it. He knew it. And the women watching most likely guessed it too.

"You don't have to answer that." Emotion pushed his words out.

"It's not like I'll be gone forever, Aaron. It's just six months, and I'll write letters. I'll send them often."

He nodded, but she could tell he wasn't satisfied.

"I'll look forward to getting them, and I'll read every one. I just want you to know, I will wait for six months." Aaron returned his hat to his head. "And, well, if you don't return, I know I'll have my answer. I'll know that maybe taming the unknown ghosts of your past is more important than the future you could have . . . here with me."

CHAPTER TWELVE

*M*arianna made her way to the train window and looked down at the small group of people—their driver, her Aunt Ida, who wore a displeased look, and Aaron. He seemed so small standing on the platform. Tears filled her eyes as she looked down at him. She had tried to apologize for the way she'd acted yesterday, but every time she tried she got interrupted by one of her siblings. She didn't know what had gotten into her. She wanted a life with him, wanted to see the cabin . . .

What she *didn't* want is for him to make things harder. Making leaving harder. Couldn't he understand that she had to go because it was the right thing to do? Not because she was trying to measure up or replace, but because, well, because honoring one's father and mother took on many shapes. Not only following the Amish way of life, but being honoring in the daily little things.

Ellie sat on her lap, and Charlie sat next to her, silent. His eyes were wide as he took in the train and the people settling into the seats next to them. Marianna had the same feeling of wonderment, even though she tried not to let it show. She'd seen trains, but had never been on one. She'd interacted with Englisch in stores, but never beyond that. Her whole life was centered around people like her. People she understood and who understood her. But being at the station and on the train, she felt like a spectacle. Once, when their neighbor's sheep had given birth to a lamb with three legs, all the kids had gathered around the pen and stared.

She felt like that lamb.

Even now she could feel the eyes of the other passengers on them. Noting their dress, watching their every move. She smoothed the long sleeve of her lavender dress and fiddled with the side hem of her black apron. A woman two rows up had already asked Dat if she could take a photo with him. He had mumbled an excuse without being rude.

The train started with a lurch, and butterflies danced in her stomach. Her body pressed backward into her seat and the floor quivered under her sturdy black shoes.

Charlie's hands gripped her arm. "Is it going much faster soon?"

"I think so." Marianna waved at Aaron, and he lifted one hand. And then, when she was still in view, he turned and walked away. Her heart sank. If only she could assure him that everything would be okay. That she'd return in six months and they'd pick up where they'd left off.

The train whistle blew, and Ellie jumped in her arms. *"Ich will hem geh!"*

I want to go home! The little girl's cry could have come from Marianna's heart as well. "It's okay. We'll be there soon. We'll have a new home."

"Nay!" Her wail increased and the other passengers didn't try to hide their stares.

"Ellie, it will be all right, *ach. Heb dich schtill.*" Even as

Marianna admonished her little sister to settle down, she couldn't deny the same overwhelming sense of loss and apprehension. Fear tightened her throat. This was happening. They were leaving.

Would they be all right?

Ellie turned, wrapping her arms around Marianna. Her feet kicked against Marianna's legs as if trying to stand. One foot kicked her thigh hard.

"*Heb dich schtill!*" Her parents sat in a row behind her, and she wished they'd do something, say something to calm Ellie.

"Mem." Marianna turned partway in her seat and looked back. Her father's arms were around her mother, and she was shedding tears. They would be no help.

She turned back around, holding her sister firmer. "Please, Ellie, look. See what's out the window. Look over there." Marianna pointed, trying to distract her, and then something caught her eye. A small red car, dented and rusted, was parked in the lot of the hardware store down the street from the train station. Levi sat in the driver's seat watching. She caught a brief glimpse of him before the train turned a corner and disappeared out of view.

"*Hem!*" Ellie cried again. *Home!*

Marianna closed her eyes to trap the tears her sister's wail brought to her own eyes.

"Would she like a cookie?"

Marianna turned, surprised at the gentle voice. A woman in a business suit stood there. Her hair was fixed up, piled on top of her head. She wore makeup. Her lips lifted in a smile.

The woman sat in the chair across from Marianna and leaned forward. Charlie's grip around her arm tightened. As if blowing out a candle, Ellie's crying stopped. She buried her face into

Marianna's neck, holding on to the strings of Marianna's kapp, not letting go.

"My grandma made the cookies last night. I visited her for her birthday." The woman pulled a plastic container from her bag and opened it. "They're my favorite."

"Ellie, look. Cookies." Marianna smiled at the woman. *Cookies* was one Englisch word Ellie understood perfectly.

Ellie turned on Marianna's lap, eyeing the woman's offering. Her grip loosened.

"They're chocolate chip. I hope that's okay."

"Yes, that sounds good. *Denke.*"

"Denke?" The woman repeated the word with care. "Thank you?"

Marianna smiled and nodded. "Yes, thank you." She took a cookie for Ellie and another for Charlie. They nibbled on their cookies in silence, their eyes focused on their laps.

"I used to be afraid of the train, but now I find it relaxing." The woman handed a cookie to Marianna and then took one herself. "It's cheaper than flying, and I can read a good book by the time I make it home. I have time to read my Bible too. Are you going far?"

Marianna had just taken a bite of the cookie when the woman asked. She chewed it and then swallowed, wiping the crumbs from the corners of her mouth with her fingertips.

"Yes, Montana."

"That's a long way. Are you going for vacation?"

"No, we're moving."

"Moving to Montana? Really? I thought the Amish stayed in the same community their whole lives." One of the woman's penciled eyebrows peaked into an arch. She was curious, but open about her thoughts. Marianna found herself liking the woman.

"Most do. That was my plan, too. But Dat—oh, my father, had other ideas."

"Well, it's good to know that God will be with you wherever you go, don't you think? It helps me to think about Him—to pray—whenever I'm scared and alone. And He's never abandoned me. When I seek Him, when I make the time to be with Him, I'm never disappointed."

Marianna couldn't help but notice the joy that spilled out of the woman as she talked. She tucked her hair behind her ear and then looked to the kids again. "I have a few coloring books and some crayons if your sister would like them. I got them for my friends' kids, but I can pick up something else later." The woman pulled two books and two boxes of crayons from her bag.

"Yes, she would like it. My youngest brother might be interested too. Josiah?" Marianna glanced over her shoulder.

The train had picked up speed, rocking side to side. Hobbling like a lame horse trying to get its footing, Josiah walked around the seat toward her. His eyes brightened when he noticed the crayons.

"Color crayons?" He sat next to Charlie. "Can we?" He looked to Marianna.

The woman's mouth circled in an *O*. "It is okay, isn't it? I know you don't watch television, but I'm not sure what else is not allowed."

Marianna laughed. "Crayons are fine, although we make our own by grinding up flowers and mixing them with candle wax."

"Really?" The woman's eyes grew wide.

More laughter spilled from Marianna's lips. "No, I'm joking. We may not watch television, but we do like to color and draw." In her mind's eye she thought of Aaron and the amazing way his sketches captured moments of life that most people took for granted and looked past. She glanced out the window. A longing to see him again mixed with regret over what she'd said. She should have gone . . . should have seen the house. Aching rippled inside her, matching the swaying of the train.

Marianna and the woman talked for the next hour. The woman asked many questions about the Amish way of life, and she told Marianna how she worked as an administrative assistant for a lawyer.

"My boss is picking me up from the train station, and we're taking clients to dinner, that's why I'm dressed like this. If I had my choice I'd be wearing jeans. I just hate wearing dresses." The woman's face reddened as soon as the words were out of her mouth. "I'm so sorry. There I go putting my foot in my mouth again."

"It's okay. I don't mind. It's all I've ever known. They are comfortable, at least I think so."

It wasn't until her father ventured over to check on them that Marianna remembered she was talking to a stranger instead of a good friend. And an hour later, when they came to the woman's stop, Marianna was disappointed to see her leave.

"I'll be praying for your family and the rest of your trip." The woman rose and gathered up her things. She carried a bright red purse and a bag that looked like it was made from some type of animal skin with a striped pattern. Marianna looked down at her own simple paper sack with just a smidgen of envy. The truth was, she'd love to have a bag like that, but she'd never be able to use it. The women in her community kept a high standard and watched each other to make sure everyone dressed as they ought. She couldn't even leave the house without her clothes and kapp perfectly pressed. They'd notice a bag for sure and then confront her on her pride for having such a thing.

With a wave the woman disappeared, and it wasn't until she was already out of sight that Marianna realized she forgot to thank her again for the cookies and the color books.

As she sat there alone, she puzzled at the woman's words. She'd say a prayer? For her? For their trip? Marianna knew she should have thought of praying, but she hadn't. She knew God was with her, watching, protecting, but the woman made it seem as if joy could be found in the asking too.

For as long as Marianna could remember, prayers to God were said reverently, silently to one's self. Yet she couldn't picture that woman sitting quietly at a table in prayer. She pictured loud, exuberant prayers. And for the first time that seemed okay. Maybe God understood the woman's heart despite the way she lived within the world? Marianna hoped so.

Surely someone so kind was worthy of God's attention too.

Dear Journal,

Sorry for my sloppy handwriting. I really can't help it. I'm writing this entry from a train heading to Montana. First of all, I can't believe I'm leaving everything behind. I've lived in the same home for as long as I remember, and soon I'll be living far from everything and everyone I know. I'm not afraid of what I will find—well, maybe a little. Mostly I'm confused. Am I making the right choice? Will I forever lose my favor with Aaron? If I stayed we'd no doubt be married soon. Maybe by next year we'd be starting a family of our own. I never did get to see the house he built. He said he did it with me in mind. That confuses me even more. Maybe if he'd made his intentions known sooner, I wouldn't be traveling on this train so far from everything.

The train is cold and drafty, and I always have one or two kids on my lap. The other passengers stare. Mem and Dat seem to be trying to deal with things in their own way. As they sit quiet, I wonder if they're thinking of Levi. I bet it's hard leaving, sort of like giving up. I wonder if it's hard leaving the graves of my sisters. This morning Mem didn't know I was up, but I saw her out there, standing under the trees planted in memory of their lives. We haven't got rain in the last week and the leaves drooped. Seemed to be sad, too.

In the sadness, though, not everything has been bad. I met an interesting woman who helped me with the kids. It was strange in the way she talked about God like He was her friend—like she could just talk to Him whenever she liked. Her eyes sparkled and she looked different than I'm used to seeing. It wasn't just the Englisch clothes and makeup. She just looked full of joy. That's the only way I can describe it. I've never thought of the Englisch being like that before.

Well, I have to stop writing, even though my mind is full of thoughts. Josiah needs someone to take him to the bathroom and everyone else is asleep.

The gentle rocking of the train lulled Josiah back to sleep, and Marianna stroked the young boy's hair. She'd enjoyed the previous quiet hours on the train almost as much as she had the conversation. It was nice, just to sit and view the countryside and tell herself it was a short trip, and she'd be back in six months. She let herself daydream about dates with Aaron Zook upon her return, and about the house he was building on his father's property. She also thought about the letter she would write him when they got to Montana. A letter apologizing for her behavior and a reminder that he was the reason she wanted to return.

But as time passed, it seemed wrong to just be sitting there. She should have brought mending, or even the embroidery she'd been working on last year but hadn't pulled out lately. She couldn't remember the last time she'd thought about so many things. She replayed her last conversations with Levi, Aaron, Rebecca, even Naomi. Her thoughts pestered her more when her mind wasn't busy, and she didn't like that. Doing things was easier. She was most secure when her hands were busy with work. They wouldn't be busy with much for a while. They had to stop in Chicago yet and change trains and then a thirty-three-hour journey stretched after that. And with each passing mile she was reminded those were miles she'd have to cross again when she returned.

As she thought about it, it seemed strange someone else would be living in their house. She also thought of a few more things she should have packed. Things she regretted leaving behind.

Marianna trusted Martha wouldn't get in her trunk. It wasn't until these quiet moments on the train she remembered her old diaries were also kept there. Most of the journals were just daily tasks and stories she'd made up with friends, but there was one special journal in which she'd written letters to God, made up of questions of things she didn't understand—like why did they need to follow the way of their ancestors? And how come she'd been chosen to be born in this family? What if she hadn't? What if she'd never learned the narrow path to get to God?

Her father's snores sounded behind her. Why hadn't she ever thought to ask him these questions? For as long as she could remember, it hadn't seemed her place to ask. Her parents guided her, disciplined her, made sure she was on the right path, but they weren't there to answer her every question. Caring and providing for their family took most of their time. When she did ask, they told her that getting all the answers would lead to pride. She supposed it was true, and just as she learned to dress and act in certain ways, she'd grown to trust that it was better to do what was required without question. And the more she did, unlike Rebecca or Levi, the more she saw they were right. Life was easier, more peaceful this way.

Yet as a girl she hadn't been as patient or understanding. One night she'd even prayed hard that God would answer her questions back. She begged Him just to write down His answers in her book. She'd promised Him that she wouldn't tell anyone if He did.

The next day there were still blank pages, but that was the day she'd met Uncle Ike for the first time. He'd been living in Canada, but having him around brought fun to their quiet home. Uncle Ike had always been quick to go on a walk with her and talk about all the things she thought about. And even though he didn't always have the answers, it made her feel better to know he often asked the same questions.

Of course that was then. She hadn't had many conversations with Uncle Ike for a while, beyond ordinary talk of life around the farm. She was mad at him in a way. If he hadn't talked her father into moving, they'd still be living life as they always had. She'd be starting to date Aaron. She could be married by fall.

Laughter interrupted Marianna's thoughts, but not the joyful laughter of hours earlier. Instead the harsh laughter of a young man about Levi's age split the air.

He stumbled through the doorway from another car. His eyes scanned the passengers, then stopped on her. Marianna looked away, focusing out the window on the large fields stretching in every direction. The waves of green rippled in the breeze in swooping waves.

Ellie still napped, and Marianna snuggled her closer. The man neared, looking at them—at her. Charlie let out a small whimper at the man's approach and rose from his seat, scurrying back to their parents. Marianna wished she could do the same.

"So what are you?" The man's words slurred. "A pilgrim?" He laughed again, but Marianna continued staring out the window, though now she did so without seeing. The hairs on her arms rose, and her heartbeat quickened. She clung to Ellie. Maybe if she just ignored him, he'd go away.

"What are you girl, deaf? Don't you talk?"

Marianna glanced at him. "I'm Amish, sir."

"Dat!" Behind her she heard Charlie call, interrupting her father's snore.

"Amish? I thought you weren't allowed transportation. Aren't you supposed to be back on the farm? Washing down them cows and getting ready to milk. Or . . ." His face neared hers. He reeked of alcohol. "Or I can wash you down. What do you have under that bathrobe?"

"Dat!" Charlie's voice sharpened.

Marianna attempted to rise, holding Ellie tight, but the man was too close. She couldn't stand. Couldn't run. She felt trapped, like an animal in a cage. Her eyes scanned the faces of the other passengers, but they were no longer staring. All looked away. No one moved. No one helped.

Marianna craned her neck to look to her father. His eyes opened a little, and then widened when he saw the man. In seconds he was on his feet, rushing around the row of chairs toward her.

"Get your hands off my daughter." Her father was there in three long steps. His face reddened, and Marianna could see the vein in his temple bulge.

The guy lifted his head, attempting to focus on her father's face. "You going to make me?"

"If I need to." Her father balled his fists and jutted out his chin.

"Dat, no. I'm fine." Marianna touched his arm, but he brushed her hand away.

"You? You're gonna stop me? You're an old man, with a big Santa beard." The young man's laugh was far from pleasant. "Do you think you can take me?"

Her father straightened his shoulders. He didn't respond but took another step forward.

The man lifted his chin, eyeing Dat, then lowered his head and stepped back. "I don't think she's worth fighting for anyways. Pilgrim hat. Pilgrim dress." Curses flew from his lips, then the man stumbled through the doors to the next car.

Marianna let out a breath she didn't know she'd been holding.

She looked down to Ellie on her lap, thankful the girl still slept. She wiped the sweat that had beaded on her brow with her fingertips. Was this going to be a regular occurrence? Fear raced through her heart. Yes, they'd be living near other Amish, but unlike where she'd come from, they'd be the minority. What would happen next time if her father wasn't there?

Satisfied the man had left, her father sat in the seat where Charlie had been. He tried to act as if nothing had happened as he peeked over to see if Ellie still slept. She did, curled up with a small fist tucked under her chin. Dat reached a hand to brush a curl off her cheek, and it was then Marianna saw her father's hand was quivering.

He released a low breath. "My girls . . ."

His whisper almost broke her heart.

"Dat, were you really going to hit him? We don't do that sort of thing." She glanced around, again, noticing they had the attention of everyone in their train car.

Dat chuckled under his breath as if pleased with himself. "Yes, I know that and you know that, but he didn't know that."

Even with his chuckle, the rope of tension refused to loosen around her heart.

Then Marianna heard her mother's voice.

"A big dog with a lot of bark and no bite," her mother mumbled in Pennsylvania Dutch. Hearing that, her father's lips curled into a smile.

Marianna smiled too. Would tomorrow—would Montana—bring more of the same? The thought brought both curiosity and fear. But the fear lessened when a sound caught her . . . a sound all too rare.

Her mother's laughter.

CHAPTER THIRTEEN

*M*arianna woke and her eyes moved to the window, then widened. The sun had risen.

The transfer in Chicago had gone smoothly, but sometime during yesterday afternoon the train had stopped, and the conductor had come through to tell them there had been some type of spill ahead. What was supposed to be a thirty-three-hour trip would now be much longer. Instead of them getting to Whitefish, Montana, last night and sleeping in the beds at their new home, they spent their second night trying to get comfortable in the train seats. But perhaps the morning light coming through the window meant they were almost there.

She rubbed her eyes and sat up, seeing a different world outside the window than the place they left yesterday. Pine trees clung to rocky cliff faces, and a river—not like the creeks back home, but a real river—roared at the base of the canyon. The color of the water was bluish-green, like the turquoise necklace the clerk in the general store had worn, one Marianna had always admired. White foam danced on top of the river, reflecting in the morning light.

She cocked her head as she gazed out the window, lifting her eyes to the sky, but the hills rose and then turned into mountains.

The sky was a sliver of blue off in the distance. Even though the view was breathtaking, her heart felt a slight pinch realizing her prairie lay far behind.

As did Aaron.

The door between the cars opened, and her father entered with long strides, his cheeks flushed. *"Sis zeit fa uff vecka, gedrett all euer stuff zahma."*

How cheerful he was, calling them to wake and gather their stuff. Marianna wished she shared his excitement.

Dat smiled at her. "We should be there in five minutes yet. Josiah, Charlie, wake up. Look at these forests and tell me if you see a bear."

Her youngest brothers slept in the seat across from her, where the pretty woman had sat two days before. They lifted their sleepy heads, hair sticking up in all directions, and put on their hats. Eyes turned to the window as the trees thinned and roads and houses began making an appearance. Those were followed by larger buildings and stores. Marianna noted disappointment in their sleepy gazes. Behind her, Mem woke David and gathered Ellie's things. The small girl had awakened at least a dozen times during the night, disoriented and scared. Only her mother's soft lullabies had calmed her.

As Marianna gazed out the window, she didn't know how she felt about Montana. The one thing in the forefront of her mind was getting off this train and freshening up. She'd worn the same clothes for the last three days. She longed to arrive at the station, find a restroom, splash cool water on her face, and run a comb through her hair.

She touched her kapp, feeling it askew. Removing it, she used her fingers to comb through her hair, refastening the strands with pins at the nape of her neck. She returned her kapp, knowing her efforts would have to be sufficient.

Five minutes later the train slowed and a cream-colored building trimmed in dark brown came into view. Large flower baskets hung along the face of the station. It looked old, like the type of building she pictured when she read stories of the old West. Clusters of people waited at the platform, but one man stood out. Uncle Ike was the only one dressed in Amish clothes.

"There he is!" Marianna pointed, and her brothers waved their hands as fast as hummingbird wings. As the train neared, Uncle Ike removed his brimmed hat, waving it and searching the windows for any sign of them.

Eager to stretch their legs, her family gathered their things and hurried toward the exit.

It was the sweet scent of the air that Marianna noticed first as she descended the train's steps. The air was sharp and clean, like none she'd ever breathed. It had a crisp nippiness, too, and Marianna wished she'd worn a sweater.

Uncle Ike spread his arms. "Welcome to Montana!"

Marianna looked to the station. To her left she saw trees and more buildings, but on her right, in the distance were mountains.

"It's beautiful, *auch,* just beautiful." The words poured from her father's mouth. Marianna turned to him and noticed his gaze fixed above the train.

She turned toward the train and was surprised to see their boxes had already been unpacked, but as she continued her gaze upward, her breath caught in her throat. There, towering over the train, were mountains bigger than she'd ever seen.

"Are those the Rocky Mountains?" David held Josiah's hand and pointed upward. "Look, Josiah." He seemed older than his twelve years, as if the train ride had matured him.

"Yes, the Rockies. Just a piece of them. Wait until you get a good look at everything around here." Uncle Ike stroked his beard. The way he looked at the mountains, it seemed he owned them all himself.

"It is beautiful," her mother confessed. "More than I thought it would be."

"Is our house near here?" Josiah stretched his suspenders.

Uncle Ike shook his head. "No, it's an hour-and-a-half drive, but a pretty one."

"More sitting?" Josiah made a face, and Marianna couldn't blame him.

"Ready?" Uncle Ike ignored her brother's complaint. "A van waits. My driver borrowed it. Should be enough room for all your things."

Marianna held Ellie's hand, and as she looked around, she noticed eyes on them. A couple with young children looked and pointed. An older woman smiled and waved, much to the embarrassment of her red-faced husband who grabbed her arm and guided her into the train station.

"So I assume there aren't many Amish here?" she asked Uncle Ike.

"Not too many. A dozen families up in the Kootenai, where we'll be. There are some Mennonites, though. Hutterites, too, but unless you travel up where we live, you'd never see a buggy in these parts."

"Will we be near these mountains?" Marianna's gaze locked on a large mountain that had lines running down it where the land had been cleared of trees.

"That's the ski park. Our community is near a mountain range to the north. Not so many paved roads or people. Everyone is excited to meet you. It's always a celebration when a new family moves in."

"It'll be nice to meet them too," Mem said, although her face showed more weariness than anything.

Her mother's words surprised Marianna. She'd expected Mem to scowl at Uncle Ike. Had something changed? Marianna thought back to her mother's laughter and her soft lullabies on the train. Even though travel was hard, maybe the doctor was right. Maybe leaving Levi and the worries of the farm behind would be good for Mem.

Marianna moved to their pile of boxes, counting to make sure they'd all arrived safely. She counted one short, and then counted again.

One was missing.

She hurried toward the baggage handler who was closing the train's side luggage panel.

"Excuse me, but there is one box missing."

"No, ma'am, I checked. There's nothing else for this stop." He closed the compartment.

"I'm sure one is missing. Can you look one more time?" She placed a hand on her hip and took a step toward him. She wasn't going anywhere until he looked.

With a heavy sigh the man opened the compartment. He hunkered down, leaning back on his heels and peered inside. "I don't see any more boxes. Only suitcases."

Marianna leaned in, half-climbing inside. "What about that?" She pointed to a box shoved behind some suitcases and turned on its side.

The man groaned under his breath and then climbed inside the storage area and pulled it out. Marianna stood as he handed it to her.

"Yeah, yer right. I suppose this is yours," he mumbled.

"*Quilt* was written on the box in her handwriting. Her heart skipped a beat.

"*Denke.*" Her words released in a breath. "I'm so glad I have this box."

"Do you need help with that?"

Marianna turned at the male voice and found a young man standing there with a wheeled cart. His hair was dark and cut short in the same style as Levi's. He had blue eyes, but they were different than Aaron's. They were almond shaped with long, dark lashes. His face was square, strong, and he had a boyish look about him. She could almost picture him hiding in the backseat of a buggy to spook the driver just for fun.

Seeing the smile in his gaze made her smile too. She patted her kapp as if insuring it was still in place. She didn't want to glance down at her wrinkled dress and apron, confirming what a mess she was after the trip. "*Denke,* but I don't think we need help. I believe our driver is coming."

"Well, if that's the case . . ." The man turned the cart and strode away. Then he paused and looked over his shoulder with a wink.

Uncle Ike approached them with hurried steps. "Mari, this *is* the driver. Yes, Ben, all these boxes, please. And do hurry. I bet they can't yet wait to see their place."

Marianna's face grew warm, and she shaded it from the sunlight overhead.

"So how was your trip?" Ben asked Charlie as he piled boxes onto the cart. "Is it true that on the train your stomach jiggles even as you try to sleep?" He chuckled and the sounds of it made the day seem warmer.

Ben. Maybe short for Benjamin? It's a good Bible name. Marianna watched him stack the boxes. The name fit him, but as he lifted the boxes and stacked them with ease, it still seemed strange he was the driver. Drivers back home were older. Most were quiet, happy to do their job without too much effort of joking around or making friends.

"Well, I had a dream I was on a tugboat . . ." Charlie started. "And—"

Marianna didn't get to hear the rest of his response. Ellie's cry split the air. Without looking to see what the problem was, Marianna darted her direction, weaving around an older man and woman who were walking to the train.

Reaching her, Marianna swept Ellie up in her arms. *"Was ist letz?* What's the matter?" She scanned her sister's face, her hands, her bare legs, looking for blood—for the wound she was certain was there.

Looking down Ellie pointed to a puddle on the black asphalt. She pointed to her coloring book that sat in the middle of the murky water.

Footsteps approached, and Marianna noticed it was Ben. His eyes were wide with concern.

"Ellie, I thought you were hurt," she scolded, embarrassed for her unladylike behavior.

"Everything okay?" Ben studied Ellie. "Did she fall?"

"No, it's her coloring book." Marianna attempted to bend down while she still held crying Ellie on her hip. "She must have dropped it."

"No problem." Ben lunged forward. His hand brushed Marianna's arm as he grabbed the book, then he turned to the side, shaking the water off in the grass.

"I'll tell you what"—he gave Ellie a warm smile—"I'll take this home and dry it out. In the meantime, I'll give you this." He stuck his hand into his pocket and pulled out a small wooden yo-yo. "Deal?"

Ellie looked at him, lifting one of her eyebrows with interest.

Then Ben turned to Marianna who held back a smile, and his eyes narrowed. "Your little sister doesn't understand me, does she?"

Marianna tried not to laugh at his sheepish look. "No, she only understands a little English, but I'll explain." Marianna explained the trade and Ellie smiled, reaching for the yo-yo.

"Do you think that'll be salvageable?" Marianna ignored Ben's bright-eyed gaze and focused on the soggy coloring book instead.

Ben lifted it up with two fingers and cocked an eyebrow at the drips of water falling from its pages. "I'm not sure, but it's worth a try."

The sounds of someone clearing his throat behind her made her jump, and Marianna turned to see Uncle Ike standing there.

"Looks as if you two have hit it off." Uncle Ike gripped Ben's shoulder. "Mr. Stone here has been a big help to me, driving me around, introducing me to folks. He's the one in fact, that showed me the house."

"Yes, so I'm the one you could thank." He puffed up his chest with a humored smile and turned in the direction of the cart he'd been attending to.

"Or perhaps blame." Marianna shot back.

Ben paused, then turned. "Blame? You blame me for bringing you to the Promised Land?"

"If that's what you call it," Marianna said, pretending she wasn't impressed by the majestic mountains. "It's only the

Promised Land if you consider what we left as the wilderness, the desert." She shrugged. "Which I don't."

The brightness in Ben's eyes faded. "Yes, well, I better get to your things. Annie from the store has threatened me within inches of my life if I don't bring you folks around for breakfast." His eyes held Marianna's for a few seconds, but instead of his humored gaze from a moment before, his look was filled with curiosity, with questions.

Marianna looked away, not sure of her answers.

Ben couldn't help but glance at the Amish woman in his rearview mirror. His passenger's eyes were on the mountains, the trees, the lakes . . . which gave him time to eye her on the straight stretches.

He'd known Ike for six months, and the man seemed to break the mold as far as Amish men went. He often showed up at their Monday night prayer meetings, and the one thing Ike had repeatedly asked prayer for was now happening. Ike had prayed diligently for his brother's family to leave Indiana and come to Montana. He'd said they needed healing from pain in their past. He'd said they needed truth.

Ben didn't know what they'd faced—Ike hadn't gone into details—but it had to be hard. His hands gripped the steering wheel tighter, and he swallowed down a lump of emotion as big as a chicken egg. He knew about pain. Knew about running. Maybe that's why he'd been so drawn to these folks when he first heard about them. And why he wanted to do what he could to help.

He could see loss in their gazes. Abe and his wife seemed older than their years, but it was the young woman who carried the weight of the world on her shoulders. She was petite, slim. Even with her Amish clothes and no makeup she was beautiful.

Ben smiled to himself, remembering her climbing into the luggage compartment determined to find her missing box. The baggage handler had been frustrated, but Ben had been enamored—so feisty for such a small package.

"Ben here is a safe driver," Ike said from the passenger's seat, turning half way to look at his brother in the back. "He's not Amish, but might as well be. He's always helping us out. Goes out of his way to lend a hand, and is faithful to God too."

Ben scoffed. "Now, I think Ike here is hoping I'll give him a discount on this trip because of all those good words." He smiled. "I like helping, that's all. Just trying to love others like God did."

"Different than our Englisch neighbors in Indiana."

Ben could feel Ike's brother Abe studying him as he spoke.

"Not that there weren't good Englischers back East, but the ones that seemed to interact with our people the most were the ones who tried to lure our young ones away—to tempt them from the right path."

Pain tinged the man's words. Had a family member been "lured away." If so it made sense why they'd come to Montana for healing—and to protect their other children from such temptation. Ben glanced at Marianna again, who sat silent, listening. She didn't seem like the type prone to wander. Then again it was hard to see into another's heart.

"If anything, I hope to encourage people into a closer relationship with God. In fact, there's a Monday night prayer meeting and Tuesday morning Bible study if you're interested."

"No—" The word spouted from the older woman's lips. "But thank ye."

Ben nodded, and Ike glanced at him out of the corner of his eye. Ike had warned him that Amish from back East liked to keep to themselves. He'd had said to take it slow and just get to know them as friends first. He supposed he'd already failed at that.

Ben turned on his turn signal and passed a small sedan going far less than the speed limit. As he passed, he realized a woman in the passenger's seat was leaning out and taking photos of cows grazing in a field. *Tourist.*

Ben told himself to be patient with Ike's family, but it was hard. His heart was so full of thankfulness to God for delivering him from the pain of his past . . . he wanted to share that hope. That joy.

Especially with Marianna.

CHAPTER FOURTEEN

he drive took them on a small two-lane road with mountains rising on both sides. Pine and birch trees lined the roads, and they saw at least a dozen deer as they drove. Uncle Ike had pointed out the small town of Eureka, which looked as if it hadn't changed much over the years. Brick buildings with tall, wooden facades lined the road. A hand-painted sign pointed to the museum. A sandwich board on the sidewalk announced the best burgers in town.

Then, just when Marianna thought they were getting close to their new community, the road turned again, taking them away from town and toward the most beautiful lake she'd ever seen.

"Ben, can you tell them about the lake? Where it got its name?" Uncle Ike directed.

Ben had been quiet almost the whole ride. While for some drivers that was typical, it seemed out of character for him.

Marianna had a feeling the way she'd responded to him had something to do with it. Regret over her rudeness throbbed in her temples, and one of her grandmother's favorite sayings came to mind: *"A person who thinks too little, talks too much."* Lately she'd gotten into the habit of speaking before thinking, and it was something she needed to mend. After all, it wasn't Ben's fault she didn't want to be here. She should be thankful he found a home for her family. He seemed to be a good driver and someone who'd be there to help her parents after she left.

"Lake Koocanusa was named by using the first three letters of the Kootenai River, Canada and the USA." He pointed. "A half-hour or so away is the Libby Dam. I think the lake's somewhere around ninety miles long."

"Ninety?" David scratched his head. "That's a lot. I bet there's a lot of fish in there. Thousands."

"Yes, I guess so. I'll have to take you guys down there sometime."

Uncle Ike nodded, but Marianna noticed her parents exchanging glances. They didn't make it common practice to let their children socialize with the Englisch. No matter how nice someone seemed, her parents knew all too well that habits and beliefs had a way of rubbing off. Once the boys reached sixteen—when they were better able to make smart decisions—they would be able to venture into the world, but Marianna knew until then the only fishing they'd do was with Uncle Ike, her father, or another Amish man.

The road turned, and Marianna sucked in a breath as they crossed over the lake on a long bridge that seemed to float in the sky over the water. She pressed her forehead against the van's glass window and peered into the sparkling blue water below. She'd never seen anything like it.

At least I'll have something to write home about. The mountains. The lakes. She wished she could write about Ben, especially the tender way he'd tried to console Ellie, not understanding she didn't speak English. That interaction alone told Marianna he hadn't been driving for the Amish very long. The drivers back home understood Pennsylvania Dutch, even if they didn't speak it well. Yet, to mention Ben to her friends would give them the wrong impression. That's the last thing she needed—for word to get out that she'd gone fancy on an Englisch driver.

Across the bridge they turned to the right, following a narrow, winding mountain road. Marianna was certain they would never reach this mysterious community—and then she spotted one house, and then two. More houses lined the road, and then an Englisch church. Not too much farther they came to an intersection with numerous buildings.

"See that small log cabin on the corner? That's the school you'll attend." Uncle Ike pointed for the boys. They stared at the small building, the muddy playground, and the simple metal playground equipment. Marianna pictured rows of desks and students hard at work on their studies.

"And just on the other side of that house is the store."

West Kootenai Kraft and Grocery, the sign read. It, too, was a log cabin. At the end of the muddy parking lot was a wooden-planked walkway, just like the ones she'd read about in Wild West books.

Ben parked the van in front of the store, and Uncle Ike jumped out of the front seat, opening the side door. David spilled out first, followed by the other boys who scanned the area as if they'd been plopped down in the middle of an adventure.

"Look at that!" Charlie ran up to a tall log post near the store. On it were arrows pointing toward various locations and the distance written on them.

"'North Pole 2,750 miles, South Pole 9,500 miles, Honolulu Hawaii 3,912 miles, Canada 2 miles.'" David grinned.

"I had no idea we were that close to Canada." Marianna rubbed her sticky eyes, still hoping to wash her face. As hungry as she was, she longed even more for a bath and change of clothes. She entered the store with tentative steps. Would her family get the same curious looks here as on the train and at the station?

An older gentleman stood behind a simple wooden counter to the left of the door, helping a customer. Beyond him were eight or ten rows of shelves with grocery items. Ike walked past those and turned right. There was an open kitchen and beyond that a large dining area. A couple tables had customers, but they barely glanced up when her family entered. A wood stove welcomed them into the dining area. Since the day had warmed up, it sat unused.

A woman with long blonde hair pulled back in a ponytail bustled out of the kitchen. A yellow scarf was tied over her hair, and she wore a white apron. Laugh lines around the woman's eyes gave away her age. She approached Mem arms wide.

"There you are. I was wondering what took Ben so long. It's good he's a safe driver, but sometimes I want to tell him to put the pedal to the metal, especially when there's food waiting." The woman swept Mem into a hug and then reached over and shook Dat's hand. After a firm handshake, she turned to Marianna, swaggering forward like a cowgirl who'd just gotten off her horse.

"Your uncle has told me a lot about you." She gave Marianna a quick hug. "He says you're a real hard worker. I'd like to talk to you sometime, but don't want to overwhelm you with too much too soon." The woman's chuckle split the air. "My friends tell me I can be overwhelming."

"You?" Ben approached and patted her back. She was old

enough to be his mother, but acted as sprightly as if they were peers.

Ben sniffed the air. "What do you have cooking up?"

"Breakfast casserole and homemade cinnamon rolls. I hope everyone will like it."

Marianna's stomach rumbled, and suddenly it didn't matter that she hadn't washed her face yet.

"Haven't had any of your cooking that I didn't like yet." Uncle Ike motioned to the dining area. "C'mon, don't be shy. Your first meal will be a free one. Annie does that so you'll get hooked on her cooking. It's trickery, I tell you."

The little kids sat at a long table, and Ben sat with them. Pushing his silverware to the side, he set to work on making a paper airplane out of his napkin. Marianna couldn't help but watch and smile.

Marianna sat with her parents and Uncle Ike. She was usually the one who sat with the kids, helping them, and making sure they minded their manners, but she didn't want anyone—Ben especially—to get the wrong idea.

When Annie hurried to the kitchen to begin dishing up the food, Mem leaned forward, clearing her throat. "Are all the Englisch this friendly around here?" Her eyes widened. "I'm not sure what to think. A free meal? It's kind but . . ."

Marianna knew how her mother's mind worked. A good deed done to her would require one in return.

"Not all. The women folk are pretty much safe, but there are some loggers that would hike a woman over their shoulders and carry her into the woods if they thought they could get away with it." Uncle Ike shuddered.

"Honestly?" Her mother placed a hand over her heart.

Laughter burst from Uncle Ike's lips. "No, ma'am, they're as gentle as they come. Although I can't say as much about a few of the rich Californians who've made their way up here and bought up lots of land. Some of them can be sharp-tongued and demanding at times. Think the whole community needs to bow to them."

The food was placed before them and the room grew quiet. Marianna saw her father's head drop, and she knew it was time for silent prayer. She folded her hands, closed her eyes, and bowed her head, knowing the others in her family were doing the same, even the little ones.

"Everything smells so . . ." Ben's voice stopped, and she knew he realized what was happening. It was even clearer now that he hadn't been around Amish much. To have one meal shared together would have instructed him on their way.

But it wasn't Ben's fault.

Frustration tightened her gut, and when she opened her eyes, she cast a side glance at her father. Would it have been too hard for her father to have mentioned something? To say something as simple as, "We are going to pray."

Her father seemed oblivious to her disapproval, and as Marianna scooped a large cinnamon roll onto her plate she glanced from Ben to Annie—who was humming as she scrubbed dishes in the kitchen—and Marianna realized something. This was the first meal she'd ever shared with the Englisch. Back home their drivers ate by themselves in their vehicles. Looking around it bothered her that it was such a big deal. Why should she even notice such a thing? Didn't God love these people, too? Didn't He call her to love others as He did?

These new thoughts made her uncomfortable. In Indiana,

where almost everyone she interacted with lived and believed as she did, she had no need to question these things.

Taking a big bite of the cinnamon roll, she felt even more unsure about this place they had moved to. Not only was she changing homes, friends, and community, but the walls protecting their personal lives had already been bulldozed over by the chuckle of a friendly driver and the quick hugs of a store owner. She felt vulnerable, unprotected.

And this was supposed to be better for her family?

Marianna swallowed. Grief pressed on her chest as she considered the loss of the place where she knew how everyone would act and where she felt safe. Even when their actions—like Levi's, like Rebecca's—weren't as she wished, at least she knew how to respond. She knew when to turn her back and when to hold on.

In a strange way, familiar conflicts felt far safer than a strangers' embrace.

Aaron tucked his hands into his pockets as he strode to his cabin. The sun had sunk over the horizon, but it was still light enough to see the grasshoppers jumping from the ground with his every step. He rubbed his eyes, and part of him wondered why he was even heading out here. He'd been up before dawn caring for his cattle. Then he'd gone to work at the Stoll's dairy only to come home to complete his dad's chores since his dad was working late at the mill. It seemed foolish to come. Marianna was gone. He'd have a house, but what good would that be without someone to share it with?

The fluttering of wings overhead told him the bats were already coming out for their evening meal. He spotted the roof of his house through the trees . . . Would Marianna come back as she said? The house should be finished in just a few months, but he wouldn't be able to move in alone. He needed someone by his side to care for their animals, help grow their food. To try to tackle all of it alone would be impossible. Aaron spit on the ground, realizing that if he couldn't make this work, he'd have to follow his dad's advice and work at the mill. He'd have no choice.

He hurried through the trees, deciding his only course of action would be to finish the house as planned and try to woo Marianna with his letters. If it came down to it, he could even hop on a train and go to Montana.

Aaron's steps paused as his cabin came into view. A light shone from inside, and he saw movement. Who could be there?

His footsteps quickened and then his heart leapt into his throat as he made out the figure of a woman. She wore the familiar blue dress, white kapp. *Marianna!*

He broke into a run and laughter spilled from his lips. She'd come back. She'd returned.

"I don't believe it. You're really here!" He darted through the doorway. Then the woman turned and a face he didn't expect was smiling at him. She lowered her head, red tinting her cheeks.

"I didn't realize I'd get that type of welcome."

"Naomi?" He rubbed his forehead. What was *she* doing here?

"I'm sorry I came uninvited. I was visiting my cousin down the road, and stopped by at the chance you'd be here." She tucked a red curl behind her ear, then straightened her apron. "I can go. We can catch up another time." With quick steps she moved to the door.

"No, wait!" He reached out his hand, stopping her. His hand brushed the sleeve of her dress and she paused.

"I really didn't mean to be a bother. I"—Naomi lowered her gaze—"Well, when Levi left I remember how I felt. I just thought you'd need someone to talk to. I know his leaving was for a different reason, but it hurt just the same." Her lower lip quivered slightly, and Aaron stroked her arm, trying to comfort her.

"I imagine that was hard." He stood there not knowing what else to say. He'd gone to school with Naomi, too, but they'd never talked much. Everyone had expected her and Levi to get married, and that's why it had been such a shock when Levi left. Aaron's sandpapered heart seemed to bleed a little more as he thought of what Naomi had gone through.

"They're family. They've been through a lot." Naomi turned to him. "It's only understandable in a way that they'd have a hard time in relationships. I bet they're afraid to love after their losses."

"Well." He cleared his throat. "Marianna and I weren't in a relationship—not yet."

She walked to a sawhorse he had set up and brushed the sawdust off the top with her finger. "My ma tried to warn me. She said there were other boys in the community who were more stable, who'd provide a woman a good home." She stopped the movement of her finger and looked to him. "I didn't listen, and now my heart is broken in two."

Aaron didn't know what to say. Marianna wasn't like Levi. She was opposite, in fact. She followed the laws of their people and cared for those in her family first. If she hadn't been such a good Amish daughter, he bet she would have stayed. It was the one time he wished Marianna had a disobedient streak in her.

"Do you agree?" Naomi interrupted his thoughts. "Do you think it's because of their loss that they left us like that?"

"I'm not sure." Aaron shrugged. "I—I guess so."

"At least we have each other." Naomi stepped forward and lifted her head, looking into Aaron's face. "I'd hate to go through something like this alone."

CHAPTER FIFTEEN

Marianna stared out the van's door at the log cabin, realizing she couldn't imagine a place more different than their sprawling white farmhouse back home. The cabin was nestled into the side of a hill, just off a pothole-riddled dirt road. A flat area to the north of the house had a fenced-in section that looked as if it had once housed a garden. Now a thin layer of pine needles covered the ground. Beyond the garden was a clothesline, a small shed, and a barn. They were all made of logs and had a weathered gray look, proving they'd seen better years.

With squeals of excitement, the kids bounded from the van and raced through the front door. There wasn't a lock on it, Uncle Ike had informed them. No need really. One had to be more concerned about bears than thieves—an idea that didn't put Marianna's mind at ease.

Her mother followed the kids into the house, and Ben set to work unloading boxes from the back of the van. There wasn't a walkway to the house. Instead four steps rose from the damp ground to the wraparound porch. Her mother paused, turned, and looked at her.

"You coming?" Mem's face reflected a simple plea. *Find a way to like it,* her wide-eyed gaze seemed to say.

Marianna looked to her father and Uncle Ike. Instead of going to the house, they headed to the barn first. Something inside told her to follow them. The barn seemed safer. Fewer emotions were tied up with that. Also with Ben unloading everything into the house, she thought it would be easier for him if she just stayed out of his way. Or maybe it was easier for her. He was handsome, she admitted to herself, and he did have a wonderful way with her siblings.

Marianna followed her father and Uncle Ike into the barn first. He flipped on a light switch and electric lights buzzed on.

"The lights are powered by a generator." Uncle Ike flipped a switch. "The owners used to have a small milking operation here and they had vacuum pumps."

Marianna scanned the large stalls that were now empty of equipment and animals. Dirty straw littered the floor and the place smelled of dirt and mold. In one corner of the barn, a wheelbarrow was turned to its side. Near one of the stalls, a hole had been dug under the wall—most likely due to some type of creature that had wanted in. A squeak sounded behind her, and Marianna turned, but whatever had been there was already gone. Other animals had no doubt filled the space after the farm animals had left. She just hoped they'd be just as quick to move out as they had been to move in.

She walked to the dusty window and glanced outside . . .

What would her father do for work? There was a forest outside, not farmland. And surely there were no large mills in this area.

She glanced to Dat, wondering if he'd would be okay without the open land. Back at their ninety-acre farm he grew two acres of sweet corn, a half acre of beans, and hundreds of tomato plants. Just last month he'd planted three acres of red potatoes, or taters as he called them. How would he feel knowing that someone else would reap the harvest of his work?

"Tomorrow I'll bring over Silver." Uncle Ike strode to one of the far stalls, and she could see it was designed for a horse.

"Silver? Like the metal?" She moved toward him. "That's a strange thing to name your horse after."

"Actually, the owner told me she was named after a famous television horse from a while back. When I told 'em I still didn't know who that was, the man tried to explain the television show." Uncle Ike snickered. "It was only after he was going on a few minutes that he remembered Amish don't watch television." Uncle Ike looped his thumbs through his suspenders and leaned back on his heels chuckling.

"Really? He didn't know that?" Back in Indiana people in the neighboring communities knew the Amish rules as well as the Amish themselves. She'd been reminded of this as a child when she entered stores where televisions played. *Just because it's there doesn't mean we indulge ourselves,*" her mother would always say. *"What would those watching us think?"* Mem always meant Amish and non-Amish alike.

"Well, I'm sure he had heard about the rule against televisions at one time, but that's something else I like about these parts." Uncle Ike used a handkerchief in his pocket to bat down some of the cobwebs that hung over the stalls. "People are people here. We are known more for who we are as individuals, not by our dress or our ways. His poor attempt at cleaning filled the air with dust, and he let out a powerful sneeze. Then, shaking his head as if to shake away the dust tickling his nose, he continued. "There's all types of crazy characters, and I don't get the feeling of *'us'* and *'them'* like I did back in Indiana."

Uncle Ike and Dat continued talking about some of the neighbors, and Marianna looked out the doorway. The van was gone. She felt bad that she hadn't said good-bye to Ben, but relieved that it was just their family again. She moved out the barn door toward the house, her shoes crunching on the dead pine needles from last fall. The needles made a carpet over tufts of green grass that attempted to poke through, and she made a mental note that raking would be a good job for the boys tomorrow, if they could find rakes, that is.

"Marianna." Ben's voice startled her, and she turned. He walked up the dirt road, hands in pockets. He waved as he neared. She crossed her arms over her chest and waited for him to approach. Why on earth was she short of breath all of a sudden? She willed her heart to calm its wild beat.

She lifted her chin and looked behind him. "Yer walking now? Did you lose the van?" She cocked her head. "I've heard of horses running off but never a vehicle so large."

His head bobbed up and down.

"I borrowed the van from the Carashes. If you pass your place, they're right down the road."

"Are you walking home?" Marianna kicked her foot against the dry pine needles.

"It's a mile and a half to the school, and I live just a little beyond that. I offered to your mother to walk your brothers there to show them the way, and then I was going to drive them back. But before I forgot, I wanted to give you this." He pulled a slip of paper from his pocket and handed it to her.

She noticed he'd written down some phone numbers.

"The top one is my home number. The bottom my cell, though it's spotty in these parts."

Marianna placed a hand on her hip. "You really don't know much about the Amish, do you?"

"Well, I know some but not much, why?"

"We don't believe in having phones. Or electricity. My uncle assured Dat this was an Amish place with no wires going to the house." Even as she said that, she scowled over the fact there was a generator and electric lights in the barn.

"That's right. There are no wires in the house. But there is wiring in the barn and you do have a phone. It's out in the shed." Ben pointed to a small building next to the barn.

Her brow furrowed. "What for?"

"The last Amish folks that lived here, well, they ran a business. Had a little milking operation, I believe. He took orders over the phone."

"They don't sound much like Amish folks. First the generator to run the milking machine and then a phone?" She clucked her tongue.

"I don't see what the problem is. Your father worked in a factory back in Indiana, didn't he? I'm sure they had electricity. They had a phone for orders, right?"

She knew her father went to work, in addition to farming, but she hadn't given much thought to the fact he'd entered into the Englisch world to do his job. "I suppose."

"This phone was for the same purpose."

"*Ja*, well, just because it's there doesn't mean we have to use it. Our Ordnung states we are not to use telephones, and in my opinion what's the difference between having the wire go to the shed and the house? I doubt we'll have a need for it."

Ben eyed her for a minute and narrowed his gaze as if attempting to figure her out. He opened his mouth and then closed it again, as if wondering what to say, and then as his eyes brightened with a challenge. She knew he'd decided to say exactly what he felt.

"Listen. Things are different here. It's not like your neighbor's house is just a stone's throw away. I'm not sure how things worked back home, but people live a ways a part. There might be an emergency. And you might need to call me sometime."

Marianna cocked an eyebrow.

"You know, if you need a ride into Eureka."

"*Ja*, of course, there's always that."

She folded the paper in her hands once, then folded it again. Back home she'd often gone to the neighbor's house to use her phone to schedule a driver. She just didn't understand why the idea of calling Ben for the same reason bothered her so.

Ben turned to the house. "If you'll excuse me, I'll go get those boys."

"Yes, of course." She squeezed the paper in her fist, realizing he was right. What would she do it there was an emergency? Who would she turn to?

Ben strode to the house with long steps, whistling a happy tune. She crossed her arms over her chest as she watched, surprised her mother was letting the boys go. They'd left Indiana so Levi wouldn't influence them, and now she was letting them hang out with this Englisch driver. Marianna shook her head and made her way to the house. It made no sense.

But then again, she wouldn't be around long enough to worry about it.

CHAPTER SIXTEEN

he house was bigger inside than Marianna expected. Nicer too. A large porch wrapped around the entire house and double doors welcomed her. She stepped through the front door and scanned the large *L*-shaped area that was a dining room, living room, and kitchen. There were two doors off the living area, and she assumed one was a bedroom and the other a bathroom. Wide stairs led upward to an open balcony. She heard squeals and the pounding of feet up there. It sounded like a stampede of cattle but was just the kids playing tag.

Ben's voice drifted down from upstairs, and a moment later he descended, three boys in tow.

David grinned at her. "See you later. We're walking to school."

"Yes, I've heard." She moved to an old kitchen table that the previous owners had left and sat down heavily on the long bench. "David, be sure you keep an eye on Josiah, yes? He tends to wander off. And if Mr. Stone needs anything translated, please help him. Mr. Stone doesn't understand Pennsylvania Dutch."

Ben walked to the door. "Translations are helpful."

The boys left, a bundle of energy racing out the door. She couldn't help her smile as they hurried down the lane, and Ben broke into a jog to keep up with them.

Mem's footsteps sounded heavy coming down the stairs. She held Ellie's hand as they descended, and the strain of the trip was evident in her face.

"Don't worry about the boxes, Mem. I'll start unpacking and find a way for us to have baths."

"Thank you." Mem approached the table and sat beside Marianna, also watching through the window as the boys crested a hill and followed the road to the other side. Ellie rubbed her eyes and then climbed into Mem's lap. Mem cleared her throat. "He's harmless, you know."

"Who?" Marianna turned and brushed stray hairs back from her face, trying to muster the energy to tackle the boxes.

"Ben." Mem smoothed a hand over Ellie's back, rubbing it in small circles.

"He's Englisch."

"Yes, I know."

"Which doesn't make him harmless."

Mem shrugged. "He wants to help. And I think we need all the help we can get."

They sat there a few minutes, taking in the view of the trees and the field across the road. Down that road somewhere was another house, and she had no doubt others lived around them, but looking around one would never know it. It was as if they were the only family in this part of the world.

"There are three large bedrooms upstairs. I thought Dat and I would take one and put the kids in the other two." Mem turned and pointed to the door off the living room. "The small bedroom should work for you."

"Yes, I don't need much. I won't be staying long, after all."

"So I've heard." Mem rose and moved back upstairs, with Ellie snuggled to her chest. The way she carried Ellie caused Mem's dress to press around her frame. Her mother's stomach was evident, small and round, like a ball under her dress. Seeing it, Marianna couldn't help but smile. Despite the fact she didn't agree with her mother's opinion about Ben, and the fact they'd had two very hard days of travel, the realization that another family member would join them by fall was something to be happy about.

Marianna rose. "You should rest, too. I'll try to find some bedding in those boxes."

"No need. The beds are already made. I assume some of the Amish from the new community took care of that. And provided the furniture, too."

"Really?" Marianna rubbed the back of her neck.

"I don't know who else would have done it."

Her mother continued up the stairs, and Marianna went to her bedroom. A twin bed was pushed against one wall. A light green blanket covered it. A wooden stand stood in the corner with a water basin. Unlike the barn, someone had paid attention to this room. And as Marianna stepped inside, she noticed a dresser behind the door sported a vase of wildflowers. Seeing that, Marianna stopped in her tracks and a tinge of anger rose. She didn't want to like this place, these people. Not even a little.

But someone was making it very hard for her to stick to that.

It took her a few hours to unpack the boxes. In that time the boys had returned and then set off again to explore the field across the road.

"Just stay where I can see you!" Marianna called after them. Then she broke down the boxes and folded them up, carrying them to the shed for storage.

Her father must have tackled the small shed first, because when she entered it was as neat as a pin. On a tall shelf sat a jar of liniment and braided rope for the horse. On two nails he'd hung extra horseshoes. And next to that hung a calendar from a local bank. A photo of tall mountains and a lake decorated this month. It wasn't until she read the name Lake Kookanusa on the border that she realized it was the lake they'd passed to get to the West Kootenai. *I really live here—in this beautiful place.*

She set the boxes in the corner and, as she was leaving the room, a sharp ringing filled the air. Marianna jumped and her heart lodged in her throat. She turned and looked to the phone, wondering what she should do. It rang again and she stepped out the door, scanning their property to see if her father happened to be there. He was nowhere in sight.

She walked back in the shed as the phone rang a third time. Even though she'd called out many times on a phone, she'd never answered one. With a trembling hand she picked up the receiver. "Hello?"

"Ah-ha, caught you." It was Ben's voice.

"Excuse me?"

He laughed. "I thought you wouldn't use the phone."

"Well, I wasn't going to. But it rang, and I didn't know what to do." She kicked the hay with her foot, trying not to laugh with him.

"I found out I'm going to Eureka tomorrow. I wanted to see if you or someone needed a ride."

She paused for a minute. It would be good to get some groceries. Tonight they'd finish off the rest of the food they'd packed for the train. Still, she was certain they could get some things at the Kootenai store. "Oh, no, I don't think so. We—" She couldn't think of an excuse not to go.

"I'm not charging. Just being neighborly."

"Thank you. I appreciate that, but I think it will take us a few days to figure out what we need."

"Sure, let me know." Ben's voice held a hint of disappointment. "There's a larger grocery store, a hardware store, and a fabric store."

"Fabric store?" A soft breath escaped her lips. She did need fabric for the back panel and batting for the quilt face she'd brought along.

"Yes, many of the ladies around here like to go there."

"I'd love to. Sometime, but not tomorrow." She fiddled with the cord to the phone.

"Another time then." Ben was quiet, waiting for her to respond.

Her fingers fiddled with the phone, and she hoped this wasn't going to be a regular occurrence, him calling. She hated the fact they had a phone, but appreciated he'd thought to call. She also was excited there was a fabric store, but at the same time she was overwhelmed thinking of all they yet had to do. She still hadn't figured out what to do for baths and laundry. Nor was she comfortable with the fact that her brothers would be heading off to school so soon, or that Ben had showed them the way.

"Yes, another time. Thank you." She hung up the phone before Ben could start talking about other things. And before she got fond of hearing his voice on the other end.

Marianna curled to her side and willed the heat from the wood stove to travel under the door. As soon as the sun set, the night had turned cold, and she hadn't packed enough warm things and only had one extra blanket. Her arms were weary from unpacking and from carrying warm water from the large heating kettle outside to the round tub in the bathroom.

Dat had gone to the grocery store for a few things, and after dinner she'd attempted to write a letter but couldn't get her mind to focus on the page. Instead, she'd pulled her quilt out of the box and eyed the pattern of the horse in the center and the loops and roses around the edge. One of the first pictures Aaron had drawn for her had been a horse like this, so it seemed only fitting to choose this for their quilt.

When it was finished, the quilt would be the perfect addition to her cedar chest. But truth be told, she wished she had it done now. Not only would it help keep her warm, it would also be good to look at. To remember—even during hard days like today—that someday she'd be caring for her own house, in her own way, with her own husband at her side.

She considered getting out of bed to open the door, but the thought of her feet on the cool wooden planks sent a shiver up her spine. Then again, cold feet for a few minutes was better than a cold body all night. Not giving herself time to talk her way out of it, Marianna pushed back the blanket and bolted from bed. In three long strides she was across the room to the door. With a twist of the door handle she opened the door, left it ajar, and then hurried back into bed, burying down beneath the covers. She waited for the heat to come, but it barely trickled into the room.

As she lay there, she heard heavy footsteps coming down the stairs. It had to be David.

"David, did you stoke the fire as Dat said?"

He didn't respond. She thought about calling out to him again when he poked his head into her room. "Did you hear that?"

"Hear what?" She snuggled deeper under her blanket.

"There's something outside. I think it's a dog."

"How do you know? It could be a wolf or a bear." She was only teasing, but from the troubled look on his face she could see he didn't find it funny.

David shook his head and then headed back into the living room.

"Where are you going?" She called louder, not caring if she woke her parents.

"It's a dog. I can hear him whining. I'm going to check on him. Maybe he's lost or hurt."

"It's not a dog, and don't you dare open that door." She really should get out of bed . . . but the thought of the cold planks on her feet held her fast.

"Yes, it is. I can see it through the window, in the moonlight. He's just a little guy."

The sound of the door squeaking open was followed by the rumble of footsteps across the floor. Marianna sat up as the sound grew louder and fear coursed through her chest. It *was* a wolf and it sensed her fear. She was sure of it. The beast was coming toward her!

She thought about praying for safety, but before a prayer formed in her mind the blur of a dark shadow caught her attention. A small animal flew through the air and landed on her bed—a wet, furry mass jumping on her. A warm tongue licked her face.

She pushed on the creature, trying to get him off her. The scent of mud and wet fur overwhelmed her, and she thought she was going to lose her supper.

Laughter spilled from her bedroom doorway, and she could make out her brother's outline.

"I told you it was a dog." David chuckled.

"A horrible, stinky dog that just covered me and my bed with mud. What were you thinking, opening the door like that? Can you light the lantern, please?"

"But Dat said to only use it in case of an emergency. We need to get to the store for more propane . . ."

"This *is* an emergency!" she shouted, attempting to grab hold of the wiggling creature. "I have a wild animal in my bed!"

She jumped up and hurried into the living room, lighting the propane lantern herself. The creature followed her, staying close to her heels. She turned, eyeing it in the light, and felt her eyes widen. It was a small gray dog, not much bigger than a large cat.

The dog lifted his head and looked up at her, tail wagging. His fur was matted and his ribs showed.

"Poor thing." She knelt next to him, and he scooted close to her leg. Ignoring how filthy he was, Marianna scratched behind his ear. "You poor little guy. Where did you come from?"

"Everything all right down there?" Dat's voice called from up the stairs.

"It looks like we have a visitor. He's so thin . . ." Marianna's lower lip pouted. "Seems as he's lived in those woods a while. I wonder when he last had a good meal?"

Dat came down the stairs, dressed in his nightshirt and rubbing his eyes. His eyes widened when he saw the creature. Dat had never been a pet person. In his opinion the only animals worth keeping around were the ones that earned their feed.

"He does look a little thin and lost." Dat crossed his arms over his chest. "I feel sorry for him, but I wouldn't get too close. Could have ticks and fleas."

"Too late. It was already on Marianna's bed." David shook his head, laughing.

"Not by my choice. It attacked me." Then she tilted her head. "Still, he doesn't seem like he has a home. Maybe we should keep him around—as a friend for the kids." She shrugged. "You know, to help them adjust."

"Tell you what"—Dat turned back to the stairs—"David, why don't you take the dog to the shed tonight and I'll look him over tomorrow." Dat yawned. "Could be the last owners left him here."

"They'd do that?" Marianna stood and then watched as David snatched the small dog up. The dog continued to look at her, ears perked.

"Maybe. Either that or he saw the opportunity to make a home with the new folks moving in."

Marianna scratched the dog's ears again, looking into his large dark eyes. Even though his tail wagged, his eyes held a gaze of hopefulness. All he wanted was a home. To be loved. Marianna offered a sad smile as David carried the dog outside, understanding. All she wanted was the same.

Dear June-Sevenies,

*I know it's a week to my birthday yet, but I received a
surprise last night—my first night at our Montana home.
I wouldn't call the small creature a gift, but he was a
surprise.*

*I was just settling into bed when David heard whining
outside. He opened the door and this small dog raced
into the house. He ran right past David and bounded
for me in my bed. He was a wiggling mess of tongue and
tail, and it took all my strength to hang on to him. And
oh what a dirty mess! He looks as if he's been living in the
woods for a while. He's thin and his fur was tangled. Dat
believes he must have belonged to the previous owners,
although I can't imagine how someone could leave their
home and also leave their small dog behind! Living on
the farm we've never had a dog for a pet before. This dog,
on the other hand, thinks he owns the whole house. He
follows me from room to room and only goes outside if
I venture out too. What an inconvenience!*

*Our house is nice, but I've discovered some things are
more primitive. There is running water in the kitchen,
but it must be a small well because that is the only
plumbing in the house. We get the rest of the water from
a large feed trough out back. It had been filled with rain
water but Uncle Ike cleaned it out and went down to the
Carashes' house to get fresh water. There is a large fire pit
out back and a kettle to heat the water for laundry and*

baths. *The washing tub is on the back porch and it's fine now, but I can't imagine what happens in winter, maybe move the whole system in the middle of the living room?*

All of us got baths and our clothes washed. Such a little thing before seemed like a big accomplishment. I washed up Trapper, too. Yes, that's what we named our dog. Charlie picked the name because he's sure the dog figured out how to trap in order to stay alive in those woods. Personally, he has so much energy I don't think he'd let himself stop long enough to die. I have to admit he is much cuter once he's bathed, but I refuse to let him sleep with me no matter how much he whines.

I've been thinking about it, and maybe I should try to get back in time for Clara's wedding. Clara, telling me Aaron is attending has me thinking this way. There's nothing more romantic than sitting at a wedding knowing that the man you fancy is sitting close by. I was worried about getting enough money before then, but Uncle Ike was telling me about the Amish Auction coming up in a few weeks. He said it's a big thing around these parts. Folks come from all around the country and bid on Amish made things, like handmade furniture, quilts, and even log homes! If I can get to town soon for supplies, I might be able to finish my quilt in time. Uncle Ike said he's seen quilts go for over a thousand dollars. Imagine that.

Well, I better go, the boys should get home from school soon. I'm curious to hear about their day. I feel like Aunt Ida—waiting on the porch for our visits, wanting to know the whos and whats. Unlike Aunt Ida, I have no one to spread the news too. I'm sure all of you aren't that interested about the latest news of the West Kootenai Amish!

Sending all my love (and a Montana wildflower), Marianna

Ben breathed in the fresh, Saturday morning air and fingered the envelope in his hand as he entered the Kootenai store, where he dropped the letter in the *out* basket. Edgar didn't comment, but the older clerk looked at the envelope with sadness in his face. One would think after seeing the same thing happen every week, Edgar would have gotten used to it by now.

"Ike's looking for you." Edgar said, returning to the Kalispell newspaper spread before him.

"Thanks." Ben headed to the dining area and even before he rounded the corner he knew he'd find Ike in the second booth on the left. Ike always sat in the second booth. Ben's feet slowed as he noticed Ike's brother, Abe, sitting across from him, sipping coffee.

Ben continued into the room, preparing to sit at a different booth when Ike motioned to him. "You can sit with us. The ladies should be gathering soon, and we men need to stick together. Besides, I have something to ask."

"Sure." Ben slid into the booth next to Ike, then motioned to Annie in the kitchen for a cup of coffee. With a grin she grabbed a mug, filled it, brought it his way, and then hurried back into the kitchen.

"Women gathering?" Abe shifted slightly in his seat as if uncomfortable about Ben joining them.

"Yup." Ike cut his scone with a fork. "The Amish ladies show up around 8:30 and the Englisch filter in around nine. They just eat and gab. You know, talking about women stuff."

"The Amish and . . ." Abe started and then stopped.

"The Amish and Englisch sit together?" Ike took a bite, chewed and swallowed. "Is that what you were going to ask?"

Abe looked to Ben, then to Ike. "Maybe." He lowered his head.

"I'm not offended really." Ben raised his hands. "I wondered the same thing too. But as Ike here has reminded me, if we're all children of God, then we have to have a family reunion once in a while." Ben elbowed Ike's ribs. "Ain't that right."

Ike nodded.

"Yes, well, that's not how I'm used to doing things." Abe lowered his head and finished eating his meal. He was at least fifteen years older than Ike, and he seemed set in his ways. Ben wanted to ask why he'd come to Montana but knew it would be important to give Abe time. He'd heard it took a long time—sometimes years—for Amish to trust outsiders.

As they sat there, women started entering. As each woman passed by, Ike introduced them to his brother.

Abe tensed up the first few times he was introduced to Englisch women, and Ben could tell from the man's face he'd never seen anything like this before—women from both sides gathering and talking as friends.

Ben wondered if Abe would tell his wife and eldest daughter about it. It would do Marianna good to get out and meet some people. She seemed bent on making this place as close to Indiana as she could get. It might work for a while to focus on tending a home and only communicating with other Amish, but as soon as the snow flew—if they stayed that long—it would be a different story. They needed each other.

All of them did.

Ben glanced at Ike. "Did you have a question for me?"

"Yeah." Ike leaned forward in the booth and rested his elbows on the wooden table, then he lowered his voice. "Is there any place in Eureka one could get an English Bible?"

Ben tilted his head. Though the Amish only read German Bibles, Ike had been reading an English one ever since he'd started attending the small Bible study Ben also attended. Most likely Abe didn't know that . . .

Ben nodded. "Yes, why?"

"Well, my brother here has already been asked to be part of the rotation for preaching. I'm not sure you know how our church works, Ben, but most congregations have a bishop who handles that duty. Because we're so small we've yet to get one, the responsibility falls on the men." Ike looked to Abe and Ben followed his gaze, noticing the older man's cheeks reddening.

"He doesn't read German," Ike continued, "and I suggested reading English might be easier."

From the tone and the expressions on the men's faces, one would think they were planning a bank robbery.

Ben hid his smile and nodded. "That makes sense. I'll be heading into Eureka soon and I'll see what I can find."

Abe cleared his throat. "But no one must know."

"Of course not." Ben folded his hands on his lap. "Your secret is safe with me."

"There is one more thing." Ike focused on Ben. "If there are passages my brother doesn't understand, can we talk to you about them? I know you've studied the Bible a great deal."

"Yes. I don't know everything, but I'll do what I can to help."

"*Denke.*"

At Abe's quiet thanks, Ben met the man's gaze—and started. Marianna had her father's eyes.

Abe cleared his throat. "This is new to me, and truth be told I don't want to make a fool of myself in front of all these folks."

"I understand." But he didn't. Not really. If Abe didn't read the German Bible well—and didn't have an English one—how much time, really, did he spend in God's Word?

Ben took a sip of coffee, pondering these people and their strange ways, wondering again how he ended up here—called to work for them. Most days he enjoyed it, but he hadn't really gotten used to feeling like an outsider. Like yesterday when Marianna did her best to ignore him once they got to their house.

As Abe and Ike turned their talk to the log-home business that Abe would soon work for, the laughter of women's voices filled the air, joined by the jingling of the bell on the front door. From his view from the restaurant, Ben watched as five women, entered. From their rosy cheeks, he guessed they'd walked to the store, talking and laughing as they went. Yet as they moved from the store area to the restaurant, their voices lowered and they eyed the room, first looking to Annie and then to him.

No matter how friendly they were, the message of their looks and quieting voices was clear:

We are among outsiders. We must be careful. We must always keep up our guard.

CHAPTER SEVENTEEN

arianna didn't know what she'd been thinking, believing she could finish her quilt in time for the auction. She hadn't even made it to town, let alone found time to work on it.

Dat cleaned up a buggy he'd bought from another family and guided the boys in cleaning out the barn. She'd shopped for Mem at the Kootenai Kraft and Grocery and a few times took Dat his lunch at his new job at Kootenai Log Homes, where he worked with Uncle Ike. Then there was all the cooking and cleaning. Now she was helping the little ones get ready for their first church gathering. They'd all woken up early to bathe and press their clothes just so.

Over the last week and a half they'd met a few members of other Amish families. Some had struck up a conversation at the store. Others had greeted Marianna and the children on the road when she took Trapper for walks. Everyone seemed nice, but she was having a hard time remembering who belonged with which family. Today would be a new experience. They'd all be in one place, and she'd really get a good look at the type of people who called this area home.

It felt good in a way to see the other buggies pulling in and parking. She let out a soft breath when she spotted all the men congregating near the front of the barn, and all the young men near the back. At least some things were the same.

Dat pulled up by the front door of the Peachy house, and Mem climbed out. Marianna followed and then turned and helped Ellie down.

Planting Ellie's feet on the ground Marianna leaned over and whispered in her ear. "You be good, you hear. These are nice people and we need to show them we're a nice family."

"Hello, hello there!" A woman's voice carried in the air like a bird's song. "You must be the Sommer family." She bustled outside with open arms, and Marianna was surprised to be greeted with a holy kiss. The round, smiling woman turned to Mem and greeted her the same way.

The first thing Marianna noticed was the woman's kapp. There was less stitching in the back and it fit loosely on the woman's head. Marianna could picture her grandmother's mouth gaping if she saw such a thing. According to Grandma, and everyone else back in their community, to have a kapp like that was a sign of laziness. There was one specific way for them to be sewn—much more intricately and better fitted. Apparently this woman was unaware of that fact. Still, Marianna forced a smile and told herself to focus on the woman's warm welcome instead.

"We are so glad you can join us today. Ike has told us so much about you. We feel as if yer old friends yet. My name is Sallie Peachy and my daughters are around here somewhere." She looked to Marianna. "About your age. I'll introduce you when I spot them. Eve and Hope are most likely checking out the bachelors. There are thirty of them around here," the woman babbled on. "They come in the spring and work through the summer in order to get their residential hunting license." She turned to Marianna. "So if you don't yet have someone special dear, there's many to choose from."

"Well, I—"

"Thank you. We are happy to be here," her mother interrupted, patting her kapp and smiling. "My husband has told me—"

"Oh my, oh dear!" Sallie stepped closer to Mem, pressing her hands on her stomach. "It looks like your family is growing, what a wonderful surprise. Oh, look over there. Come, I'll introduce you to the other women, and we'll check the schedule to see when church is at your house."

Mem nodded, and Marianna's eyes grew wide at Sallie's energy. She'd been looking forward to sitting back and observing everyone today, but she knew this woman wouldn't allow that.

"Come inside." Sallie motioned again, leading them through a screened-in front porch. It was simple, made of bare sheets of plywood. Chopped wood for the stove lined the walls. "We set out extra seats for we knew your family was coming, and around these parts when the snow melts we also know there will be extra guests. Everyone seems to have someone visiting this time of year. Especially with the auction coming up next week yet."

Marianna nodded following the woman into the living room area where other women were already sitting. She opened her mouth to mention her eagerness over the auction, but before she could say anything Sallie sucked in a breath and started in again.

"You are such a pretty thing. I'm sure you'll have no trouble gaining the affection of one of the bachelors, if not more. Your name is Marianna, right? Your uncle told me a little about you. How old are you, my dear?"

"I'll be twenty soon. On June 7." Marianna spotted two young women in the kitchen who looked to be younger versions of Sallie. She guessed they were her daughters, Eve and Hope. Before she had a chance to ask to be introduced, laughter spilled from Sallie's lips and Marianna looked to Mem, wondering what was so funny. Her hand tightened around Ellie's.

"Mari, I think today is June 7." Mem looked to the woman to see if she'd guessed correctly.

"*Ja*, it is. How someone could forget her birthday I'll never understand." Sallie clicked her tongue.

Marianna forced a smile, but deep down she wondered the same. In a few days she'd no doubt get a large envelope, filled with birthday wishes from all her friends, but the realization that no one from her family remembered pierced her. How much she'd lost when they moved! Levi, Rebecca—*they* would have remembered. Many in her old community would have remembered, too. Aunt Ida always embroidered special towels or pillowcases as a gift for Marianna to put in her trunk.

She sat on the backless bench and pulled Ellie on her lap, telling herself not to look around, not to notice all the differences lest she break into tears. An emptiness expanded in her chest as she realized how many miles spread between here and the only community she'd ever known. Tears lined her bottom lids as she imagined all the families gathered around the tables for lunch. The laughter. The familiar faces. The many birthday wishes. She imagined Rebecca showing up at church, as a gift to her, and surprising her with a large slice of homemade pie. She bit her lip wondering if Aaron would have snuck a small gift, too. Maybe a hand-carved trinket, a drawing, or handmade card just to let her know she was in his thoughts.

Then again . . . for the first time since she could remember, Mem hadn't seemed especially broody today. Marianna's birthday also brought sadness, since it was the anniversary of her sisters' death. Yet today Mem had acted like everything was normal. She'd fixed breakfast and cared for the kids without evidence that her heart was breaking in two.

But even that wasn't enough to blow away the dark clouds that had moved over Marianna's heart.

Her knees quivered, despite her best efforts to keep her feelings inside. She did her best through the singing. She attempted to focus during the silent prayers, but it was hard to keep the tears pent up when the preacher was introduced for the day, for it wasn't a preacher at all, but Mr. Peachy. He was tall and wide with a red beard that seemed to bounce when he spoke. After leading them in silent prayers, he explained to the newcomers that since their community had no bishop, no ministers, all the men took turns sharing a word from the Scriptures whenever church was hosted in their homes.

Though she kept her eyes focused forward, Marianna reached over and poked Mem's side and she felt her mother stiffen beside her. They'd been here less than two weeks and each day they found a difference between this community and the one they left. Although it was challenging, they could dismiss most differences, but this . . .

Ellie must have felt Marianna's stiffness because she scooted over and moved onto Mem's lap.

Marianna crossed her arms over her chest and listened, but the words didn't sink in. Instead she thought of something else. If the men in the community took turns preaching when church was in their home, then that meant her father would have his turn too. She looked across the room to where her father sat. She could only see part of his face, as he looked ahead and though she couldn't see his expression, she clearly noted his fists clenched on his lap.

Obviously, he wasn't happy with this. The question was, was it enough to get them packing and heading home?

The rest of the service followed an order similar to what Marianna was used to, and she had to admit the people were nice. Many women approached to talk to her as they got out the food after service and laid it out for all the men. Eve and Hope introduced themselves and offered to come by and visit that week and show her the way down to the lake. Marianna agreed. She'd spent so much time caring for others she liked the idea of taking Trapper down for a walk along the lakeside.

At least I can enjoy the time I'm here.

They were climbing into the buggy when a woman approached. She was half the size of Mrs. Peachy and her voice was half as loud. Marianna liked her.

"I'm sorry to bother you yet, I'm Deborah Shelter. I know you're heading home, but I'm sure you've heard of the auction. It's a fundraiser for our school. The whole community helps, and I was wondering if I could ask fer your help that day. I wouldn't ask 'cept I've heard you plan to be part of our community for a while, and I know your sons benefit from our school."

Mem straightened her back. "Yes, of course. How can we help?"

The woman's face pinched up, and Marianna could tell she didn't like to impose. "Well, if you're not too busy, we'll need someone to help with the quilts. Caring for them. Taking them to the auctioneer and such. And another to help with the food . . ."

"I can help with the quilts." Marianna leaned forward in the seat. "If that's okay, Dat?"

"*Ja*, of course." Dat stroked his beard and looked to Mem.

"I could help, too."

Marianna knew that's what her mother's answer would be. After all, what would it look like if she refused?

"Wonderful. Since you're planning to be around a while, this will give you a chance to meet pretty much everyone from these parts." The woman clapped her hands together so softly they didn't make a sound. "If you'll be at the store at 8 o'clock on Saturday, we'll be all set." The woman chatted with her mother for a few more minutes, telling her how all the money for the auction went to the school and for a much-needed firehouse, and Marianna noticed that Mem answered in as few words as possible.

As they drove away, the buggy wheels followed the dirt road, dipping and rising through the potholes, and Marianna couldn't help but recognize the tension between her parents.

"So yer telling folks we're gonna be here a while?" Mem's words pushed out through clenched teeth. "More than one woman told me she was happy we'd committed to a longer lease on our home."

An angry electricity flashed between her parents. Months ago the tension had been over them coming. Now it seemed it had shifted to the idea of them staying. Until today Marianna had believed her father when he'd said they'd only come for a year. But it seemed the community members were hearing otherwise.

And the frightening thing was, as they continued down the road, listening to the squeak of the buggy as it rolled along, Dat didn't deny that claim.

Dear Mari,

It was strange to address this letter and know that it was going to find you at another place. My intent is to wish you a Happy Birthday and to let you know how your old brother is doing. I'm fine I suppose. I've been better. I wanted you to know first that I broke off my relationship with Naomi. I've been thinkin' a lot of what you said that night a month ago, and I realized it is the truth. Naomi wouldn't think of leaving if it weren't for me. She's a nice girl, but I keep wondering what would happen to her if things don't work out with us. I'd hate to put her into the position of having to go back to her family home in shame. She says I broke her heart, but she'd find a new suitor. I don't have a doubt about that. Philip Beiler has always fancied her, and he's already been baptized into the church.

Write and let me know how things are. I got a new job, and I still have my friends, but my heart feels like it's only hanging by a thin string every time I think Dat, Mem, you, and the kids aren't at the place. I've tried twice to drive by but turned around. It makes me happy to know you'll be around before long, and I'll be able to throw gravel at Aunt Ida's window.

Tell David he's the man under Dat now.
Your brother,
Levi

CHAPTER EIGHTEEN

The air was cold and the first rays of sunlight crept over the mountains. Today would be a big day at the auction. Dat was excited that one of the log cabins he'd worked on would be auctioned off.

More than once she'd also heard him telling Mem, "Just wait. Don't get mad at me for wanting to stay longer than a year until you spend a day with the community. Until you see for yourself what Ike's been talking about, and what I've been witnessing at work."

It seemed Dat counted on this day making Mem like it here so much she wouldn't want to go back. The only problem was, Mem had volunteered to help with the food, and to Marianna that didn't sound like an enjoyable way to spend the day.

Marianna's small purse rested on her lap. In it was the money she'd saved up from caring for Mrs. Ropp's kids. She guessed she'd need money for food, and it would be nice to have it if something else caught her eye.

She sat on the porch fiddling with a long stick between her fingers. Trapper sat at her feet, his eyes focused on the stick. She twitched it to the left and his eyes followed. She lifted it a few inches, and he took a step back, waiting to run after it as soon as it was thrown.

"Want it?" She grinned and lifted it over her head, then she turned her body to the right, launching the stick in the direction of the barn. Trapper bounded after it and returned a moment later, setting it at her feet. She picked it up again, but her mind wasn't on their game. Her mind wasn't even on the morning's auction. Instead, it was on the letter Uncle Ike had brought in last night from town.

Marianna had read Levi's letter a dozen times, and each time the ache of missing him deepened. Growing up they'd never been close. Levi had been quick to pull her hair, throw rocks at her on the way home from school, push her into the creek, and then laugh as she scrambled up the muddy bank. But that was then. Things had changed since they'd gotten older, and not seeing him much over the last year had made her miss him in ways she hadn't expected.

Her heart ached for Naomi too. Marianna thought back to the excited look in Naomi's face over her hopes of being with Levi. Though they both would have broken hearts for a while, Marianna knew he was doing the right thing. And there was something else: Clearly, Levi knew the Amish way was right. Otherwise he wouldn't have made the sacrifice for Naomi to stay. Marianna had thought about sharing the letter with her parents. Maybe it would give them hope. But instead she folded it up and placed it in the dresser drawer underneath her underclothes. They hadn't mentioned Levi since they left, and she didn't want to be the one to sour their moods.

The sound of the horse's hooves and the crunch of the wheels on the road, alerted her to the buggy's approach.

She rose, grabbing her purse, and led Trapper to the house, putting him inside. He whined at the door wanting to stay out, but she knew better. More than once he'd followed the buggy to town, darting around the slow moving buggies and cars. She couldn't risk that. There would be too many automobiles, too many distracted people today. As much as she found the dog a hassle, she was also getting used to having him around.

Since she had to be there before anyone else, Uncle Ike said he'd give her a ride. He must have noticed her introspective mood when she climbed into the buggy, but he didn't mention it. Instead, he filled the silence with information about the day.

"You're not going to believe it when you see it. I think this is going to be the biggest auction yet. There are two large fields filled with RVs. Annie at the store told me last night she's met folks from Washington State, North Dakota, and even New York."

"They all come here? For this?"

"*Ja*, partly for the items, and partly for the event. When yer Aunt Ida heard about the price some of these quilts fetch, she sent me four of hers. Said she could only get half as much back in Indiana."

"Did you bring the quilts?" Marianna looked to the seat behind her, but didn't see them.

"Oh, I dropped them off last week. They need them that soon to get ready. Each quilt will get a number, and they make up a sheet of all of them, jest so people can see who made them and where they came from."

As they neared the store, Marianna could see that Uncle Ike wasn't joking about all the people. They rolled over the hill, and she saw cars already parked on the side of the road. The sun still hadn't crested over the mountains, yet there was already a line of folks who'd parked and were walking toward the store.

When they neared, Marianna noticed there was only one other buggy parked near the auction area.

"Where is everyone? Did the Amish forget to show up at their own event?" She chuckled, feeling the sadness of Levi's letter give away to the excitement of the day.

"No. I believe almost everyone will be out in these parts today. Most of them walk, though, since it's close. Or ride their bicycles."

Marianna cocked an eyebrow, not wanting to tell her uncle what she thought about that. Bicycles were another thing that hadn't been permitted in their Indiana community. Everyone, it seemed, rode them here.

After Uncle Ike parked, she hurried to the store where she was supposed to meet Mrs. Shelter. Entering the front door, she looked around for the woman and then heard voices in the restaurant. Turning the corner near the wood stove, Marianna stopped short. Dozens and dozens of quilts were laid out. The room was filled with color, and Marianna couldn't help but draw in a deep breath, placing a hand over her heart at the bright beauty in the room.

The Amish had many rules about their dress. They even had rules about keeping a plain home, but one place the women enjoyed expressing their artistic nature, and their creativity, was in their quilts. She'd never seen so many at one time. Never seen so much color and design swirled together.

"Here's another of my helpers." Deborah Shelter approached and took Marianna's hand into her thin ones. "I'll need your help taking these quilts to the main auction ring. Each quilt has a number on it, telling you which order. You have one job most important."

"And what is that?" Marianna looked around, seeing the others were also listening.

Mrs. Shelter's lips slipped into a thin smile. "Make sure they don't drag on the ground."

"Yes, of course." She chuckled.

After being schooled on the system, Marianna gathered up three quilts, protected in clear plastic bags. The one on the top was a blue and cream Boston Commons quilt similar to one Rebecca had on her bed. Seeing it, an unexpected longing flooded her. The day would be fun, she was sure. But how much more fun would it be to experience with a friend. Marianna hadn't heard from Rebecca since she'd arrived, and a heaviness weighed her steps.

As she transported the quilts outside, the warm June air carried with it scents of pine needles and a hint of the light morning rain that had blown away, over the mountains, much to the thankfulness of those attending the auction. The sound of a vehicle echoed through trees and from the corner of her eye she spotted a small, yellow truck with a blue camper on the back pulling in behind the store. Her steps slowed when she saw Ben driving. He waved and smiled, and then jumped out of the driver's door nearly the same instant the truck came to a stop.

"Hello there, Marianna. I'm glad you could be here for your first auction . . . but you're dragging."

"Oh no!" Marianna looked down and sure enough the quilts were dragging. She lifted them up, thankful the plastic still protected them.

Today Ben wore a red plaid shirt rolled up to his elbows. He looked like a lumberjack. Yet, he wasn't like any mountain man she'd met yet, and unlike any Amish man either. It was his confident steps that impressed her most—like he owned the ground he walked on. And then there was his eyes, crystal blue like the Indiana sky after a spring rain.

His smile broadened. "Here, let me take those. I don't want to hear that tongue lashing you're going to get when Deborah sees that plastic dragging. I think you managed to get a little mud on the plastic, but it's not anything we can't clean up."

"Thank you." Heat rose to Marianna's cheeks. "I'm so sorry." She allowed him to take the quilts from her.

"No worries. I have some old towels in the back of my truck. I'll wipe all the mud off the plastic, and she'll never know." He winked and then hurried to the truck.

Marianna wondered if she should follow him or stay where she was. Her eyes fixed on the man carrying the quilts with a hop in his step, and her feet felt as if they were glued to the ground. She wanted to follow him, wanted to strike up a conversation. She wanted to see him chuckle the way he had the day they'd first met, and that was the problem. She'd never thought much about the Englisch and especially had never wanted to spend time with one of them as she did with Ben.

He opened the back of the truck and used an old towel to wipe off the mud and then turned with a smile. He looked taller than she remembered, and for the first time she noticed a dimple in his chin.

"Thank you for saving me." She smiled back.

She hadn't seen him since that day he'd driven them from the train station. Hadn't talked to him since he'd called on the phone, offering her a ride to Eureka. Thinking back, she wished she'd accepted his offer. Being here at the auction gave her a longing to finish her own quilt. Would it be too forward to ask if she could get a ride into Eureka the next time he went to town?

Ben carried the quilts for Marianna and then headed to the farthest auction ring where two other Amish women were setting up displays.

Numerous buyers were already there—mostly Englisch—looking over the quilts, studying their design, and taking notes on their favorites. As soon as her quilts were hung, Marianna thanked Ben for his help. But when she turned back to the store to get more, instead of heading off in a different direction, Ben followed.

"So do you quilt?"

She liked the way he matched his stride to hers. "I do. I have one I'm trying to finish."

"Too bad you couldn't have gotten it done before the auction. You probably could have fetched a good price for it. I'm sure it's nice."

"I like it, although it's not as fancy as some of these. I thought about finishing it, too, but I haven't had much time, helping around the house and all. But even if I had finished, I wouldn't sell it. I've decided to keep it." She didn't want to tell him she wanted it for her cedar chest, for her future home—a home not in Montana.

"I was sort of surprised to see you helping." He chuckled. "You've hardly arrived, and they've already put you to work." He slowed his pace, as if not wanting them to get to the store too soon.

"I like work. I'm used to it. As my grandmother always told me, idle hands lead to the devil's work."

"Yeah, my grandma used to say the same thing, but I didn't quite believe it. She always wanted me to help her pick beans, but as a twelve-year-old I thought the devil's work sounded more fun."

"Did you grow up around here?"

"No, not at all. I grew up in Southern California, as different as can be from this area."

"Sunny?"

"Yes, and busy. Cars filled the roadways and there are people everywhere."

"So how did you end up here of all places?" Marianna clasped her hands in front of her, listening.

"I first came two years ago to do some brush clearing for the Forest Service. It sounded like a fun summer job for a city guy. My dad didn't want me to go, but my mom convinced him I just needed to go away for a while and find myself. I felt different being here, but when I went home . . ." He lowered his head. "Well, some things happened that changed my life. Some bad things. I knew if I stayed where I was, I'd get into more trouble, so I ran." He spread his arms. "And this is where I came."

"It sounds like this place is special to you." She paused her steps. She knew she should reach for the door, enter, and continue her work, but something inside urged her to stay for just another minute. She enjoyed talking to Ben. Felt like he had nothing to hide.

"The place is special, but mostly because how it turns my thoughts." He looked around them. "When I look at mountains like that, I have to believe there is a God who is caring, artistic, and a bit on the wild side. I wanted to get to know more of His heart and knew this was the place to do it."

She paused and looked at him out of the corner of her eye.

Goosebumps rose on her arms. The way he talked about God was so . . . moving. Confusing. Disturbing.

All of the above.

Sometimes at home her parents mentioned things they were thankful for. But to talk about God this way, with such . . . passion and vulnerability?

Never.

For the most part, she heard about God when she was at church. Even at home they always prayed silently. Marianna thought about the woman on the train. Like her, Ben talked as if God was a friend he'd see later that afternoon. It was all so confusing!

Time to change the subject. "So do you work now?"

"I do. I've done some logging. I deliver log furniture, and lately I've been a driver for a few Amish families. What I'd really like to do is get more steady work—like building log homes. My dream is to buy some property and build a place of my own."

Marianna nodded, and her mind took her back to Aaron. A pang of regret struck her heart . . . she should have gone to see his cabin. Did he still work on it? Still think of her? She'd only written him one letter since arriving. She needed to write more. Maybe later today she'd write and tell him about the auction.

They continued to put out more quilts in the main auction ring, Ben walking alongside her, carrying them and helping to display them, as if that had been his plan all along. Other ladies also helped put up displays, including Eve and Hope Peachy. They wore matching light blue dresses that looked new, and Marianna wondered if they'd been sewn for this occasion. As she worked, Marianna couldn't help but notice the eyes of the other ladies on her and Ben.

Marianna rubbed her eyebrows, knowing why. She was an Amish girl spending all this time with an Englisch guy.

She spread out the quilt in her hands and turned to see Hope talking and whispering to another girl, looking their direction. Marianna felt as if her collar was rubbing, and she ran a finger along her neck. It's not like she asked Ben to join her. It wasn't even as if she needed his help. She'd answered a few of his questions, and then asked a few of her own. She turned back to the store for the second time, and he trailed her, just like Trapper did at home. Tension built in her shoulders and she paused her steps.

Ben stopped beside her. "Is everything all right?" Ben stopped beside her.

"Actually, no." She crossed her arms, refusing to look back over her shoulder.

"What's wrong? Did you put the wrong numbers on those quilts?"

"I was just hoping to finish my work alone." The words slipped out of her mouth, and Marianna couldn't believe she said them.

He looked to her and a puzzled expression filled his face. "Wait a minute, it's because I'm not Amish, isn't it?"

"Well, it's not only that. It's just that mostly folks don't spend time together talking like this unless they have intentions." Her cheeks warmed at speaking of such things.

"You mean guys and girls can't just be friends?" Ben took a step closer to her and leaned down, his voice almost a whisper. "Is that why we're getting all these looks?"

"It's not how things work. It was the same way back in Indiana. Men have their work and women have theirs. And, well, single men and women really don't spend time together unless they're courting."

"Maybe we should start courting. That'll fix it."

Marianna's eyes widened and laughter spilled from Ben's lips. She refused to respond to his joke and instead took a step backward. "Don't you have other work you need to do?" She looked around, eyeing the men who were hauling log furniture. "There has to be other more exciting things to do around here—other than hanging out with me."

"But you make me laugh." Ben stood with his feet planted. He seemed to have no intentions of heading off to find something else to do.

"Excuse me?" The words came out a whisper.

"I'm serious. You made me laugh the first time I saw you, demanding that baggage worker on the train climb in there and get your box. And your insistence that you weren't going to use the phone . . ." Ben ran a hand through his short brown hair and smiled, as if replaying the memory in his mind.

More Englisch had arrived and filed in the gate. They, for the most part, seemed oblivious to the Amish girl talking to the Englisch guy, but for the tension she felt, it was as if she stood in the middle of them naked. She knew she should dismiss his statement and walk away, but something inside her wanted clarification.

Marianna jutted out her chin. "But those things aren't funny."

"Not really." He crossed his arms over his chest. "But in a way, they are. I don't know much about the Amish, you're right, but I did have my ideas. I have to admit part of me wasn't looking forward to going to the train station to pick up your family. I expected everyone to be somber and quiet. I thought you'd jump if I spoke to you and that you'd be afraid to look me in the eye. I was surprised—and glad—to find I was wrong."

"Maybe I should have been more like that. The way, well, the way we've been acting this morning isn't really acceptable." She looked over Ben's shoulder at the Peachy girls, who had finished with the quilts and were now handing out a handwritten list of auction items, which someone had photocopied for them.

"I see." Ben looked behind him and followed her gaze. "That's a bummer then."

A . . . bummer? Marianna couldn't help but lift her lips slightly. She'd never heard the word before, but she could easily guess what it meant. "Really, why is it a bummer?"

"Because a month ago I loved this area. Everything about it. But it wasn't until you showed up I realized even a place as wonderful as this could get better."

This definitely had to stop! "Yes, well, thank you then."

Before he could speak another word, Marianna spun on her heel and hurried to the store—and, she hoped, safety. She didn't need to hear more—especially considering everything inside her felt lighter. And she couldn't deny the reason.

It was because of Ben's words.

Chapter Nineteen

ay no attention to his words!

All day long Ben's words had kept drifting through her mind. And all day long Marianna had scolded herself. Ben was just being nice. Just being a friend. He didn't mean anything by what he said. He couldn't.

She tried to enjoy the biggest day of the year in the West Kootenai. For a while she walked around with Dat, who carried Ellie on his shoulders and held Josiah's hand. That lasted a few hours until both kids grew tired, and Dat decided to take them home for naps.

After he'd left, she walked around the place alone, watching the people. And—though she didn't want to admit she was doing so—keeping an eye out for Ben. It was maddening! The number of people and all they were doing made her senses ten times more sensitive than ever before. Three auctions took place simultaneously. Unlike back home the auctioneers were Amish. One man was the best. He spoke loud, describing the auction items with fervor. A crowd gathered, their faces brightening as they looked at the items displayed.

The noise of the auctioneers and the buzz of people talking filled the air. Above her the sun warmed her kapp, and in the distance the mountains seemed to be especially majestic, even though she guessed they'd been just as pretty yesterday.

She sniffed the air, the aroma of homemade donuts making her stomach growl. Children ran in every direction. And every now and again, she'd see David and Charlie within the pack, running around the tables that held small items to purchase. It reminded her of the way they played with their friends back home.

If one were to look at her brothers, running around and laughing with the other boys, he'd never guess David and Charlie had just moved there less than a month prior. Her brothers knew the names of all the kids and played with them as if they'd always been the best of friends.

Crowds of smiling people surrounded her. Amazing how much time had been put into preparation for the auction. Each visitor received a sheet of paper with a list of all the auction items and where they came from.

Walking to one of the auction circles, she gazed up at the loft of the big barn. Two quilts hung from the rafters, and she scanned down the list to see who'd made them and where they came from.

"Mrs. Orlie Kauffman, Lone Star Quilt from Shipshewana, Indiana," she read aloud. "Mrs. Harley Troyer, Broken Star Pattern, Rexford, Montana."

The auctioneer rattled off a slew of numbers, and she was amazed how everyone kept track of what was happening. Her mind was too distracted to do that.

The scent of barbecued chicken filled the air, and Marianna's stomach growled. A long line waited to get a plate of chicken, coleslaw, and mashed potatoes. Should she join it? Looking closer, she spotted her mother behind the table, scooping up large heaps of mashed potatoes, placing them on plates with a smile. One of the other ladies turned to Mem, and she must have said something funny because laughter tumbled from her mother's lips.

Marianna paused in her steps. She tilted her head . . . her mother looked so different. So much younger. Marianna couldn't help but smile too.

Mrs. Peachy approached, following Marianna's gaze. "You can get a free meal if you'd like, for all your hard work helping." She wrapped an arm around Marianna's shoulders.

Marianna didn't tell her that it wasn't the food that had drawn her so. "That's wonderful, thank you much."

"Enjoy yourself, and think about making some quilts. You can sell them next year, and I'm sure get a good price."

"I like that idea."

The woman squeezed her shoulder again and left, and a sinking feeling came over Marianna. She wouldn't be here this time next year. If all went as planned, she'd be attending the classes that led to baptism and preparing to make two major decisions in her life: to give herself fully to the church and to a husband.

Trying not to let it bother her that she didn't have anyone to share the day with, Marianna walked to the end of the food line, but the sinking feeling expanded, echoing inside her. She looked to her mother again, now busy chatting with the man Marianna recognized as the clerk at the grocery store. Again her mother smiled, and it wasn't the forced smile Marianna had come to know so well. Her mother was enjoying this day—just as Dat anticipated.

Marianna saw two young girls run by, and for a moment she thought one of them was Ellie. But neither was. Both were older, even though they had the same dark hair and full cheeks. They continued on, catching up with their mother, who strode across the field and chatted with another Amish woman. As she watched, Marianna thought of her older sisters. If only she could have seen what Marilyn and Joanna had looked like. Why hadn't she been brave enough over the years to ask more about their personalities? They'd be twenty-five and twenty-seven by now—no doubt mothers with children of their own. Did Mem and Dat think about that? Consider not only their lost girls, but the generations also lost?

She took a step forward in line, and as her mind turned to that long-ago accident, too-familiar feelings flooded her. How different would her life have been if they'd lived? How different would she be if she weren't always trying to make up for her parents' loss? Hadn't always known, even as she did so, that she was never enough.

She looked around her. Would Joanna's beautiful singing have filled the air, bringing admiring glances and smiles to her parents' faces? Would Marilyn be hosting a table full of the bounty of her garden, making their parents proud of their daughter's skill?

She was one person replacing two. How could she ever be good enough to take their place?

She couldn't. No matter how hard she tried.

She continued to watch the girls, and the loss hit her afresh. One day they were there, her two sisters, running and playing like these girls. And the next day—they weren't. How her mother must have missed their laughter. Had she woken up in the morning thinking about making breakfast for them, only to realize they were gone? Had every child singing, every chubby hand bearing flowers broken her heart anew? And what about Dat and Levi? Each with their own memories of her sisters, memories of that nightmarish night. Marianna's stomach ached at the thought that those two she loved so dearly carried such terrible images with them always. The remembered presence of her sisters had no doubt filled their Indiana home.

No wonder each of her family members had, in their own way, run.

A tap on her shoulder from behind made Marianna jump.

"Miss, are you in line?"

Marianna looked ahead and realized there was a gap between her and the person in front of her.

"I was." Marianna blinked twice, trying to chase away the moisture clouding her eyes. "But I think I've changed my mind. I'm not hungry." With quick steps she left the line. Not knowing where else to go, she approached another auction and attempted to focus on the sale. She tried to push the picture of those two beautiful girls walking hand in hand out of her mind.

It worked for a while. Just like she sometimes got caught up in the gentle rhythm of a buggy's wheels on the roadway, she became entranced with the sound of the auctioneer's voice. With the flow of the people around her, with the beauty and the colors of the quilts. She was so focused, in fact, that she didn't notice the tall man approach, standing beside her.

"Excuse me, I was wondering if you could help me a moment?" He ran a hand down his shaved face and his eyes locked on hers.

"You need help?" Marianna eyed the man, and leaned back as she studied his face. The look in his eye made the hairs on the back of her neck rise, but she told herself she was overreacting. After all, what could he do to her in the middle of a crowd?

"Yes, I'd like to buy a quilt for my fiancée, and I thought you'd tell me which one you like best." He sidled up to her, and when his arm brushed hers, she took a sidestep.

"They're all beautiful." She scanned down the line of the half-dozen quilts that remained. "Well, except for the one with the cactus. I don't care for that pattern much."

"Do you like the red and yellow one?" He pointed to one with a Dutch tile design.

"It is very nice." She took another step sideways, creating more space between them.

"Nice? I need something better than nice."

"Well, I don't know—" Her words died in her throat when the man's arm wrapped around her shoulder.

"Excuse me, sir. I really don't—" She tried to pulled back, but his grip was strong.

"If you were getting married soon, which one would you want to spend your wedding night under?" He squeezed her shoulder and pulled her toward him. "Or maybe you don't want to wait."

Marianna pulled to the side, trying to brush his arm off. "Sir, please . . ."

Out of the corner of her eye, she saw a blur of red.

"I don't think that's the way you treat a lady."

The gruff voice barked near Marianna's ear, and she released a relieved breath.

Ben.

The man turned his head, jutting out his jaw, but didn't let her go. "What did you say?"

Ben moved in front of them, reached out, and gripped this

man's arm, breaking his hold on Marianna. "I *said*, don't believe that's the way you treat a lady.

"Hey, now, I was being friendly."

Ben pushed himself between the man and Marianna, focusing on her face. "You okay?"

She couldn't keep the gratitude from showing in her eyes. "Yes, thank you."

A growl started from the man's chest and parted his lips. "Are you turning your back on me when I'm talking to you?"

"Yes, I suppose I am," Ben called over his shoulder, then his hand cupped her elbow and led her as if it were the most natural thing in the world. Ben guided her away, toward a table where young girls were selling homemade lemonade.

"You can't walk away!"

Ben ignored the angry call and continued on like no one was talking to him. "Would you like a cup of lemonade, Marianna?"

"Yes, thank you." Her ears were perked to the man behind them, and she almost expected him to follow. But when she glanced back over her shoulder, he was stalking off in the opposite direction.

"Don't worry, he's not from around here. He'll be gone in the morning, blown out of town like tumbleweed." Ben forced a smile, but she could see concern in his gaze.

"It's not the first time something like that has happened." But Marianne had to admit this was even more unsettling than the encounter with the man on the train. At least she'd known for certain she'd never see that man again. "But how do you know he doesn't live here? What if he's new?" She didn't want to think she'd run into someone like that again, perhaps when she was walking to the store. She didn't want to imagine him following her home.

"If he's new he won't last, but I really think he came for the day. I know most everyone around these parts, if not all."

"So it's not normally this busy around here? I thought it was always like this," she teased, feeling her heartbeat slow. Her balled fists relaxed.

Laughter spilled from Ben's lips. "No, not even close."

"I don't understand how someone could act like that and think it's not a problem." She rubbed her arms, attempting to erase the rest of the tension.

"Some people don't have social manners." He shrugged, paying for the lemonade and leaving a generous tip in the girls' jar.

She accepted the cup he handed to her and took a long drink. She hadn't realized how thirsty she was until the cool liquid slid down her throat. She sighed. "No social manners. Sort of like me this morning?"

"Actually, I'm the one who needs to apologize. I didn't realize there was such a dividing line. You'd think I would have figured that out after living here a year. I've never been good about staying within those lines." He moved his hand as if pretending to color a picture in the air. "Just ask my first grade teacher. Speaking of which"—Ben used his free hand to pull a few sheets of folded up papers from his pocket—"I wasn't able to save the whole coloring book. It was a mess, but I did save a few pages that your sister colored on." He set the cup on the table and then unfolded the pages. "I thought this one was especially good."

Marianna looked and noticed that it was a drawing of a farm with a barn, rolling hills, and a dog. Ellie had colored those things and then added in some trees and taller mountains. She'd also drawn two stick figures. One was a taller woman—or so she guessed from the kapp and dress—and the other a small girl. They both had large smiles.

There was a brown tinge to the paper where it had gotten wet and tear marks along the side where Ben had pulled it from the book. Marianna smiled. To her the picture was as pretty as any of the quilts.

"Do you think she was drawing Montana?" Ben pointed to the mountains on the page.

Marianna grinned. "I think she was trying to, but it's strange."

"What is?"

"Well, that she and Mem are smiling. We hadn't even been here yet, and she drew both of them with large smiles." Marianna put the page with the others and then refolded them, holding them in her hand. "Ellie wasn't too happy when she first got on the train. Maybe somewhere along the way things changed, and she had a feeling of what it would be like."

"Or maybe she just planned on it." Ben took another sip from his lemonade. "She's a smart girl, maybe deep down she knew the first step was planning to be happy."

CHAPTER TWENTY

*M*arianna had retreated to the cool of the store and was looking at the display case of refrigerated beverages when she noticed Eve and Hope approaching.

"Hi, Marianna. Are you enjoying your day?"

"Yes, it's great fun. I've never been to anything quite like it."

"You don't have auctions back home?" Eve flipped her reddish-blonde braid over her shoulder and took a bottled iced tea from the case.

"We had auctions, but usually with Englisch auctioneers. "Also, I've never been to one that opened with a prayer—a spoken prayer, that is." All the Amish she knew back home only prayed silently, reverently.

"Yes, I know." Hope shook her head. "That's one of the things about living here. Amish move here from all over the United States, and each bring their own traditions and ideas. We were only ten or so when we came, but we noticed differences. I'm sure you have too."

"Yes, but nothing too different . . ." She let her words trail off, knowing it would sound prideful if she pointed out examples.

After all, she didn't want them to believe she thought the way she'd grown up with was the only way.

"One thing that alarmed us at first is how nice the Englisch are." Eve was as talkative and bubbly as her mother.

Hope continued the thought. "They talked to us all the time, and we weren't used to it. Sort of like Ben did today, with you."

Marianna felt heat rise to her cheeks despite the fact she was standing in front of a refrigerated case. "I'm not used to it, but he seems nice enough." She shrugged. "I think he knows I'm new and is trying to make me feel welcome."

An Englisch woman neared the display case, scanning her choices, and they lowered their voices.

"He is just being nice, and you don't have to worry. He's not fancy on you. He—" Hope turned to Eve and scrunched her nose as if wondering if she should continue.

"What? What were you going to say?" Marianna looked from Eve, to Hope, and back to Eve again.

"Well, we shouldn't mention anything, but Ben drove us to Eureka yesterday, and the whole way he talked to our dad about wanting work building log homes. He said he'd get experience and get money for his own place."

"And . . ." Marianna knew what they were alluding to, but she wanted to hear it from their mouths.

"And since both your uncle and your father work there, we think he's trying to make a good impression."

Marianna lowered her head, hoping she hid her disappointment. No, it was more than that—her sadness. She took a breath. Their words seemed to wrap around her neck like a tight scarf, cutting off her air. She didn't want to care what Ben's motives were, but that didn't make the breaths come any easier.

She thought about that first day at the train. How eager Ben had been to help. She thought about him walking her brothers to school, and how he'd helped her twice today.

Of course, it made sense.

"Thank you for telling me. I'm not used to this. Back home I didn't interact with Englisch much."

"We know how odd it feels." Hope pouted, sticking out her bottom lip. "All the Englisch around here are talkative. They are friendly too. But we'll pass on to you what our dad has told us many times, *Such as the tree is, such is the fruit.*" Hope shrugged. "I guess you can't trust the Englisch too much, not knowing what's in their hearts."

Marianna grabbed a bottle of cold water, placing it against her neck, wondering if she could handle going out in the heat.

Hope let out a long sigh. "Like I said, we thought you should know." Then she clasped her hands in front of her. "But what we really came in to do is look at fabric. Seeing all those quilts out there inspired us."

"They have fabric here? I thought you had to go to Eureka for that."

"Oh, haven't you been to the craft room? That's our favorite part of Kootenai Kraft and Grocery."

"Can you show me?" Marianna scanned the room, wondering how she could have missed that.

"Sure."

They walked toward the front register, but instead of continuing toward the front door, they made a sharp left to an open doorway. Marianna was sure she'd seen the door, but she hadn't thought much of it.

They entered, and the room was full of people, mulling over tables covered with colorful tablecloths and filled with all types of handmade crafts—aprons, grocery bag holders, pot holders, stationery, handmade soap.

In the center of the room were two dozen bolts of fabric and bolts of quilt batting. Marianna's hand moved to the small purse she wore. She'd brought some money in case she needed food, but she hadn't realized she could get her quilting supplies here too.

Eve and Hope *ooh*ed and *ahh*ed over the new fabrics that had come in, trying to decide what to buy, but Marianna's eyes focused on the ideal fabric for her quilt. It was a creamy white color that almost looked like it was polka-dotted, but as she stepped closer she realized they were tiny pink rose buds. She smiled. Buds promised the bloom to come. Did she have the money to spend on it? She wanted to finish her quilt, but she also knew she needed to save as much as she could for the train ticket home.

Hope and Eve laughed, and Marianna looked up to see them looking out the store window toward a group of Amish men. She could see from their shaved faces they were bachelors. They'd gathered near some log furniture that would soon be auctioned off.

Only moments later the two women waved good-bye to Marianna and hurried outside. Marianna supposed that even the prettiest fabric couldn't compare to an attraction like that.

Marianna turned to the fabric again. She picked up the edge of it, feeling it between her fingers when she saw Annie approaching.

"Excuse me, Marianna?"

"Yes, ma'am."

"Oh, sweetie, you don't need to call me, ma'am. Annie is just fine."

Marianna smiled. "Okay then."

Annie waved a hand toward the fabric. "So, did seeing all the quilts make you want to start your own?"

"I'm working on one already. Just need a few more things to finish." Marianna pushed the bolt back in place.

"Good for you." Annie sighed, looking out the window and watching two women carrying quilts toward their cars. Then she turned back to Marianna. "I have no talent, and I don't even have time. For the last few years I've been wanting to get out there and bid, but I'm too busy running this place."

Marianna looked around, noticing even more people trying to fill the small craft room.

"You wouldn't consider selling me the quilt you're making, would you?"

"Me?" Marianna pinched her lips together. "Well, that's very thoughtful of you to ask, but I'm keeping it for my cedar chest, back in Indiana."

"Is that like a hope chest?" Annie stepped aside to let a woman by.

"Yes, I suppose so, but if I make another quilt I'll let you know."

Annie touched Marianna's arm. "Sure, honey, you do that. And . . ." She stepped closer. "There's actually something else I wanted to ask, too. I was hoping to talk to you today, and when I saw you coming in here I thought it would be the perfect time."

Annie's face was red, no doubt from working in the kitchen, and strands of moist hair curled on her forehead, softening her features. "I was talking to your mother this morning, and she mentioned you might be looking for a job? Said something about saving up for a train ticket?"

Marianna felt her brow lift. Even though that was the plan, she hadn't talked to her parents about it recently. If anything, she thought her parents would discourage her from working so she wouldn't be able to return home.

"Yes, that is correct." She lifted her chin. "I hope to return to Indiana in the fall."

Annie winked. "Your ma told me about your special friend back there, and I believe we could both help each other. I'm looking for someone to help in the bakery—for the next few months. Summer is our busy time, with all the Amish families visiting their kin and the vacationers. I can't keep up."

Marianna forced a smile. She knew how to bake, but back home she'd enjoyed being outside, tending to the animals or in a rocking chair caring for the kids. She offered a half smile, remembering how her mother had wanted her in the kitchen more. After all, as her Grandma used to say, *kissing wears out— cooking don't.*

"I'd love to help you. I'm glad my mother suggested it."

"Oh, good. Do you think you could be here by 6 a.m. Monday?"

Marianna's eyes widened. A job meant she could buy the fabric and still save for the ticket.

"Yes, that will work. Is there anything I need to bring?"

"Your skill and your smile, oh, and if you have any recipes. We're always on the lookout for new ones."

"I have some good ones, and I brought my grandma's recipes, too."

"Great, see you Monday."

"See you Monday." Marianna lifted the bolt of fabric, eager to talk to Dat about a quilt frame.

The day was turning out better than she thought.

Marianna hadn't considered how she'd carry two large bags, filled with quilting supplies, home until she'd paid for her purchase. She'd bought her items and started the mile and a half walk, leaving the people, the smells, and the voices of the auction behind.

She'd gotten off the main road, to the smaller road that would take her to her house when she heard the sound of a vehicle. She quickened her steps afraid to turn, wondering if that man from earlier had followed her.

Holding her breath, she dared to turn and was thankful to see Ben's truck pulling up. Not only was it someone safe, but she could get a ride.

She held back her smile. He'd been doing that a lot today—showing up when she needed him most. Of course, that's what one did when he was trying to get on someone's good side.

The truck pulled up beside her, slowing down to a stop. He rolled down the window on the passenger's side. "So you need a ride?"

She opened the door. Earlier that morning when she saw him, she'd felt nervous in his presence. But now, knowing he was being kind to her because he wanted a job took away all those butterfly feelings in her stomach. She'd let him be genial. She didn't mind the help, as long as she knew it wasn't going anywhere. "Thank you. I'd appreciate that."

"What do you have in the bag?"

"Fabric for my quilt. And batting too. It's not heavy, just bulky." She lifted it, showing him.

He chuckled. "Did being at the auction today inspire you?"

"Sort of, although I've wanted to finish my quilt for a while." She set her bags on the seat between them and closed the door.

It wasn't more than a mile to her house, and they rode in silence. Marianna enjoyed the cool breeze through the window, and she curled her aching toes in her black shoes.

The truck stopped in front of the house, and as she climbed out she heard Trapper's bark. Marianna turned and looked toward the shed area and beyond it to where the mangy mutt exploded from the trees, like a furry ball from a cannon. Within seconds he was at her feet, a wagging fuzz ball.

"I see you have a friend there."

"If that's what you call him." She chuckled.

"He's excited to see you."

"He always is." She sighed, trying to hide her smile. Trapper yipped and then looked at her, his head tilted and ears cocked. Large dark eyes softened her heart. She enjoyed being sought out, even if it was by a flea-bitten stray.

"Come here, boy." Ben whistled, and the dog bolted around the truck.

"You know him?" She slammed the door shut.

"Well, I did. I thought he left with the Litwillers when they moved east." Ben climbed from the truck, then sighed. "Although I can see why they didn't take him."

"What do you mean?" She walked around the truck and watched as Ben squatted down and scratched the dog behind his ears.

"It was their oldest daughter, Patty's dog. She was almost your age when she passed away."

"She died?"

"Yes, a boating accident. A group of young people were crossing the lake in their rowboat when a large motorized boat hit them. Everyone else was okay, but Patty didn't know how to swim."

"That's so sad." Marianna placed a hand over her chest. She could understand far better than Ben knew. For the second time today the loss of her sisters struck deep. A deep ache pulled at her stomach, and she looked at the mutt with new compassion. "I imagine my room used to be hers. No wonder the poor animal reacted in such a way."

"For a while after she died, this doggy would sit on the shore, waiting for Patty to cross back over. He used to wait there, you see, when she and her friends went on the lake. He was too hyper for them to take, so he'd sit at the shore and wait."

"Didn't Patty's parents bring him back here? Bring him home?"

"They tried many times, but he went back to the lake. Many other folks around here tried, too, but he'd run away and head back to the shore. I haven't seen him since the Litwillers left." Ben turned his attention back to the dog. "Looks like you've been on your own for a little while, a little skinny and dirty."

"You should have seen him before we gave him a bath. We've done our best to clean him up, and he seems pretty happy here."

"So your parents don't mind a surprise addition to your family?"

"Well, Trapper's never given us a choice."

Ben lifted his head and his blue eyes twinkled. "That's a nice thing to do. I'm sure Trapper would love to have a family again."

A lump grew in Marianna's throat as she imagined the little dog waiting on the shore by the lake. Her heart ached as she thought about all her friends and family she'd left behind, but at least she understood what was happening. The poor little dog had no idea. All he knew was that someone he loved wasn't around anymore.

"So I have to ask, what was his name before? What did Patty call him?"

Ben pinched his lips together as if trying to remember and then he nodded. "Oh, I remember now. She called him Monty—short for Montana. They moved here, too, when she was a teenager, and she loved the place. She said as soon as she got here, it felt like home."

CHAPTER TWENTY-ONE

arianna awoke and yawned, remembering it was Sunday off. Since they only met every other week, today they didn't have church. Usually she enjoyed the day off from church, but today she woke with an unsettled feeling.

What was wrong? Was she bothered because of that man at the auction? She'd spent the rest of yesterday watching, hoping not to see him. But she hadn't. And by the time she came home, she'd all but forgotten about him.

She turned to her side and noticed the bags of fabric that she'd soon pull out. She also spotted Trapper lying on the braided rag-rug on her floor. He must have heard her stirring because he opened one eye and yawned. Then seeing she wasn't out of bed, Trapper closed his eyes again, content to wait.

Closing her eyes, she searched through her mind. Why this strange feeling? So many good things had happened yesterday too. Annie from the grocery, and the young girls at the lemonade stand. And Ben . . .

Her eyes open. Ben. That's where the uneasiness originated.

For as long as she could remember, the leaders of the church had told her she was privileged to be Amish, and that the world outside the Amish was evil and corrupt. That was easy to believe when she spent most of her time within her community. She attended church with people she'd known her whole life. All her neighbors were Amish. She'd done most of her shopping at an Amish store. Rarely had she taken trips to Englisch shopping centers. Only once—when she was eight—had they gone on vacation outside of Indiana, and she hadn't dared to look too long at the Englisch, let alone speak to them.

But now . . .

Now that she was getting to know them, something didn't seem right. She'd grown up without questioning that the Amish were the only ones with the real chance to get into heaven, but now she couldn't help wondering. What about everyone else? They were good people. It was plain to see. Didn't God see that too?

She sat up, fluffed her pillow, and then settled her scarved head against it.

Not that she would be prideful enough to say *she'd* go to heaven for sure. She'd done her best and tried to follow all the rules. She said her daily prayers, was humble, and always followed the Ordnung. She'd obeyed her mother and father—even choosing to come here and leave her friends and family and Aaron behind. She'd done all she knew, but it was still God's decision to choose whether she entered His kingdom. But at least she had a chance. What about everyone else? If God was a God of love, it didn't seem fair they had no opportunity.

Perhaps what bothered her even more were her thoughts of Levi. Since he was in the ban, she knew he was cut off from God. Her mother and father never spoke of his fate, but she knew—

everyone knew—that if Levi died this day, it would doom his soul to hell and he'd have no chance of salvation. Her heart ached at the thought.

As she lay there, she could hear her parents stirring in the kitchen. The scent of bacon mixed with the aroma of coffee, and if she closed her eyes she could almost imagine she was ten again. A bird sung somewhere outside the window, and she thought of the birds back home. Some things were different—too many things—but she was thankful some things were the same.

"So they're asking you to preach in a couple months?" Her mother's voice carried through the open door. "I don't know what type of backwoods place you brought me to, Abe Sommer, but it seems to me these Amish like being away from the bishops. Thata way they don't have to follow the Ordnung to a *T.*"

"They're laid back and relaxed, that's all. They have plans for a bishop coming. They've had them before, but after the last one left they haven't found a good replacement. Give it time. It'll happen."

"Yes, well, as far as I'm concerned the Bible says nothing about relaxing your way into heaven. As far as I remember, God's Word talks about putting your hand to the plow and not looking back."

"Didn't you see, there's no plow around here." Dat spoke in a playful tone, and Marianna imagined the twinkle in his eye.

"I still don't like it. You getting that English Bible and all."

Marianna stood and walked to the doorway, standing against the wall. She didn't want them to know she overheard, but she couldn't make herself close the door.

"I can't read German well, and I do have to preach . . ." She heard Dat shift in his chair. "And have you ever thought Jesus didn't speak German? Where did one get the idea that's the only language for Scripture?"

Marianna's door opened wider, and she jumped. She looked down to see Trapper sticking his nose out, trying to open the door the rest of the way to get out.

"Shhh!" Marianna reached back and pulled him back into her room, but it was too late.

"That you, Mari?"

Mem had heard her. Marianna tightened the belt on her bathrobe and then walked into the kitchen. "Good morning."

"It is a good morning." Dat nodded and smiled, but when she looked to the table she saw his German Bible sitting there. Where was the English one they'd talked about?

"Marianna," her mother said. "There's a letter from Mrs. Zook. It arrived in the mail yesterday, and I forgot to show you last night."

"For me?" Marianna rubbed her forehead.

Mem shook her head. "Well, she wrote to our family but she wishes you a happy birthday."

Marianna looked to the open letter at the table and then sat. Her mother continued to make breakfast and her father flipped through his German Bible, but she could tell they both waited for her to read the letter. Waited for her reaction.

June 15
Dear Friends,

Greetings in love. I was hoping to write in time for Marianna's birthday, but even though the summer days are long I did not get it done. Thank you for your note from Montana, Ruth. It was thoughtful you had us in mind. Montana does sound like a beautiful place. I can't imagine living by mountains like that.

Many people have heard that things are quite different there than here. We heard your new church does not have a bishop. I hope this matter is taken care of soon. Bishops are not perfect people, but their authority is necessary. We also were surprised that Abe was already put into the rotation to preach. He wasn't yet a deacon here, and now he'll speak in front of the church? Do you worry you are not really honoring our fathers and mothers like the sixth commandment says in the Ten Commandments if you do not stay with the system of leadership we have been taught?

It is still not too late to return to Indiana. The Mosers have not married yet and your house remains vacant. Perhaps it would be a fitting birthday gift for Marianna? Please come back. We miss you and are praying for you.

Aaron is doing well. He finished the roof on his cabin. I wish Marianna had a chance to see it before she left. Please tell her to write. I would enjoy a letter.

With fondness,
Mrs. Norma Jean Zook

Marianna put down the letter and then looked at her parents. "It sounds like there's a lot of rumors going around back there." She glanced at Dat.

"Not rumors if they're true," Mem said, whipping up pancake batter in her large white bowl. She didn't look at Marianna, she didn't have to. Marianna knew she felt conflicted about going back.

Marianna thought about talking to her parents about Dat preaching. She also thought about telling them about Ben, about his friendship, and about the job he wanted, but as she looked to them, it felt good to be here. To enjoy the morning without the kids yet. To see her mom smiling as she cooked, smiling despite her talk with Dat, despite the letter. It was a new thing to see her unruffled by things that would have bothered her before.

There was a special glow about her mother. Her face looked brighter. Her stomach was larger, a round ball.

"Mem, it looks like your stomach's bigger. Eat too many mashed potatoes yesterday?" Marianna rose and poured herself a cup of coffee.

Mem looked down and rubbed her stomach. "Yes, it looks like it grew, doesn't it? This always seems to happen in the sixth month. It has since the first bab—" Mem looked away, then she glanced back at Marianna. "It has with each baby. Three months to go."

Marianna took a sip of her coffee. What all would happen in three months? Not even a month had passed yet since they'd gotten here, and she felt changed already. She had a different vision of the world. She also looked forward to getting to know some of her new friends, especially Annie. Working at the store would insure that.

A month ago when she was still in Indiana, the thought of working with the Englisch would have frightened her, but now she thought it might be nice to step out of her safe world and spend time with people not like her—at least until she returned.

Mem put the last of the cooked bacon on a plate, and Marianna stood.

"Going back to bed?"

"No, Dat, I'm going to get out Grandma's recipes. I thought it would be nice to find a few to take in to work tomorrow."

"Good idea. I bet Annie would like those Oatmeal Butter Crisps. They always were my favorite."

She headed for her room and Dat called after her, "Better yet, maybe you should make some today, to test them. The baby would like those too, won't she, Mem?"

Mem's laughter filled the air. *"She,* is it? You know, Abe Sommer, you've never guessed the sex of our children right, not once."

"There's always a first time."

Marianna could hear the smile in her father's voice and she couldn't help but smile too.

Ben sat at the picnic table overlooking Lake Koocanusa and opened his Bible to the passage God had placed on his heart. He happened to run into Abe Sommer at the post office yesterday, but he knew it was no accident.

"I've been meaning to see if you had time to talk to me—you know, about the Bible," Abe had said.

Ben looked down to his highlighted passage, praying God would give him the right words. If he had time he would have met with Ike—to get a better idea of what the Amish believed, but since he didn't, Ben had to trust God would speak through him—to speak truth and love in a way Abe hadn't heard it before.

In the distance Ben could see Abe approaching on foot. He carried a paper sack tucked under his arm, and Ben guessed the Bible was inside.

Abe wore a serious expression as he neared, and he sat down at the picnic table across from Ben without the slightest smile.

"There's a Scripture I've been wanting to share." Ben pointed to a passage in Romans.

"Actually there's one I want to talk to you about." Abe opened his Bible to Acts. "It's talking about two groups, I know, but I'm wondering if this message is for us. It has me confused."

Ben read the passage Abe was pointing to. "'Now the Bereans were of more noble character than the Thessalonians, for they received the message with great eagerness and examined the Scriptures every day to see if what Paul said was true.'"

Ben looked up to Abe. What was confusing about that?

"Are we supposed to do that too?" Abe's tone was solemn. "Should we examine the Scriptures to see if what we hear is true?"

For a second Ben thought it was a trick question, but when he looked into Abe's eyes he saw earnestness there. "Yes." Ben nodded. "We should read the Bible daily. We should know what's in there and then, when others tell us a message is from God, we can tell if it really is true."

Abe stroked his long beard, then he looked to the lake. "Before I moved to Montana, I can't remember more than a few days ever reading the Bible on my own. One of the bishops when I was a boy got on a man from church for doing too much reading. Said we were at risk for pride by trying to know too much."

Ben breathed in a breath of fresh air. "I don't think that's how God sees it. His Word is a message to us. Each of us. I know when I write letters and send them back home, I'm happy when those who love me read them."

"Can I confess something?" Abe glanced up from under bushy eyebrows.

"Yes, of course." Ben nodded.

"I've read the Bible every day since I got it." He pursed his lips. "And the truth is, the more I read . . . the more I want to."

"That's a good thing." Ben couldn't help but smile. He also didn't understand what he'd been so nervous about. God didn't need him to preach to Mr. Sommer. God was already speaking to his heart. He just needed to be here, to encourage him, and to let him know he was on the right track.

Aaron sat on the new porch steps he built and scanned the field, waiting for Naomi. He'd asked for the day off from the Stoll farm, and he was looking forward to finishing the wood floors in his cabin. When he mentioned it to Naomi last Sunday at church, she'd volunteered to bring him lunch. Later, at the youth sing, she hinted she wouldn't mind spending the whole day with him. Then came right out and asked if it would be okay. At first he was unsure—after all, what would Marianna think? Then again, if she really cared she would have taken the time to see the house. She would have written more, as she promised she would.

He rose and entered his cabin, finding his sketchbook he kept tucked under a box of sandpaper. He flipped through the sketches until he found the one he wanted. It was her, sitting on the grass the day of the barn raising. Aaron's heart ached as he looked at her face. He brushed a thumb lightly over her captured smile. He knew he'd get in big trouble if anyone saw the drawing— capturing her graven image like that. But he had to do it. Had to put to paper the face he always saw in his mind.

"Anyone home?" he heard Naomi calling.

Aaron closed the book, tucked it back under the sandpaper, and turned to find her standing in the doorway.

Naomi laughed. "You look surprised. Did I come at a bad time?" She carried a lunch pail in each hand.

"No." Aaron stood and turned. "Just looking over my house plans."

Naomi nodded, but still had a look of uncertainty on her face. "All right then." She forced a smile, and for some reason she looked paler than usual.

"Sorry I'm late." She placed the lunch pails by the door. "I wasn't feeling well this morning. I think I got a touch of something from my little brother. He was sneezing all the way home from church the other day."

"Thanks for lunch . . . and for coming." Aaron tucked his hands in his pants pockets, not knowing what else to say.

Naomi stepped forward and reached a hand toward his face, but just when he thought she was going to stroke his cheek, she straightened his shirt collar. "I'm happy to come, Aaron." Her eyes fixed on his. "We are much more like, you and I. I'm not sure why we didn't spend time together before." Naomi crossed her arms over her chest as she scanned the room. "Same values. Same dreams . . ."

"I suppose we were focused on other things." Aaron looked down into her face. His heart pounded. Mostly because he remembered when he'd looked into Marianna's eyes, just like this. If he'd only been so bold to kiss her when he had the chance.

Taking his hand from his pocket, Aaron reached up and took Naomi's hand from his collar. He placed it on his face, feeling the warmth of her skin.

But Marianna wasn't here. Was she?

CHAPTER TWENTY-TWO

The scent of bread rising greeted Marianna as she hurried through the back door of the restaurant. The lights were bright inside in contrast to the still, predawn sky. Annie stood by the sink, humming as she rinsed out a cake pan.

"Good morning," Annie chirped. She turned to greet Marianna, and her long blonde ponytail swung over her shoulder as she did.

"It *is* a good morning." Marianna entered and hung her coat on a hook by the back door. "It was a nice walk. Quiet and still, and smelled like last night's rain." She approached Annie, who was separating bread into rolls.

"We have a busy night tonight. The restaurant will be closed to the public. A private party has rented the place."

Marianna went to the sink and washed her hands, then jumped in and helped Annie without being asked. "The whole place? What can I do?"

Annie stood back watching. "Thata girl. I knew you'd do a good job." Then she wiped her hands on the dish towel hanging around her waist. "Yes, the whole place. The owner of Kootenai

Log Homes is having an anniversary party for his parents. I'm cooking a special dinner, and there will be live music too."

Live music? She'd often heard songs playing in stores, but the only music she knew well was the hymns sung in church without instruments.

"Ben Stone is going to play. Have you heard him on the guitar yet?" Annie glanced over her shoulder and shook her head, as if remembering again that Marianna was Amish. "Of course you wouldn't have, but if you ever get the chance, you should—for the sake of his being a friend and all."

"Ben?" Marianna rolled the piece of dough in her hand. "He doesn't seem that type."

"Oh yes, he was at college on a music scholarship before he moved to these parts. I met his parents last summer. They came up for a visit and didn't seem none too happy he'd give up all he had to live in the woods."

Marianna lowered her head and continued her work. She couldn't help but think of Aaron and how different he was from Ben. Aaron was someone who did all his parents asked. He worked hard to honor them. Yet, she still couldn't help but wonder if it would be possible to come tonight. To help. And maybe she'd even hear a bit of Ben's music as she worked in the kitchen.

She opened her mouth to ask, but the back door opened and an older gentlemen strode in. He waved to them and then hurried to the front, turning on the lights. Marianna had often seen him as she shopped.

"That's Edgar Miller," Annie explained. "He's worked at this store since it first opened thirty years ago. He's more friendly as the day goes on, but in the morning the only thing on his mind is getting everything ready to open." Annie chuckled. "I'm sure the folks up here would think the world had stopped on its axis if Edgar didn't have the front door open and the front step swept at least thirty minutes before the time the sign says."

"I've talked to him a few times. He seems very nice."

"Yes, he is." Annie pulled out a second large mixing bowl and moved to a small box on the counter that Marianna assumed held recipes. "Edgar's up in age so there's a few rules to working with him." Annie looked up from the recipe box to meet Marianna's eyes. She lowered her voice. "Don't ask him to carry anything heavy and don't ask him to do more than one thing at one time. He's known to put receipts in the fireplace and kindling in the filing cabinet." She chuckled and shook her head. "And don't get me started about the bread he was supposed to put in the oven and the ant traps he was suppose to put on the back porch. What a mess."

As if knowing they were talking about him, he walked into the kitchen, with a broom in hand. "I thought I saw a new face."

Marianna smiled. Edgar's forehead was wrinkled above his white, bushy eyebrows.

Annie rolled a ball of dough. "Yes, but remember she's *my* help not yours, no matter how busy things get up front," Annie joked.

"That's fine, I appreciate she's in the kitchen. We've been selling all our sweets before noon," Edgar explained to Marianna. Then he cocked his head and leaned forward on his broom, focusing on Annie. "And did you remember to ask her?"

Marianna looked from one to the other. "Ask me what?"

"Oh, when Edgar heard you were coming, he wanted to see if you had any new recipes. He says he's craving something different. Guess he's getting bored with my cinnamon rolls and scones."

"Cookies are my favorite." Edgar stroked his chin. "Customers like them too."

"Well, then you're in luck. I happened to bring a recipe today. It's in my coat pocket. They're my father's favorite—Oatmeal Butter Crisps."

"You gonna make them today? Is that what I heard? Please tell me that's what I heard." Edgar's eyes widened.

Marianna couldn't help but chuckle. "I don't think that's up to me."

Edgar looked to Annie again. He lifted an eyebrow in expectation.

Annie sighed. "I have a feeling if I don't ask you to make them, Marianna, I'm going to hear about them all day. And . . ." She paused and stroked her chin. "That might be nice to go with the homemade vanilla ice cream I'm whipping up for tonight's dessert. Do you think you could make some? Also could you come tonight? I know it's your first day, but I could use the help with serving—"

"Yes, of course." The words spouted from Marianna's lips, and she placed a hand to her cheek. "I mean if you need me."

"Get to work then," Edgar said, carrying his broom to the front door. "I need something to sample. Better for me to taste test them. Then you can give it Ole' Edgar's stamp of approval." He winked.

The room was quiet, and the heady fragrance of baking cookies filled the air. In the corner was the stool Annie had set up for Ben. He must have been by when Marianna went home for a few hours to check on Mem and to tell her parents she was working late, because when she returned his guitar rested on the stand. She walked to it, running her fingers over the strings, wondering when he first started to play. She sat on the stool and tilted her head, looking at the words painted on the front of the guitar in a fancy script. Set Free.

What would it feel like to have the freedom to pick it up and play?

She looked around again, knowing that the cookies—her fourth batch that day—still had a few minutes to bake. People shouldn't show up for thirty minutes at least.

She pinched her lips together, and then told herself it wouldn't hurt to hold the guitar. Feel it in her hands.

Marianna reached down to pick it up before she talked herself out of it. It was lighter than she expected. She held it so her left hand was around the long part and her right hand prepped to strum. She closed her eyes and imagined herself having a guitar like this and sitting in the trees behind their home. She wondered what it would be like to listen to the forest and the birds, matching their tune. It was a beautiful thought.

"So you want me to show you how to play?"

Ben's voice made her jump. Her eyes popped open, and she noticed him near the kitchen. He wasn't dressed as a lumberjack today, not even close. Ben wore pressed black slacks and a blue shirt, looking very much like the Californian musician Annie had told her he'd been.

"Oh no." She held the guitar out in front of her, handing it to him. "I was just, uh, looking at it."

He took long strides toward her, grabbing another stool and pulling it behind her. "No, really, it's okay. I can show you how to strum."

She pulled it back toward her, not knowing what else to do. He scooted even closer, pressing his chest against her back and wrapping his arms around her.

"Okay, so we're going to take your fingers and place them on these strings." His left hand moved her fingers so that each of her four fingers covered a string. Then his hand covered hers.

Marianna blew out a soft breath, then she swallowed hard. A thousand tingles sparked to life under his touch and then spread. Heat gave way to excitement. Then fear. Both battled for control.

"Now with your other hand." He took her right hand and curled her fingers, then with a gentle motion they strummed as one.

"Have you ever played before?" He tilted his head and looked at her. She was afraid to turn her head. If she did their faces would be within inches of each other, their lips close enough to touch.

"No. I—" She didn't know what to say, what to do. For the first time in her life Marianna wished she wasn't Amish. Wished she could enjoy the beat of his heart against her back. Enjoy the closeness of his touch and play a simple song without a veil of guilt dropping over her. Suffocating her.

She shook her head. "It's not allowed." His breath was on her neck, her cheek. He smelled like soap and like the forest outside. She took a deep breath—taking it in, and then chiding herself for doing so.

The front door opened and footsteps neared. Marianna turned to see her father's face.

Marianna scrambled to her feet, her cheeks burning. She held the guitar out to Ben. Her whole hand shook. "Our church doesn't believe in playing musical instruments." Her knees quivered and she'd never felt so much shame. "You need to take this."

Ben's eyes fixed on hers, and Marianna saw a loving tenderness. It was different than Aaron's gaze—deeper. It was more intimate than when her father looked into her eyes. Ben took the guitar from her, placing it in the stand.

The timer in the kitchen buzzed and relief washed over her. "The cookies." She turned and hurried to the kitchen, relieved to get away.

Marianna pulled the cookies from the oven and then leaned on the counter, her hands pressing on the cool surface. She didn't want to go back out there. Didn't want to see all the questions, the care in Ben's eyes. She was afraid of her father's accusations. *How would she ever explain to Dat? What would she say?*

She thought back to the last time she'd attended church in Indiana. She remembered Viola and her confession. What had Viola thought as she'd listened to those records? For a moment did Viola feel free? As much as she didn't want to admit it, Marianna enjoyed the feel of the guitar in her hands. Even more than that, she had never enjoyed the touch of another as much as she enjoyed Ben's arms around her. She ran a hand down her neck, feeling feverish. It was as if the fires of hell were nearing, reminding her of her misdeed.

Not only had she broken the Ordnung, her father had seen it. What would he do? What would he say?

Footsteps sounded behind her, and she busied herself using a spatula to remove the cookies from the cookie sheet, placing them on a cooling rack.

"So, do you need any help in here? Getting things ready?" Her father's voice was lower than usual, tight, and she could tell he was fighting back his anger.

"Oh, no, I think I'm doing okay." She bit her lip. "Unless you want to pour the punch into the punch bowl."

One of the cookies fell back onto the cookie sheet, and she tried to pick it up and put it on the plate. The sheet was still hot and it burned her finger. "Ouch."

"You hurt yourself?" Dat asked.

"No, just a little burn." She hurried to the sink.

Her father neared. "If you keep acting that way, keep getting close to that young man, you *will* hurt yourself. I saw you at the auction, walking around together, talking. And now . . . today."

"It was nothing. We're just friends. That's all it will ever be. That's all I want it to be."

Lies. She lied again but didn't realize it was a lie until the words were out of her mouth.

Marianna stood in the doorway and watched as Ben approached the stool, settled down into it and then picked up his guitar. The last guest had just been served their meal, and all eyes turned to where he sat. The conversations stilled, until the only sound was the light clink of forks and knives against plates.

"First of all, congratulations to Mr. and Mrs. Grandell. Fifty years of marriage is a celebration indeed, something I hope I can celebrate someday."

Applause filled the room and the older couple blushed as they looked to each other. When the applause died down, everyone's attention again turned to Ben.

"I'm going to play a collection of songs this evening. The first one is called *D'Cinnamons, Selamanya Cinta,* which is a fancy way of saying romantic guitar solo."

Chuckles erupted around the room.

"So, men, if you have someone special here tonight be sure to take a moment and stare into her eyes."

An "Ahhh" flittered through the crowd.

"Thata way she'll be so focused on you she won't notice when you steal her cookie." Ben sniffed the air. "Don't they smell wonderful?"

Laughter filled the room again and then quieted as Ben started playing. The song begun off slow, yet each chord took on life, moving around the room like a living thing. Marianna clenched her hands, wishing she could release the emotions building inside. What was happening? It was almost as if the music was being absorbed inside her, filling her up.

She looked around the room at the smiling faces. One couple was locked in a fixed gaze. A woman fanned her face.

Another woman sat alone with an older couple. Fresh tears flowed down the woman's cheeks, and Marianna wondered if she was thinking of a lost love. Then there was Annie. Annie stood just outside the doorway where Marianna was standing. She swayed from side to side, ever so softly, as if imagining herself in the arms of someone she loved.

The song told a story. She pictured a young couple walking through the woods, enjoying the beauty around them, enjoying each other.

She looked back to Ben. He seemed to be watching the crowd as much as they were watching him.

Then the music rose in depth and emotion, and Marianna found herself fighting tears. Just when she thought they'd spill over, Ben turned to her. Their eyes locked, and for a moment she felt as if she was the only one there, the one he played the song for.

She swallowed hard, looked away, and took a step back. Walking back into the kitchen, she fanned her face and then looked for something to busy her hands.

As quietly as she could, she laid out small dishes and placed two freshly baked cookies into each one. Her fingers quivered as she plated the cookies, and a couple of them crumbled, scattering crumbs on the floor.

Brushing the crumbs from her fingers, she hurried to get a broom and dust pan and swept it up. As she rose, the dust pan hit the oven and made a loud clang. Marianna froze, hoping the guests didn't hear. With the cookies set, she got out the homemade ice cream and began scooping it up, placing the dishes in the large freezer until it was time for them to be served.

Footsteps sounded behind her, and Annie entered. She stepped close to Marianna and leaned in to her ear.

"We still have time for that. Why don't you enjoy the music?"

"No." Marianna frowned, interrupting. She hadn't meant to be so abrupt. Her mind scrambled for another excuse. "I was trying to get everything ready. I've been away from home most of the day. I wanted to get back to Mem as soon as possible. She might need my help."

"I understand. But I wish you could stay to enjoy the music. It's hard to believe we have someone so talented living here, don't you think?"

Marianna nodded. "He plays beautifully." She wanted to say more, but couldn't. As she looked away, she was sure Annie could read her emotions, even though she was trying so very hard to hide them. Hide them from Annie.

From herself.

CHAPTER TWENTY-THREE

he song was still there, replaying in her heart.

It had been months since that night she heard Ben play, and she'd only stayed to listen to the one song, but that didn't seem to matter.

In the days and weeks since her arrival in Montana, Marianna had settled into a simple pattern, going to work, going to church, helping Mem, walking Trapper, and counting the weeks until she returned to Indiana.

Mem's stomach continued to grow, and as summer slipped into fall Marianna began to question if she'd be able to leave as soon as she thought. The kids were a handful, and with Marianna working in the store all day, the chores piled up. She did her best at night, but she was always behind. That's why she told Mem she'd stay until after Christmas—or at least that was one of the reasons. The other was she couldn't imagine being away from her family during that time of year. And somewhere back in her mind she hoped that more time would give her a chance to sort out her feelings about Aaron.

And about Ben.

She felt guilty as she walked back from Mrs. Peachy's house after a day of quilting—she hadn't written Aaron in a month. But how could she, when her thoughts were so often on another?

Today, as the ladies cleaned up their things, they offered to help Marianna with her quilt next, but she came up with an excuse. Because, out of all the chores she did, quilting was *her* time. She usually snuck in a few hours on Sunday afternoon to sit and quilt. Focusing in on the needle, moving in and out of the fabric, she could forget about the cares of the world and find a sense of peace.

Today they'd worked on Hope Peachy's quilt, stopping only to enjoy a hot dish lunch. In the four hours she was there, she learned nearly everything there was to know about the people in the Kootenai community—except for Ben. No one mentioned him, and Marianna didn't bring him up. She saw him sometimes when he came into the grocery store, but they rarely exchanged a word.

After that night at the restaurant, Dat had started using Danny Noel to drive their family to Eureka for shopping or to Libby for Mem's doctor's appointments, and no one had asked why. Marianna didn't have to ask. She knew Dat wanted to keep them apart as much as possible. He no doubt feared, as she did, that her feelings for Ben could grow into something unacceptable, unthinkable.

She crested the hill within a half-mile of their house, walking with slow, heavy steps. By the time she reached the front of the house, Trapper would sense she was there and run to her, greeting her with a bark, wagging his tail so hard his whole body moved with it.

In the distance the mountain peaks jutted into the sky, the

tops of them hidden in white, puffy clouds. Overhead an eagle soared, and Marianna wondered what it would be like to join him—to lift into the clouds and leave the stuff of earth behind? It was a pleasant thought.

A soft breeze tugged at the lower branches of the pine trees, but all she could think about was the corn stalks waving in the wind back home. Did those she left behind think of her as often as she thought of them? Or did their small community continue as it always had? She hoped in a way they missed her. That she was worthy of being missed.

Her limbs felt as if they weighed a hundred pounds each, and she could barely lift her hand to brush her hair back from her face. It wasn't anything at the quilting that had bothered her—she'd put on her best smile for that. Instead, she'd dreamt about Levi last night and couldn't shake the heavy feeling from her chest.

In her dream they were back home, climbing the tree that hung over the river. He'd been ahead of her and the limb had quivered under their feet. She could see he was unbalanced, but her body couldn't move fast enough to reach out and steady him. She saw him fall, tumbling downward. She'd woken up then, heart pounding. She'd woken to her own sad cry filling the room.

She didn't like that dream. Not one bit. Yet replaying it in her mind made her think of another . . . a dream she first had in Indiana, that had replayed at least four or five times since she'd been in Montana. It was a dream of a man standing beside still waters. There was peace at that place, and he was calling to her. She never saw his face, but she felt his love. At times she thought it was Aaron. Other times her father. Sometimes, when she let her mind wander, she imagined it being Ben. Or maybe it was Levi? Did Levi need her? Did the love of a brother beckon her to return?

She'd written him two letters in the last month but hadn't heard back. When she asked Uncle Ike if he'd heard anything, he'd shaken his head.

"Nothing different 'cept that he's working and living in the same trailer with some friends," Uncle Ike had told her. She lowered her head and kicked a rock down the dirt road, wondering if another letter would do any good.

A few minutes later she crested the last hill near her home, and as expected Trapper darted toward her.

"There you are." She knelt down to pet him, barely able to scratch behind his ear before he zipped around her, circling her once, twice, three times.

She walked to the house. It was so quiet today. She opened the front door, and there were no greetings from her siblings. No sound of footsteps. Her heart began to pound. Her mother still had two weeks until it was time to deliver, but many babies came early.

Marianna rushed back out the front door, and then hurried to the barn. At least the buggy was still there, and as she looked to the field across the way she spotted Silver grazing near the line of trees.

She went back to the house. Could Mem have gone into labor? Maybe they were on their way to Libby even now, which was sixty miles away, with their driver. If that was the case, surely they'd have left a note. It wasn't good that the doctor and hospital were so far away. There was a midwife in the West Kootenai, but considering her mother's age, even the midwife recommended she give birth in a hospital.

Ben popped into her mind—she still had his phone number. She'd placed it in the shed after he'd given it to her but had yet to use it. Today though, that might be different.

A piece of paper was on the table, she rushed toward it and then released a slow breath as she read the note:

Mari,

I got a bit of energy today and the kids and I walked to the Carash's house down the road to pick raspberries. You can join us if you'd like.

Mem

Marianna sat onto the bench at the dining room table and willed her heart to stop its wild beat. She patted her kapp and then rested her face in her hands, letting out a slow breath. Mem was good. The kids were fine.

It took a moment for her to feel settled—or at least as settled as she could be until the baby was born. And when she stood, determined to make dinner, she noticed a letter on the table, addressed to her from Aunt Ida. At least someone back home was thinking about her.

Liebe Kind,

I am here on my porch stitching on my quilt and thinking how much I missed you at our last quilting. Have you had a chance to work on your beautiful quilt?

In a recent letter from your father he told me
you changed your mind and decided not to come in
November, but rather after Christmas. That decision
does not sit well with me. It is worrisome enough for
a young woman to travel alone, but what about the
weather? Wouldn't it be better to leave when it is yet fall?
I promise you and I will have a lovely holiday, just the
two of us. Perhaps we will invite the Zook boy over to visit
a spell. I'd love to hear about that cabin he's building yet.
Maybe he'll give us a tour.

 As I wrote your dear mother, I saw your brother Levi in
town yesterday. I hope and pray he will soon give himself
up to what the bishop and the church want. He would be
such an example to other youth who have turned their
back on the ways they've been taught. As we all know, the
spirit of obedience is much better than the spirit of I'll-
do-as-I-please. I am concerned about his mother—your
mother. Little children step on one's lap; tall ones tread on
one's heart. I hope her heart is holding up.

 Please write quickly and tell me if you can indeed
come in the fall. The sooner the better in my opinion.

Aunt Ida

Marianna folded up the letter and returned it to the envelope,
trying to imagine leaving in the fall. Could she do it? Could her
heart handle returning and being that far from her family? She'd
panicked when she'd returned home and didn't know where they
were. However would she return to Indiana alone? Would it be
like this every day, worried about Mem and the baby? Wondering

how the children were getting along. Suddenly even December seemed too soon.

Just then something caught her eye. It was the English Bible, sitting on the window sill. She'd seen Dat reading it a few times, but every time she came around he put it away. Did he worry that she too would accuse him, just as Mem did, and remind him that reading the German Bible was the Amish way?

Marianna rose and picked up the Bible, surprised by the soft leather of its cover. They had an old German Bible, but she had never read it. Although she'd been taught how to read some German, it was a more difficult, older language than the Pennsylvania Dutch she'd learned to speak since childhood. She looked out the window, down the country lane, checking to see if her family was returning yet. When she saw that they weren't, she took the Bible and moved to the front porch, sitting on the top step, enjoying the warmth of the sun upon her.

Her hands ran over the cover, and she opened up the first page. She paused, noticing an inscription there.

To Mr. Sommer,

God's Word transformed my life, sir. I hope you don't find it too forward of me to give you this English Bible as a gift. No pay is required. I hope it helps with your sharing of the Word in your church services.

With respect,
Ben Stone

Marianna's hands quivered as she read Ben's name. She knew her father spent some time with him, mostly during deliveries at work, but it startled her that they had the type of relationship that Ben could give Dat this—and that he would accept it and read it.

Marianna turned it over in her hands, noticing a bookmarked area. She opened it and discovered it was marked on Psalm 144. Her eyes went first to a section her father had underlined.

"I will sing a new song to you, O God; on a ten-stringed lyre I will make praises to you."

Heat rose up her arms, then filled her chest. The sun seemed ten times brighter, and she felt hot and prickly all over. Her mind took her back to that moment months ago at the restaurant. She'd been plagued by that moment ever since. The music had moved her in ways she couldn't explain, and many times she was thankful she hadn't officially been baptized into the church. For if she had, she would have to submit to a confession and be disciplined like Viola. To listen to music, to enjoy it, to be moved by it simply wasn't allowed.

Something else bothered her too. It wasn't just the fact that she was caught being so intimate with Ben, but she was also bothered that her father had never brought the incident up again. He'd stopped using Ben as a driver on family outings, but he'd never talked about the episode.

She looked to the Bible again and reread the passage. The reference to the harp confused her. She'd grown up learning musical instruments were forbidden. To play an instrument was considered worldly. Her people believed when one person received attention for playing an instrument, it was contrary to the spirit of *Glassenheit*, humility. It also stirred up the emotions of the listeners—another thing that was not allowed.

Marianna had always thought the main emotion that would be stirred was one of jealousy. To see someone's talent might make you covet it and wish the talent were your own. But as she'd listened to Ben playing that night at the restaurant, jealousy wasn't the emotion that had stirred her. Desire perhaps. And even a little bit of awe and joy. The sound of the music had moved her, as if filling her soul and lifting her. It had warmed her. Challenged her. Focused her in ways she hadn't thought it could.

Marianna rose and pushed those thoughts from her mind, telling herself to stop thinking about that. About him. And as she did, a new emotion filled her. Anger.

She closed the Bible and stomped into the house, slamming the Bible back on the window sill. Suddenly she was mad at everything. Mad at Ben for making such beautiful music. Mad at him for buying the Bible for Dat. Mad at her father for not talking to her about what had happened and causing her to carry the guilt and shame on her own. Mad at the church for forbidding music, while at the same time mad she'd even questioned that they did.

Most of all she was angry that they'd come to Montana in the first place. Things were good in Indiana. Everything had order. She knew what to do and knew how others would respond. She knew what to expect. And she liked it that way.

Just an hour before, she questioned if she'd be able to leave after Christmas, but as her emotions turned she wondered why she'd stay.

She looked to Aunt Ida's letter again still sitting on the table. *"Please write quickly and tell me if you can indeed come in the fall. The sooner the better in my opinion."*

As the frustrated anger grew and filled her, Marianna couldn't agree more. She needed to leave. And soon. This place wasn't doing her any good. If she left, she could spend time with Aaron. She could see his cabin, and they could spend time going on walks or drives, getting to know each other better. Then she could forget about Ben Stone. She could also keep her mind on the things she should. This world tugged at her, trying to pull her away from all she knew. To return *would* be the answer. To return meant safety, security, familiarity.

She grabbed up the letter and took it to her room, placing it on top of her dresser. Then she looked to the bed where her quilt was. She'd finished most of the hand-stitching and just had a little more to do.

She'd work hard and finish it, because she wanted to take it with her, and because she couldn't imagine staying any longer than was necessary.

Chapter Twenty-four

ave you brought any more cookie recipes with you?" Edgar poked his head into the restaurant kitchen where Marianna worked.

Marianna put down the measuring cup, trying to remember if she'd counted off three or four cups. She decided it had only been three, then turned to him, forcing a smile.

"I did." She lifted an eyebrow and placed a hand on her hip.

"Really what kind?"

Marianna took a deep breath. "I won't tell you until you're ready to try it—it's a surprise."

"Surprise? You're gonna make me wait?" Edgar grumbled and then waved a hand in her direction. "See if I do any favors for you."

He acted as if he were mad as he stomped back to the front register, but she could make out the smile he was trying very hard to hide.

Marianna turned back to her recipe, hurrying to the refrigerator for eggs. She finished mixing the batch of peanut butter cookies and then stuck them into the oven. Annie had gone to Kalispell to get more supplies, and Marianna knew she would be back soon.

"Better get this place cleaned up." How had she managed to make such a mess? She scrubbed the whole kitchen and pulled out the first batch of cookies, sliding the cookie sheet onto the top of the cooling tray, just in case Edgar thought of peeking. She put another batch into the oven and then noticed the floors were the last thing that needed to be clean.

Picking up the floor mats, she took them outside to sweep them off. As she exited the door her shoulder bumped into someone who was opening the door to enter.

"I'm so sorry." Marianna took a step back, nearly dropping the mats. Ben stood there, his face only inches from hers.

"Am I in your way?" He hopped down from the porch and it was then she realized the back steps were gone. Somehow he'd managed to dismantle them while she'd been busy at work in the kitchen.

"No, I just had to sweep these off." She plopped the mats on the porch and stepped back inside for the broom. A twinge of excitement at seeing him shot up her elbows and she ignored it. He was just a guy—someone she could count on as a friend and nothing more.

Ben used his tape measure to measure the back porch. Then he walked over to a long piece of lumber, using a pencil to mark it off.

"Building new steps?" she asked, even though it was obvious he was.

"Yep. Annie was worried about Edgar going up and down the old ones. These steps will be wider, with a nice handrail. I told her I'd do it in exchange for some of your cookies. Those oatmeal ones are my favorite. I bought out all she had left that night after the concert."

"That's kind of you." Her broom brushed over the mat at half the speed she usually swept, and her eyes were fixed on Ben's. "I've been meaning to tell you how much I liked your music. It was very moving."

He glanced up at her and then his lips tipped up in a smile. "I could tell you liked it, and seeing that was even better than the cookies."

"Do you have any more concerts coming up?"

"Not unless you count Megan Carash's tenth birthday party. She requested Disney tunes." He chuckled, but Marianna just eyed him.

"Not familiar with those I suppose," he stated.

She laughed. "No, not really."

They worked side-by-side for a few minutes, and neither said a word. Then she opened her mouth, getting up the nerve to tell him something she'd been thinking about since she first heard him play. "It doesn't seem like you fit here. You're a good musician. Shouldn't you go someplace else where there are more people who can listen to your music? Then you could just do that, and you won't have to work making deliveries and building porches on the back of country stores."

"Is my music any less special if one person hears it?" Ben straightened and tucked his pencil behind his ear.

The question surprised her. "What?"

"I used to perform in large concerts with my high school band. Yes, I have to admit it's a good feeling when I played and would scan the large crowd and realized all those eyes were fixed on me. But there's just something different about playing in the restaurant—or smaller gatherings. It's not a crowd I'm playing for, but friends—old ones and ones I'd just met. And when I see their smiles, I really get to see them. I can also see the happiness in their eyes. It's not the roar of a crowd on their feet when I'm finished, but I can feel the pleasure of those I'm playing for. And in a strange way it gives me a glimpse of what God must think."

Marianna paused her sweeping and leaned forward against her broom. Being here, talking with Ben, the uneasiness of the last few months seemed to vaporize just like morning dew on mountain meadows. "What do you mean?"

"Well, He's God. And there are a lot of people in this world who think He's a pretty cool guy. There are people from your community who love Him in a quiet, reverent way. There are others who are more bold and vocal about their faith. But I have a notion what makes Him feel special isn't just the fact that all those people think He's great. But rather when you or I are praying, and thinking about Him or singing to Him or thanking Him for his mountains and trees, that He takes joy in the intimacy of the moment. It's that personal connection, I bet, that brightens His day."

Marianna felt both drawn to the words Ben was saying and uncomfortable about them. In all the years she'd gone to church and lived in her community, she'd never met someone who talked about God like He was right there, caring about the events of her day. She'd never thought about a God who would make a sunrise to please her for that moment. Or bring her a wiggling, active dog to make her smile.

She placed a hand to her throat and tried to imagine what the bishop would think of that. And, without warning, the face of another came to her mind. Levi. What would he think if he met Ben? Marianna was sure Levi would like him. She couldn't imagine her brother not being drawn to his outgoing personality and his smile. But what would Levi think to hear Ben talk about God like this? She knew when her brother left the community and refused to join the church, in his mind he was leaving God behind too. But did it have to be like that? Could you have one without the other? Ben seemed to prove one could.

The door creaked behind her, and Marianna was pulled back to the realization that she was supposed to be sweeping out the mats. She looked down at the broom in her hands realizing it had stopped quite a while ago.

"There is a beeper going off in the kitchen, and since I didn't put anything in the oven I supposed it's calling to you," Annie chirped.

"Oh the cookies!" Marianna set the broom against the porch railing and hurried inside.

As she approached the kitchen, the smell of burnt cookies told her that the timer had been going off for a while.

"Oh no." She hurried to the oven and opened the door. A puff of dark smoke exited, and she grabbed an oven mitt and pulled them out.

"Looks like an afternoon sacrifice to me." Annie chuckled. "Burnt to a crisp."

"I am so sorry. I can't believe I put them in and just forgot. I'll buy more ingredients to replace—"

"Marianna, whoa." Annie held up her hands. "It's just one batch of cookies. It's not the end of the world." Annie approached and placed a hand on Marianna's shoulders, giving it a squeeze. "I'll either have to get a louder timer or tell that Ben Stone to come inside if he wants to talk, so you won't get distracted." Annie winked.

Marianna placed the cookie sheet on the cooling rack. Heat rose to her cheeks. "I'm so sorry. I don't know what's gotten over me. I can stay later to make up time we spent visiting too."

"Marianna—" Annie's tone was sharp—"look at me."

Marianna lifted her head and focused on Annie's green eyes.

"I'm going to give you an order and I want you to follow it, you hear?"

Marianna tucked a wayward stray of hair back under her kapp and nodded.

"Stop trying so hard." Annie's tone softened. "This job is yours until you choose to leave. And if you choose to stay, it's still yours. Enjoy yourself. Relax. Take time to listen to the music. Play around in the kitchen with some recipes. If you spend fifteen minutes chatting with a friend, it's not the end of the world. I bought this store so I can service the people in the community. Sure they come for cookies and for groceries, but they'll come around just as often to visit for a spell. To tell us about their garden, and to just see how you're adjusting to life in the West Kootenai."

Marianna nodded, and even though she could hear what Annie was saying, it didn't make sense. From the time she was small, she'd been trained how to work and how to do it efficiently and quickly. She learned not to be slothful or wasteful. She also knew that anywhere at any time others watched. From as long as she could remember, her mother rose at 4 a.m. every morning to get started on laundry. What a shame it would be to have neighbors passing by on their way to town to shop or to work and not have the laundry hung.

"Yes, ma'am. I mean Annie," she said, wondering if God was sort of like that—wanting her to enjoy life instead of just trying to do everything right. It was a nice thought, but one she'd have to adjust her thinking to believe.

With a forced grin, Marianna pulled the cookie sheet off the rack and moved to the trash can.

It was just then that Edgar entered. He sniffed the air and then scowled as he looked at the burnt cookies on the tray.

"If that's the new recipe, I'd go back to the old one," he huffed. "I like my chicken barbecued, but definitely not my sweets."

CHAPTER TWENTY-FIVE

arianna watched her mother move around the kitchen with both eagerness and efficiency. Her stomach stuck straight out, full and round. Mem smiled as she cooked dinner—Haystacks, which was one of Dat's favorites. Marianna was working on another of Dat's favorites, Betty's Salad. She didn't know which Betty came up with the recipe, or how long ago, but it was one of the first things she'd learned to make. The broccoli and cauliflower were already chopped up and next she worked on the bacon.

"The kids enjoyed the day out. Tomorrow we're thinking about going down to Lake Koocanusa, just to skip rocks." Her mother hummed while she worked, which made Marianna feel better about her plans of leaving. Mem enjoyed it here. The kids did too. They were settling into their days without her since she worked.

"Mem, it seems like you're settling in. Are you happy here?" Marianna asked, chopping the bacon into small bits.

"I didn't think I would like it, but I have to admit I feel freer. There aren't so many eyes on me. And . . ." Mem's voice quieted. "The future doesn't seem so bound to the past here."

Marianna nodded, wondering what Mem was going to say when she told her that past—that whole life—was what was driving her back. Back to Indiana.

Just this morning she'd used the phone in the shed to make two calls. One to the train station to check on the price of a ticket in one month's time, and the other to Annie at the store. Annie was out for the day, but Marianna knew she could talk to her tomorrow.

Yesterday at church she'd also talked to Hope and Eve Peachy, who agreed that between them they could cover every day of the week until Christmas to help Mem. They'd also stated a good price for their work. Now, if she could just get Annie to agree on buying her quilt, to pay for the help, everything would be worked out. Then, three weeks after the baby was born, and Mem was back on her feet, she'd be free to return to Indiana.

Trapper scratched at the door, wanting to go out for a walk, and Marianna sighed. "After dinner, I promise."

"Mari, why don't you go ahead now. The kids are occupied, and I'm almost finished over here. Jest leave that and I'll finish it up. Dinner will be ready in an hour. You should get out and enjoy yourself. You've been working awfully hard lately."

Marianna looked to her, unsure if she'd just heard her mother correctly. Still, she wasn't about to argue. She set out behind the house with Trapper by her side. He enjoyed long walks up and down the road, and sometimes in the forest, but he wouldn't go unless she was with him. It was if he were afraid to turn around and find her gone.

An uneasiness settled over her chest . . . How would Trapper take it when she returned back to Indiana? She glanced at him, noticing the way he pranced beside her, blissfully unaware of the change to come. Her lip quivered, and she pushed those thoughts out of her mind. She didn't need to think about that now. This day held enough worries of its own.

The air was cool in the forest. The wind whispered through the pines, and Marianna moved on, farther into the woods than she usually went.

The dog trotted beside her, prancing as if they were on a grand adventure. Up ahead she spotted a small tree that had been gnawed off six inches above the ground. And then ten feet beyond that, another tree.

For the briefest moment she considered turning around and getting the young ones to join her, but the quiet of the afternoon did something to her soul. It soothed her. And even though she was alone, she felt a strange feeling someone was with her. Not in a scary way, but perhaps that God was looking down from above, happy that she was enjoying His creation. She smiled, thinking Ben would like that thought.

The ground was damp. Layers of dead pine needles and aspen leaves covered the earth, making a soft carpet. The air smelled damp, too, and alive. Birds sang, happily enjoying the sun's rays that arched over the mountains, falling upon the trees, and drenching them like golden rain.

"Look, more chewed-off trees. There has to be a beaver dam near."

Trapper wagged his tail in agreement. In her mind's eye she pictured the busy beaver gnawing on the tree, watching it fall, and then clamping down his teeth and carrying it through the woods over and around varied obstacles. The enormity of that task both overwhelmed her and also caused her to marvel at how nature had been created to care for and nurture its own in such unique ways. The ground rose in front of her, cresting to a small hill. Marianna hurried up it, and Trapper barked in excitement as if also anticipating what was on the other side.

Marianna neared the top but then paused. Her heart was pounding and she didn't understand why. It wasn't because of the exercise. This place was less than a quarter mile behind her house. There was a hint of excitement, but there was something more. A deep knowing. A feeling that she'd been here before. A returning to a special place, but that made no sense. She'd never traveled back this far in these woods. She'd never seen . . .

Then, like a fuzzy memory filtering into her mind, Marianna remembered the recurring dream. The special place had come to her many times. The dream of still water. The man's voice calling her. Drawing her.

Marianna placed a hand over her heart. She could feel its wild beating and wondered if she was going crazy. Maybe there would be just a forest on the other side of the hill. More trees?

"I suppose there is one way to find out." She patted her leg as a signal to Trapper and continued on.

It was the scent of water that greeted her as she crested the hill. And then the glimmer of light on the forest floor. Laughter bounced from her lips as she spotted a worn trail just to the left of her. The trail was one the beavers used when they dragged the trees to their pond.

And there, on the south end of the pond was their lodge.

"Look, Trapper!" A joy filled her that she couldn't explain. It wasn't just the lodge that made her so happy, but she had a feeling this place had been created in part for her—that she'd been drawn here.

She walked closer and saw the lodge was much larger than

she anticipated. A squirrel raced up a nearby tree, causing her to laugh again and as she did, tears rimmed her eyes.

Her hands pressed to her face, and she didn't attempt to hold the tears in. It was a beautiful place. Not the same beauty as a pasture dotted with colorful wildflowers. Not the same designed loveliness as rows of cornstalks waving in the wind. Instead, it was an untamed place that reflected a peace she didn't realize she'd been missing until now.

Her heart grew warm. Her throat tightened up and thickened with emotion. She swallowed it down, while at the same time lifting her head to the sky and wondering how she could have dreamt of a place she'd never been to?

It was foolishness she knew—or was it? She thought about Ben's words.

"I thought I'd come for a summer job, but then when I got here, I knew I couldn't leave. How can I not believe there is a God who is caring, artistic, and a bit on the wild side when I look at mountains like that."

She bit her lip, remembering how she'd hardly heeded Ben's words. Now she felt the same sense of awe with a bit of perplexity.

Why her? Out of all the people in the world to get to experience a place like this, why them? Why her family? Ike had been instrumental at telling them about Montana, but they were the ones who set out. Just as she grew up feeling special that she'd been blessed to be born into an Amish home—to be told and warned of the outside world—she also felt that she'd been given this gift.

Marianna neared a fallen log and sat upon it, feeling the dampness seeping through her skirt. Movement from the water caught her attention, and she looked to see that two ducks had landed on the surface, and gliding across the water, appreciating the fact they had the whole pond to themselves. Even though she couldn't see their legs, she knew their feet paddled with intensity. And even though she couldn't see the beavers inside the lodge, she knew they were there. Safe, warm, protected. A smile touched her lips.

Trapper rose from where he sat beside her and trotted down to the water, lapping it up and then looking back at her with curiosity as if wondering why she hadn't joined him.

"You go ahead. I'll just sit here a while." He too was another gift that had been forced upon her. One she couldn't imagine not having.

The ducks continued to swim in circles. Ripples flowed out from their bodies. Marianna yawned and told herself the next time she returned she'd have to bring a blanket to spread on the forest floor. It wasn't that she was tired. Instead, the feeling was one of fullness. The same type of feeling as if she finished a delicious meal or had just read the last page of a satisfying book.

After what seemed like an hour passed, she rose and decided to return before Mem sent out a search party of her younger siblings for her. She didn't want to worry them, but more than that. She didn't want to share her special place, at least not for a while.

She carried the peace home with her.

Marianna arrived just in time for dinner and through the meal she couldn't help but laugh and joke with her siblings. She couldn't help but smile.

All through dinner Marianna noticed something was different with Mem. Her mother had a strange look on her face. A look of surprise maybe. Or uncertainty?

By the time dinner was done, and they were cleaning up the kitchen, her mother's legs were shaking like the aspen leaves outside the window.

"Are you having contractions?" Marianna took her arm and led her to the softest living room chair.

"Yes, through dinner. My labors usually go slow, but this one . . ." Mem face scrunched up and her breaths quickened. "It's coming fast, like when I had you, Mari."

Dat lowered the newspaper he'd been reading. The kids, who'd been putting together a puzzle in the center of the living room turned and eyed Mem. David and Charlie were old enough to remember Ellie's birth, but the younger two looked both worried and surprised.

"Outside kids," Dat called. "Everyone go play in the barn for a while. David keep an eye on Ellie and Josiah."

"Time to get the midwife?" Marianna's voice was no more than a whisper, but both Charlie and David paused and looked back.

Mem nodded. "Yes, but I don't think we'll have time to drive to Libby. It—" She placed her arms around her stomach. "The pains are coming so fast."

Marianna didn't need to hear more. As Dat led Mem upstairs to their bedroom, she hurried to the shed to call Jean, the midwife, explaining the situation. And by the time she returned to the house, it was her father's cries that startled her.

"Mari, boil some water and sanitize our scissors. Then bring up extra towels. I think the baby will be out soon!"

She was just heading upstairs when the midwife arrived. Marianna could barely hear her mother's soft moans, and the woman hurried past Marianna.

By the time Marianna entered the room, Mem was lying on the bed and the baby's head was crowning.

"It's okay, Ruth"—the midwife put on gloves—"it looks like we're going to have a baby in a few minutes. Just go ahead and push on the next contraction."

Dat was on her mother's left side, and Marianna rushed to her right. She grabbed Mem's hand, and Mem squeezed tight. Then she pressed her chin to her chest and pushed.

Marianna was expecting a long process, as it had been with both Josiah and Ellie, but another push later and the baby slid onto the bed. Dark hair covered her head. The midwife checked the baby's mouth, and then placed the little one on Mem's chest. Marianna stepped forward with a towel.

"Okay, Marianna, rub the baby down with the towel. All over really well."

Tears streamed down Mem's face.

"Look at your beautiful baby, Ruth." The midwife clamped the cord and then snipped it.

"Is it a boy, a girl?" Dat's voice squeaked, and a smiled filled his face.

"A girl." The midwife gave him a wide smile. "I just caught your daughter. Marianna, do you want to take the baby and wash her up while I tend to your mom?"

"*Ja*, of course."

A few minutes later Marianna cradled the small baby in one arm as she heated another pan of water on the cook stove. The baby's eyes squinted, trying to open, attempting to adjust to the light. With a soft flutter of her eyelashes, her eyes opened, and she looked around. Her brow was furrowed as if she was just trying to figure out what had happened.

"Look at you, beautiful girl." Marianna locked eyes with the small baby whimpering in her arms. "Oh, don't fuss like that. You've just been born into the most amazing family."

Marianna washed the baby, careful to watch her cord. Then she diapered and dressed her. She lifted the baby to her, tucking the soft cotton blanket around her as she did.

"Hello there, wee one. Look at you. Are you wondering where you are? Who's holding you?"

Marianna returned. Mem was cleaned up and had a peaceful look on her face.

"I think you should name her." Mem curled to her side. Her hair was damp. Moist curls clung to her head.

"Me?"

Mem nodded and her eyelids drooped.

Dat approached and ran his finger down the baby's arms. "I agree. So what's the perfect name for this beautiful girl?"

Marianna thought of the afternoon. She considered the peace she felt beside the still waters. She marveled how easily the baby was born. She thought about how Mem had been lately, how she'd settled into this place with a smile.

"Joy." Marianna looked to her father. She glanced out the window at the cluster of pines and through the open window could hear the laughter of her siblings carrying up from the barn. "I believe her name should be Joy."

Dear Marianna,

*My mother told me about the birth of your sister. How
exciting! Your family must be happy for another girl—to
make up for the ones they lost.*

*My wedding was beautiful. It seemed nearly everyone
from the county turned out. I did miss your mother's fruit
tapioca at my wedding lunch. Many others commented
that they missed it too. Everyone is thankful your family
will be returning in the spring. We are even more glad
that we don't have to wait as long to see you.*

*Frank is a wonderful husband, and I'm finally
settling into the life I'd always dreamed of. I know it has
been your dream too. We hope to start a family this year.*

*My mother said that she has heard all types of news
about Montana. She says that the Amish there ride
bicycles. She also said you're working in an Englisch store.
I hope it's not too difficult for you. I am sure you will be
happy when you return and don't have to do that again.*

*I wasn't sure if I should mention it, but I did see
Aaron Zook at the wedding. From what I hear his cabin
is nearly complete. That's all he talked about. The part
I didn't want to mention is all the time he spent with
Naomi. At first I thought that they were just comforting
each other about their losses—with you in Montana and
with Levi in the world. But the way they looked at each
other. And they way they laughed and talked. Many
people raised concern. Some of the other Junes said they*

*would never tell you, but I thought you should know.
I would want to know.*

*Please let me know when you return. I'd love to get
together and learn about the Wild West.*

*Sending all my love,
Clara*

Aaron grinned as he stepped through the door of his cabin
and saw Naomi sitting there. A blanket was spread on the floor
and she leaned against the wall. Her face was lowered and he
grinned wider, knowing she was playing shy. She did that sometimes, when he took her hand too fast or kissed her too hard,
she'd pull away and act as if she were uncertain of where their
actions were leading.

He hurried over to her and sat down on the blanket, facing
her.

"What are you thinking about, Naomi? Or were you going to
nap? Is that why you have the blanket on the floor?" He grinned.

"No." She lifted her hand. "I wasn't thinking of napping." Her
cheeks reddened and she looked away. He followed her gaze to
the box of sandpaper. On top of it his sketchbook was open to the
drawing of Marianna. Aaron sat up on his knees.

"You got into my things?" Anger filled his chest.

Naomi didn't respond. Instead she looked to her hands folded
on her lap. "Do you still love her?"

Aaron swallowed hard and looked to the windows. Then
past them to his father's fields of tall corn. "I thought I did when

I first built this place." His words came out hard. He looked back to Naomi, knowing he should tell the truth, but also knowing it would hurt.

"And now?" Naomi's hands covered her face.

His anger lessened as he saw her pain. She'd done nothing to deserve this . . . she'd already been hurt. He sat there a few minutes, silent. He told himself to make an effort. She'd done so much—had been there during his hardest days.

Aaron reached for her hands, pulled them toward him, and kissed her fingertips. "I'm not sure."

A sob split Naomi's lips and her shoulders shook. "I still love Levi." She gulped down her emotions. "I'm trying not to, but I do."

Aaron's heart ached for her, and he wanted to make things better. He didn't have the same feelings for Naomi as he had for Marianna, but she was here. And that said something all its own.

"Naomi, listen." He leaned forward and kissed her forehead. "I care for you more each day."

"Is that enough?" She turned her head, making it clear she didn't want his kisses to lead to anything else.

Aaron leaned back, not knowing what to say. She was here, but his heart was someplace else. In Montana.

Maybe . . .

A thought formed, then became resolve. He knew what he had to do. He would go there. To Montana. And find her.

Maybe then . . . he would know.

CHAPTER TWENTY-SIX

arianna cried until she was sure there wasn't another tear. She sat on a log down by the beaver pond, but it no longer felt warm or inviting. A cold had settled in the air, and even with her coat on, the breeze chilled her to the bone. She crumpled up Clara's letter and stuck it into her pocket, knowing now why Aaron hadn't written. Perhaps his interest was turning to another—someone close, not thousands of miles away.

Annie had given Marianna the week off to help with the baby, and she'd done the best that she could. She still hadn't told her parents about her plan to leave early. There were a few nights, especially the night the baby was born, when she questioned if she should return. But this letter confirmed it. She needed to go back. Needed to show Aaron that she hadn't abandoned him. Needed to focus on the life she'd always dreamed of—like Clara said—and not pay attention to all the confusing thoughts being here had brought up.

She was just about to rise and leave when she heard footsteps. Marianna swallowed hard and frustration filled her. Couldn't she get away from the boys for just a little while? Was it wrong to want time alone?

But as she watched, another figure crested the hill. It was Ben, and he had his Bible in hand. He stopped and his eyes widened in surprise as he saw her.

"So you found my spot?"

"I was just about to say the same." She wiped her face, hoping her tears weren't evident.

The ache that she felt burdened her chest, and she wondered why she hadn't taken Aaron's care for her more seriously. She'd made a mistake. One that could cost her all she wanted most. Anger rose up again, but not because of anyone else. She was angry for herself—angry for the emotions that welled up just seeing Ben there. Why did he have to be so handsome? So wonderful? Why did Aaron have to be so far away?

Ben neared, his footstep crunching the dead leaves on the forest floor. The wind chilled and Marianna blew in her hands warming them.

He paused before her. "Mind if I join you?"

She looked up at him and shrugged. "I suppose not—this is your spot after all."

Ben sat on a fallen tree and placed his Bible on his lap. "I'm glad I have a chance to talk to you, alone. There's something that's been bothering me. Something I need to tell you."

"You don't really like my cookies as much as you said you do?" She offered a sad smile.

"I wish it was that simple. I need to clear something up. Remember when you asked about why I was here?" She picked up a golden leaf from the forest floor and twirled the stem between her fingers.

"Yes," she whispered.

"I didn't tell you the whole truth. I think you should know."

Marianna sat, waiting.

Ben lifted his chin and looked to her. "I worked up here one summer and then went home. I was living my dream, Mari. My band was a hit. I had a girlfriend in every town. I had money to do what I wanted."

She crossed her arms over her chest, not sure if she wanted to hear this. Not sure if she wanted to change the image of Ben she'd built in her mind.

"My band included four other guys. We lived together in an apartment. We went to school during the day and drank every night. On the weekends we'd have parties. I thought I was having the time of my life—" Tears filled Ben's eyes, and she thought he would stop. Instead, he cleared his throat and continued.

"One weekend we were having a ton of fun. We'd stocked up on alcohol for a big football game, but I don't think we ever got around to turning on the TV to watch it. One of the guys, Jason, was upset because he and his girlfriend had just broken up. He usually didn't drink and said he'd have a beer that night to make himself feel better. Every time he'd have a sip, one of us guys would top it up." Ben offered a sad smile. "I'm not sure why he didn't realize he never drank that beer even halfway down, but he didn't."

Trapper whined beside Marianna, as if he were listening to the story. She stroked his fur and then turned her eyes back to Ben.

"We let him finish that one beer and then he kept drinking more. We thought it was funny—he was always the one who'd tell us not to drink too much.

Well . . ." Ben lifted his head and looked to the treetops. "Jason passed out that night and we left him on the couch. I think one of us even snapped some photos to tease him the next day. The thing was, there was no next day for him. He died that night. From alcohol poisoning."

Shock race through her. "Oh Ben, I'm so sorry."

"It wasn't two weeks later I left that lifestyle and headed up here. It took a while, but I found God in this place. I hated myself until I accepted His forgiveness."

They sat there for a while, both staring at the ripples of the wind on the surface of the pond.

"All of us had to go to court and had to confess our part in Jason's death," Ben finally continued. "His family didn't want jail time. Instead they asked us to do something instead. Each week I'm e-mailed a name of a minor caught with alcohol. Each week I have to write a letter to that person and tell my story. His family wanted to make sure Jason would never leave my mind."

Marianna didn't know what to say, but she moved over and sat next to him, close enough for their elbows to touch. "Is it difficult?"

"It used to be, but now I see it as a chance to share God's love. He's changed me. I'm not the same person who left that place. He's given me peace, joy."

Marianna nodded, understanding in a way. And then her body stiffened as his hand reached over and took hers.

"I care for you, Mari. I—"

"No," the word escaped her lips and she stood. "You can't say that."

"But why? Surely you know . . ." He looked up at her. "I know what this means—you being Amish . . ."

"You don't." Marianna turned away. "You can't know." She touched her fingertips to her lips. She cared for him, but she knew that could lead to nothing good. To care meant she'd have to leave the Amish community . . . and her parents. They'd lost her sisters. They'd lost Levi. She couldn't walk away too.

And it was then Marianna knew what she had to do.

"I care for you, Ben, but I'm going back to Indiana. There's someone there who loves me very much. An Amish man."

Ben stood, approaching her. "And do you love him?"

Marianna didn't answer. Instead, she said, "I'm thankful, though, that I came here. I feel I've found God here in new ways. And I have you to thank."

"Mari . . . can't we talk?"

She shook her head, and then she took two steps forward.

"Can you at least look at me?"

She shook her head and continued on. To turn, she knew would be to see his face. And that . . . would be her undoing.

Ben could not be her choice. She had to go back to Aaron. She had to make sure Naomi didn't steal away her dream.

The next day at work Marianna approached Annie.

"Are you still interested in buying my quilt? I've decided to sell it after all."

"Really?" Annie put down the cup of coffee she'd been sipping on. "What's happened? Why have you changed your mind?"

"I've decided to return to Indiana. In two weeks."

"That's mighty soon."

"Yes, in a way it is, but I've been thinking about it for a while."

Annie nodded. "I see. Then in that case you better book the tickets. The price goes up less than two weeks out. Also, this time of year, the tickets sell out."

"Really? But that means I'll need a ride to Whitefish to buy the ticket."

"Oh no, I can book them on the Internet with my computer." Annie hurried to the back office of the store. Marianna followed. "If you tell me what you want I'll put it on my credit card. Then we'll just take it out of the money I'll owe you for your quilt."

Marianna bit her lip. "*Ja.* I would like to do that."

The process seemed too easy. Marianna told Annie the day she wanted to leave, and Annie pulled it up.

"You're in luck. There's only one ticket left, but it's nonrefundable." Annie pushed her blonde hair over her shoulder. "Are you sure you want to do this?"

Marianna nodded. "Yes." She closed her eyes and pictured Aaron's face. She thought about the home he was preparing for her. She thought about her cedar trunk and all the days she'd spent thinking about her life. That life. She opened her eyes again. "Yes, I am sure."

Ordering the ticket was the easy part. Marianna had a harder time letting her parents know.

She waited until the children were in bed. She pulled out her quilt with plans to embroider Annie's name in it, but the quilt remained in her hands untouched.

Mem rocked in the rocking chair, breastfeeding Joy. "You've been quiet all night, Marianna. Do you have something you wanted to talk about?"

"I've decided to head back to Indiana sooner than expected. I . . ." She lowered her head. "I asked Annie to book the ticket."

Dat sighed. "Figured it was coming. You've been different. The last few days especially. You remind me of the look a horse gets when she's on her way home. She could still be fifteen miles away, but when she knows she's heading homeward it might as well be one mile."

"I understand." Mem's lower lip quivered as she placed Joy against her shoulder to burp. "You are a grown woman. You have a good future back there to look forward to." Mem wiped away a tear. "Thank you for coming, for helping. I couldn't have settled in without you."

Marianna thought about reminding her parents that they'd only be apart seven or eight months. After all, her parents' plan all along had been to come for a year. But Marianna couldn't get herself to ask if that was still the case. She was afraid of the answer.

She'd seen changes lately. Her mother was more settled, content. This was becoming home. Marianna was afraid that hearing them say they would not be back in May would cause her to rethink her own plans.

And she needed to go back. Needed to let Aaron know that she was ready to start their life together.

If only . . .

If only she could ease the ache brought on by her thoughts of leaving. If only she could forget about Ben. The way he looked at her. His relationship with God.

But she couldn't. Any more than she could understand why not.

Marianna set the large laundry basket by the back door and yawned. If it hadn't been for the fact that Joy would need laundered diapers soon, she'd still be in bed. Knowing that after she left Mem would need help with the laundry, Marianna had also woken the boys. Both of them sat at the kitchen table looking at her.

"Why aren't you at work again?" Charlie rubbed his eyes.

"Did you like it better when I worked?" Marianna sorted the clothes into piles.

"We didn't get up this early." Charlie swung his feet.

"Well, I told Annie that I needed to work at home and not at the store anymore. I need to get you two in shape. Mem's going to need all the help she can get after I leave. I was thinking that David can do the laundry, and Charlie start the fire to heat the water for the washer."

"But laundry is women's work," David complained.

Marianna looked at him, lifting her eyebrow.

"Never mind."

Charlie moaned. "Do I *have* to?"

"Didn't Dat show you how to do it yesterday?" Marianna gathered up all the baby things and put them into a basket.

Twelve-year-old old David elbowed his younger brother. "*Ja*, you need to start helping around here more. Mari's going to be leavin' soon and Mem needs our help."

Eight-year-old Charlie looked out the window, and his eyebrows frowned as he looked into the darkness that was just starting to lighten.

"Can we wait? No one needs hot water this early."

"Mem does for bathing the baby and the laundry." David stood. "Right, Marianna?"

"There ain't no Amish neighbors close by. No one's watching to make sure she gets those clothes out on the line before breakfast like in Indiana." Charlie walked closer to the window and looked around. Then he pressed his fingers to the glass and looked harder, as if trying to find some excuse for not having to go into the dark. Charlie placed his hat on his head and sucked in a breath, as if trying to get up the nerve to go out.

Marianna cocked her head and eyed her brother. No one had told Charlie that's how things had worked back in Indiana. No one needed to. Everyone kept their eye on their neighbor not to compare themselves . . . but just to make sure everyone was livin' as they ought.

As she looked at her brothers, with their ruffled hair and wide eyes, a twinge of sadness made Marianna's breaths heavier. She sucked in air, surprised by the small burden that piled on her chest over the thought of going back. Folks around the Kootenai kept an eye out too, but mostly to see if one needed an extra hand, needed help lightening their load.

David cuffed Charlie, sending his hat spinning from his head and skittering across the wood floor. "You're such a little kid. Are you afraid of the dark? Scared a deer might attack ya?"

"No!" Charlie turned and grabbed up his hat.

"That's enough, David. Jest because he wanted someone to go out with him doesn't mean he's scared. Maybe he just wants company. Did you think of that?"

"I don't want no one to come with me. Not anymore." Charlie opened the door and looked outside. "I can light the wood fire all by myself."

"No, I'll go with you." She slipped on her shoes. "But tomorrow you're going to have to learn how to do it alone."

The air was chilly as they stepped outside. Knowing winter would be coming on soon, Dat had placed the washing machine up on the back porch. The large kettle for heating the water for the machine still sat in the middle of the back yard, and Dat had already put wood under it last night. The large storage container was set up next to it.

"I'll put water in the kettle while you light the wood. Remember, don't use too much of the gasoline. Only a splash is needed to get the fire going."

"Will David have to do all the laundry?" Charlie asked.

"Yes, all of it."

He smirked. "Then I guess starting one little ole' fire isn't that bad."

CHAPTER TWENTY-SEVEN

arianna pulled a wet shirt from the basket and grabbed a clothespin, preparing to shake it out and hang it on the line. A screech filled the air and at first she thought it was the cry of an eagle. It was a second cry that followed that she recognized.

Charlie's cry.

"Mari, help!"

She ran, spotting David grabbing up a bucket and running to the water container. It was then she saw—

Charlie's right leg was engulfed in flames.

"Charlie!" Her screams filled the air as she raced to him. The knot in her belly pulled tighter as she picked up her brother and tossed him into the water container. He sunk to his waist, which put out the fire, but his screams filled the air.

Marianna turned to David, and her mind tried to piece together what was happening. "Go to the phone. Call . . ." She struggled to remember what to do. "Call Ben. On his cell phone. Tell him to get Dat and bring him home. His number is posted. Tell him it's an emergency." Marianna's whole body shook and she saw that Charlie was shaking in the water, from pain. From cold. It took everything within her to get brave enough to pull him from the water.

She lifted him, carrying him like one would a baby, and hurried to the house. Mem came to the door, eyes wide. Her face blanched and she looked as if she would faint.

"The fire—he must have got gasoline on his pants." Marianna moved to the sofa and placed Charlie on it. His right leg looked completely blue, but as she looked closer she realized that the fabric of the blue pants he'd been wearing had melted into his leg. Her stomach wretched. She wondered if there was any real skin left underneath?

Her brother moaned and his eyes flickered closed.

"Is he going to be okay?" It was David's voice.

"David, you're supposed to be calling Ben. Go do it. *Now!*" she shouted at him. She'd never shouted that loud before. Hearing her, the baby woke and cried in her cradle. Mem sat at the table her face in her hands.

As if being pulled from his daze, David darted out the front door and sprinted to the phone in the shed.

Charlie's eyes fluttered closed again but his cries continued.

"It's okay, Charlie. Help is coming. It'll be all right," she said over his cries, but she didn't know how this would ever be all right. The sight of him on fire filled her mind and her shoulders shook. She noticed he was shaking too, and she ran to her bedroom. The first thing she saw was the quilt. Grabbing it, she took it to the living room and wrapped it around her brother.

Then she sat, pulling her brother's head onto her lap, noticing

the stench of burning flesh. The front door opened, and she could
hear Josiah calling her. She'd forgotten than he and Ellie had been
playing with Trapper near the barn.

"Josiah, go get Ellie and come in the house. Get to your
bedroom and stay there until I come for you!" She stroked
Charlie's hair. Josiah listened and retreated, and Marianna felt her
strength recede too.

A moment later he returned with Ellie.

"Is Charlie going to be okay?" Josiah's question came out in a
terrified whisper.

"Yes." She answered with more confidence than she felt. "Go
upstairs now and hurry."

Her brother and sister looked to her and then to their mother
and thankfully obeyed.

Charlie lifted his hands to her as if wanting to sit on her lap,
but Marianna was scared to hold him. His leg looked like a log
that had been smoldering in an outdoors fire pit overnight and
would crumble if she tried to move it.

"Dear God!" She couldn't have stopped the prayer if she tried.
Which she didn't. "Please help my brother!"

She lifted her face toward the sunny window. "God, we need
You here." It wasn't until the words were out of her mouth that she
realized she'd spoken her prayer. But instead of shame at praying
out loud, she felt a strange sensation coming over her. It was as
if God's arms were reaching through the window on the rays of
sunshine. Tears pooled in her eyes, and she attempted to wipe
them with the sleeve of her dress.

Her hand trembled—this time not from horror over the
accident, but a peace she'd never experienced before. A heavy,
thick sensation filled her chest, as if a breath of God's care

were filling her up. And at that same moment Charlie's screams stopped, replaced by soft moans. She looked behind her to where David had gone.

"Please, God, please. Let him get through to Ben." But even as she worried about those things, confidence replaced the panic flooding her. Help would come. Charlie would be okay.

"Dear God . . ." The prayer poured forth as she begged for His presence, His protection. The sun brightened and the feeling of God around her, inside her, heightened too. It was not like anything she'd ever experienced. God—the God she used to know—was someone who watched to make sure one did as he or she should. But . . . was this the God Ben knew? If so, how could she have missed Him for so long? How could she never have been taught He could be so real and active in one's life? So full of peace even in pain?

She pulled Charlie to her lap. His whimpers stopped and his arms wrapped around her. With a heavy sigh, he rested his cheek on her chest.

"God is with you, Charlie. Taking care of you."

He didn't answer but simply nodded.

She didn't know how long they sat there but started when the sound of a truck engine filled her ears. Marianna couldn't see the road from where she sat, but she heard it stop. Heard a truck door open and shut, and then heard Ben's voice.

"Mari!" Ben shouted.

"In here." *Thank You, God! Thank You!* Sobs burst forth, and she stroked her brother's damp hair back from his pained face.

Ben rushed into the room, followed by Dat. The weight of the moment lifted slightly, but the peace remained. She met Dat's shocked gaze. "He was lighting the fire. He must have gotten gasoline on his pants." Marianna tried to explain.

Ben ran forward, sinking on his knees at her side. "Don't worry, Mari. Everything's going to be okay."

"Yes, I know, Ben." She gazed up into his eyes. "In a strange way I know."

She expected her father to follow Ben to the couch, but as she looked up she saw him with Mem. He was holding her, rocking her. Mem's whole body quivered and she had a faraway look in her eyes.

"It's okay, Ruth," her father said. "This isn't the same as the girls. He's injured but he'll be okay. Charlie will be all right."

Marianna watched Ben's truck drive away, and she pulled the quilt to her, hugging it to her chest. It was wet. It smelled of fire. And she knew that even if she had to pay Annie back with all the money she'd saved from working she wouldn't be able to sell the quilt now. It no longer represented her future. It represented her life here—the peaceful moments when she worked on it. And now, God's presence even in the pain.

Ben was driving Dat, Mem, and Charlie to the hospital in Libby. He said he'd call when he heard anything. Before Ben left he gave her a hug and told her she was brave.

She didn't feel brave. She felt both amazed and sad. Sad to see Charlie's pain. Sad to see her mother's pain resurfacing. Amazed how God had carried her when she cried out to Him.

It was then, as she turned back to the house, she realized she hadn't seen David lately. He'd made the call, but she had no idea where he'd gone after that.

Marianna looked in the house first, and then in the fort he'd been building out back. Panic gripped her throat as she hurried to the barn. On her first walk through the barn, she didn't see him, but then as she scanned the loft she heard the jingle of Silver's harness. Marianna hurried to the stall to see David there, sitting in the corner of the horse's stall.

"There you are. I was looking for you." She leaned against the stall door. Her hands still quivered from the emotion of the moment.

David didn't respond, didn't lift his head.

"They're taking Charlie to the doctor. I'm sure he'll be fine."

"I don't think when someone catches on fire they'll be fine." David dug his heel into the straw.

She opened the stall door and hurried to him, kneeling before him. Silver looked to them out of the corner of her eye, curious.

"I'm not going to lie to you and tell you it's not a horrible burn, and I don't know what's going to happen, but I need you to know something." She tried to lift his chin, but he didn't move, didn't look up. "Listen to me." She lowered her head and waited until he lifted his eyes. "I want you to know that what happened isn't yer fault."

"Yes, it is."

"No—"

"It is too!" David shouted in her face. "He asked me to help him light the fire. He was scared. If I would've helped I would have noticed he spilled the gas and—and he wouldn't have caught on fire."

"You didn't light the match, David. You meant no harm. You were just being a kid. Levi used to tease me like that—make me do stuff on my own—and I've done the same to you more than once.

You should have been kinder, yes, and we'll work on that. But these things happen. God is watching over Charlie, but I think He wants you to know something too."

David looked into her face, his gray eyes filled with tears.

"It is not your fault. You cannot take back the past. And going into the future you cannot work hard enough to make up for it."

Even as she said those words, Marianna thought of Mem's face. Her legs trembled, remembering Mem's tears.

"I've tried for many years to make up for our sisters' deaths. The day they died was the day I was born." Her voice cut out. She cleared her throat and tried again. "But I didn't cause them to die, and I shouldn't be sorry I was the one to survive."

She pulled her brother into her arms. "God has a plan, David. He did then. He does now. God has a plan."

She was waiting on the front porch when she saw the headlights coming down the road. Ben had called ahead telling them that though the burn was bad, it would heal over time and they were coming home.

When the truck stopped, Dat climbed out, carrying Charlie. Mem was next with the baby and finally Ben.

Dat walked up the steps and turned to Ben. "Can you fill Marianna in? I need to get Ruth to bed. I'm going to set up a bed in our room for Charlie too."

"Yes, of course."

Ben approached and she stood.

"We should go inside where it's warm," he said.

She looked down at the quilt. "I'm fine if you are."

Ben pointed to his jacket. "Yes, I can handle it." He sat on the top step beside her.

"So they say he's going to be okay?" Marianna looked to him, noticing the way the moonlight touched his face.

"Second-degree burns. It could have been worse. Your fast thinking in putting out the fire really helped."

"So did Charlie say what happened?" Marianna pulled the quilt tighter under her chin.

"He said he put gas on the fire, but he didn't know it spilt on the ground and on his leg. After he lit the fire, the flame jumped out of the fire pit and followed the line on the ground. He tried to stomp it out, and that's when his leg caught."

"Poor little guy." Marianna let out a shuttering sigh.

"The doctor wants to see him in a few days to change the bandages and check his leg. I think we'll be making some trips to Libby. But the truth is, I'm not as worried about Charlie as I am your mom. She just kept crying. Something about the girls?"

Marianna looked to the moon that was full and bright and she wondered if it had been that bright on the night of her sisters' deaths.

"Yes, I had two sisters that I never knew. Their names are Marilyn and Joanna. They were in a buggy and semitruck accident. Dat fell asleep and the horse crossed a big road. A semi hit the buggy and my sisters . . . they were gone in an instant."

A shuddering sigh escaped Ben's mouth. "I'm so sorry."

"My mom was pregnant. The trauma put her into labor. That was the night I was born." Marianna lowered her gaze and dared to look at him. "They lost two daughters and gained one. My whole life I didn't think it was a very fair trade."

"But you can't think about it that way . . ." Ben's voice was filled with sorrow.

"I know. I'm learning that. I was saying the same thing to David today, and I realized I needed to listen to my own words. But it's hard when it's planted so deep in your heart, *ja*?" Marianna reached up and touched her kapp. Just as she'd learned to live as an Amish girl, she'd also grown up with a feeling of trying to do enough to make up for all her parents lost.

"Marianna, I know this will sound strange, especially since you don't believe in praying aloud—"

"Actually, I do." She met the surprise in his gaze with a smile. "When Charlie was hurt, I found myself praying. The words just came out . . . and I felt Him, Ben. God was there."

"Good." He smiled as if she'd just figured out a secret he'd known all along. "Can I pray for you too? Can I pray that God will continue to lift your burdens? Your mom's burdens?"

She nodded. "Yes." And then she stretched out her hand to him, knowing she needed this. And as Ben prayed for healing, for releasing of all the pain of the past, a new sensation came over her. She felt his touch—his hand on hers. But she felt something more too.

A sweet, deep peace, like still waters, in her soul. The same type of peace as before, but this time a united peace. God wasn't just with her. He was with *them*.

Tears filled her eyes once more.

CHAPTER TWENTY-EIGHT

arianna held the printed out confirmation of her train ticket in her hand and stood before the boxes of her things. She heard footsteps behind her and saw that it was Dat, entering the room.

"I don't know. Maybe I shouldn't go now. Mom has the baby and well, Charlie needs so much extra care."

Dat inclined his head. "Some of our neighbors—both Amish and Englisch—have already offered to take shifts. And." He stepped forward and placed an arm around her shoulders. "I hear the Peachy girls are going to come help out. Thank you for doing that for Mem."

"Only for a few weeks. I wish it was longer, but I used some of that money to pay Annie back for the deposit she gave me on the quilt." She stood, looking at her boxes. They held nearly the same things she'd packed when she came, except that the quilt was finished now. Marianna decided not to sell it to Annie. She decided not to keep it either.

She had yet another plan for the quilt.

But unlike her boxes, Marianna carried within her so much more than when she arrived. So much she couldn't explain. More peace than she'd ever had.

More questions too.

"Didja ever think when you left Indiana that you'd hesitate about returning?"

Dat's question brought a sad smile. "It's not that I'm hesitating about going back to Indiana. I'm just questioning if I should be so selfish and think about myself and not what my mother needs."

"I think what your mother needs most is peace of mind that you are following God's call for your life." Her father ran a hand down his face, and she could tell the words were hard for him to say. "As much as we'd love to have you here, you have a life of your own that you need to start. If Aaron Zook is the man you love and want to spend the rest of your life with, as you keep saying, then you need to go there. It's what we've always wanted for our daughter. To find a good man. To start a good home."

Marianna nodded, but her mind was no longer on Aaron Zook. It was Ben's face, his smile, that filled her mind. She thought of the way he'd cared for Charlie after the accident. The way he'd dropped everything to help her family. She smiled, remembering the way he'd returned over the last few days to check on her brother, and the way he held Joy in his arms and prayed over her. She also thought of the feeling of his arms around her that night at the restaurant. His hands over hers on the guitar.

Tingles danced up and down her arms, and she opened her eyes, shocked she'd let her mind go there. Yes, she needed to leave. There was no question now. Aaron was waiting, and that was a good thing. But even more important, she'd be leaving Ben—locking the door on her wayward emotions. To continue to entertain those thoughts meant to turn her back on everything she believed in and lived for. He was Englisch. He was forbidden. And he was here.

Which meant she *had* to board that train.

"That does make me feel better that our neighbors are going to help Mem." Marianna forced a smile. "It gives me a peace of mind to be heading back."

Her father's eyes searched hers, and she hoped he couldn't see what she really felt. The pain of leaving the people she'd grown to care for so much. And the question burning at her.

If it was Aaron that she loved.

"Do you smell that?" Uncle Ike sniffed the air. He'd come to join them for Marianna's good-bye dinner. And while she appreciated it, Marianna wished Ben would have come too. Wished she'd had a chance to tell him good-bye.

Charlie elbowed David. "I told ya that you should shower. The smell must be you."

"Oh, c'mon." David rustled Charlie's hair, then he sniffed the air. "It's not me. Smells like smoke."

"It does." Uncle Ike looked out the kitchen window and scanned the horizon.

"Do you think someone's burning a slash pile?" Dat asked.

"Hope not. It's high fire warning. And if a forest fire started . . ." Ike didn't need to finish for worry to flash across all the faces circled around Marianna.

"We should head out and see." Dat rose from the dinner table and moved to the front porch. The rest of the family followed.

"Look!" Mem pointed to a column of smoke rising into the air.

"That looks like it's comin' from Carashes' place." Dat jogged down the porch steps and hurried up the road. Ike and David followed. Marianna quickened her pace to keep up with them. Mem stayed behind with the little ones and Charlie.

They hurried up the dirt road, crested the top of it, and turned a bend. It was then Marianna spotted the flames, bright orange flickering the Carashes' barn. Mr. Carash was trying to put it out with a garden hose. The rest of his family watched helplessly.

"Someone needs to call the fire department in Eureka!" Dat called out. Without hesitation David ran back toward home. Toward the shed.

"They won't get here. Not in time." Uncle Ike shook his head.

"Mari, why don't you head back and tell Mem it's the barn," Dat said. "We'll see what we can do to help."

Marianna nodded, not wanting to turn back. Tears filled her eyes as she thought of her friends' loss. And then the tears came even faster when she realized they *were* her friends. She knew them, cared for them. She talked to Mrs. Carash every time she came in the store.

Marianna wiped her face and then hurried back toward their house. Fear softened her knees. Her mother and Charlie were waiting on the porch when she returned. David exited the shed and said the fire department was on its way, but it would be forty-five minutes at least.

Charlie looked at her, wide-eyed. "What are they going to do until the fire truck comes?"

Marianna cleared her throat and sniffed, trying to be brave for her brothers but not doing a very good job at it. "I suppose they'll have to watch it burn."

Another loss. Another heartache. Things like this happened in Indiana too. So why, this time, did it hurt so much?

Marianna moved to the porch and Trapper jumped into her lap. Not knowing what else to do, Marianna turned to what was becoming as natural as breathing. She prayed.

CHAPTER TWENTY-NINE

wice during the night Marianna walked up the hill, only to have her heart broken even more to see the barn burn. Even when the fire department arrived, they could only wet down the area around the fire to make sure it didn't spread. The barn was already too far gone.

Mr. Carash had managed to get his livestock out of the barn. The cow was found in a nearby pasture, but the Carashes' three horses had run off. A dozen men from the community had gone into the forest to help find them. Including Dat and David. Including Ben. They'd been gone all night and hadn't returned. She'd walked down to the Carashes' house one last time, just in case they were there. They weren't. Ben's truck sat parked not far from the burned down barn.

Marianna took a deep breath of the Montana air, now filled with smoke. She looked to her watch—a parting present from Edgar. If she didn't leave soon, she'd be late for the train.

As Marianna hurried back toward their house, she saw Annie was already there. Her small, blue car was parked outside.

Inside she found Annie sitting at the table with Mem. They were drinking tea and talking about the rebuilding of the

Carashes' barn. They talked as if they were old friends, and Mem seemed content as she bounced Joy on her knee. There were toys scattered on the floor from the older kids, and dishes in the sink, but Mem didn't seem to mind. She was just enjoying Annie's contagious smile.

Annie turned as Marianna came in. "There you are. I thought maybe you'd changed your mind."

Marianna crossed her arms over her chest and then readjusted her kapp. "No, just checking on everyone before I left."

"Did you see them? Are they coming?"

"No, Mem." Marianna sighed. "I'll go to the neighbors when I get to Indiana and call Dat just to let him know I'm okay." She shrugged. "I hate good-byes."

"It's not a good-bye." Her mother rose and moved to her. "It's a see you later, *ja*?"

Marianna stroked Joy's soft cheek. "Yes, of course. Who knows, maybe I'll even make the trip back for Christmas."

"Your Aunt Ida won't like that. Not one bit." Mem grinned.

Marianna smiled. "I know. But it's okay. She'll just have to accept it."

"Did you get a chance to talk to Ben yesterday?" Annie jingled her keys in her hand.

"Ben?" Marianna felt her forehead fold.

"When he left the store yesterday, he told me he was on his way over here. Maybe he went to help at the fire instead."

"Yes, I think he did." Marianna crossed her arms over her chest. "But when you see him will you say good-bye for me? And"—she hurried to the box sitting next to the couch—"will you give him this?"

Marianna pulled the quilt from the box. She'd stayed up late the last two nights finishing it.

Annie's eyes widened. "Your quilt? Are you sure?"

Mem cleared her throat. "Mari, really? I don't think—"

"For his help. He's been so kind. The way he helped with Charlie—and in other ways." She thought of their talks about God, about the Bible. And his prayers . . . But she said none of those things. Instead, she met her mother's still-suspicious gaze. "My motives are pure."

Mem looked at her, staring deep into her eyes as if trying to determine the truth. Moisture filled her eyes as if she was realizing the reality of Marianna's leaving. Or maybe . . .

Maybe she saw within Marianna's gaze that her daughter's motives weren't as pure as either hoped.

"You've always had a kind heart." Mem rose and turned to the window, gazing out at the mountains in the distance. The message was clear. She didn't agree with Marianna, but she didn't object either.

Marianna turned back to her boss. Make that former boss. "I hope you don't mind, Annie. I'll make you another quilt."

Annie laughed. "I don't mind, but I'll hold you to that."

Marianna looked to the freshly laundered quilt one last time. She looked to the stitching, remembering Ben's words: *"If our Creator so carefully designed this mountain valley and filled it with such beauty, how could you not trust in His extravagant love?"*

She'd thought about those words so many times as she finished the quilt. She'd put so much care and attention into the colors, the patterns, the stitching—and it was only fabric. How much more thought and care did God put into her?

She wasn't a replacement for her sisters and she never would be. God had a good design just for her.

She just wished she was more confident that her design included going back to Indiana. She'd found God in a new way here. Ben had given her glimpses of the type of friend God could be. The quilt seemed so inadequate as a thank you—but it was all she had.

She returned the quilt to the box and then hurried to her mom, pulling her into an embrace with Joy pressed between them. "I'm going to miss you . . ."

"You don't have to go."

"I know." Marianna swallowed. "I don't have to, but I need to. I need to go back and . . ." She couldn't finish the sentence. And see if she still fit? If Aaron still cared? To see if the presence of God that she felt by the still water of the pond could be found there, too?

She bent down and kissed the top of Joy's soft head. "Don't grow up too fast." Then she turned and noticed Charlie, Josiah, and Ellie standing in the hall. They'd woken up to tell her good-bye after all.

She lifted her skirt so it wouldn't tear, and then knelt on one knee, opening her arms to them. Ellie and Josiah rushed forward, and Charlie limped over to join them. "Be good for Mem and Dat, *ja*?"

Even as she released them, her heart ached. Was she was making the right choice? She stood and turned away. Right or not, the decision was made.

"I'm ready."

They walked to Annie's car, and Annie put her boxes in the back. Marianna climbed in. Trapper whined at the door and she stroked his fur one last time. Tears filled her eyes. "I'm so sorry I have to leave you." Then she pushed him away and shut the car door, staring down the dirt road, straight ahead. She didn't look back to see if Mem and the little ones waved. She didn't let herself dwell on the fact she hadn't said a last good-bye to her father, Uncle Ike, or David. That she hadn't been able to hand the quilt to Ben herself. To see him, one last time . . .

"If we hurry, we can make it on time." Annie started the engine, and the car picked up speed. "Sometimes the train is late. Let's hope it is by a few minutes today."

"Yes. That'll be good."

Marianna's hands gripped the armrest as the small car sailed over the potholes. And she lowered her head. In a strange way she'd even miss those stupid holes in the road. After all, they led her to her family.

To her home.

A few dozen people waited outside the station, lined up and prepared to board the train. Her boxes had already been checked, and Marianna's hands were empty except for her ticket and a small satchel her mom had packed with food for the trip.

"I got you something." Annie held up a paper bag. "It's a new book about two boys who get lost in the woods near West Kootenai and spend the winter there. I've read it three times and thought it would keep your mind occupied during the ride."

"Thank you." For the briefest second she remembered her dreams and her own refuge in the woods. She forgot to say good-bye to that place too.

"Say good-bye to Edgar for me. And all the customers too." Marianna watched as the attendants opened the doors and motioned her to board.

"Call me when you get there. Or write." Annie brushed her long blonde ponytail over her shoulder and gave Marianna a hug. "Just find a way to let me know you're okay. And come back soon with new recipes. My customers will love it!"

Marianna nodded, sure that if she tried to respond she'd start crying.

"Now get on, will you." Annie patted her back and gave her a push forward. "I need to get back to the store to check on Edgar. Got to make sure he didn't put the ice cream in the oven and the cookie dough in the freezer." She chuckled, and Marianna forced a smile.

"Okay, I'll see you soon." Then, before she could change her mind, she hurried to the train, up the steps, and into the closest open seat. Her legs quivered, and her stomach felt sick. She'd left Indiana awash in anger and a feeling of injustice. But as a whistle blew, and the train prepared to pull away from the station and she turned to focus on the seatback in front of her, sadness and a deep missing of her family and her friends gripped her heart.

"Dear God, am I doing the right thing?"

In her mind it made sense. She smoothed her apron, and then touched her kapp. She'd grown up knowing what was right. Her whole life she'd had one goal . . . but now? *Lord, I need wisdom. I need to know I'm making the right choice.* Marianna closed her eyes, not wanting to see the station disappear behind her. Not wanting to see the mountains. *God, if I'm making the wrong decision, please show me.* She felt someone sit beside her. She thought of the man on the first train ride and her stomach clenched. Fear tightened her neck and she opened her mouth, preparing to cry for help. Then opened her eyes.

Dat?

Her father sat there next to her, smiling.

"What are you doing? The train. It's going." She looked out the window and saw the station already behind them.

"I bought a ticket. Just made it." He rubbed his beard.

Confusion filled her mind. "You're coming back to Indiana with me?"

"No, I'm not. The ticket's to West Glacier. It's about a thirty-minute ride. I thought it would give us a chance to talk. I'm sorry I wasn't there when you left."

Her chest filled with joy. Dat was here. He'd come. She wrapped her hands around his arm. Her father sat up straighter, and though she knew physical touch wasn't common among the Amish, she didn't want to let go. She held her breath, wondering what her father would say if she told him that his being there was the answer to the prayer she'd just prayed!

"I understand why you weren't there, Dat. With the fire and everything. Did you find the horses?" Why was she talking about that when she had a dozen other questions to ask? Why had he come? Was it just to stay good-bye?

"We found one of the horses. Two are still lost, but there is a group still looking."

"I'm sorry they lost their barn." Marianna knew she was rambling, but it was hard to believe her father was sitting next to her.

"Me too, but I think they will be all right."

"Too bad there wasn't more Amish. They could do a barn raising."

"Oh, the people in the community are already talking about that. You know something, Mari, I don't think you have to be Amish to help your neighbor. The folks around the West Kootenai do a good job of that, Amish or not."

"Yes, they do."

They sat in silence for a moment, and then Dat turned to her. "Are you sure you want to do this?"

Words crowded into her throat, then caught.

Dat's tone softened. "Maybe you should come back home for a while. Give yourself time to think. When I saw you'd left your quilt there . . . well, I knew I had to come talk to you. You were leaving an important part of you, and I had to make sure you still felt this was right. We still have a place for you. You don't have to leave."

"I can't go back. I'm . . ." She swallowed. Should she tell him? Should she be honest? She looked into his eyes and knew the answer. "I'm afraid."

"What are you afraid of?"

She didn't answer his question right away, and not because she worried what he'd think. Instead she didn't want to verbalize all the things that had been going on in her mind. As long as she didn't actually say them, it was as though they couldn't be real.

Finally she blew out a breath.

"I'm afraid I'll get too familiar with the Englisch. I'll forget how things are supposed to be. I'll forget what it's like to live in a real Amish community, where the boundaries for what is right and wrong are clear. I'm afraid that I'll stray from the right path and not know it."

"Are you afraid that you'll lose Aaron?" Her father's voice was gentle.

Marianna lowered her head. "Yes, I'm afraid of that, too."

She was also afraid about her feelings for Ben, but she still couldn't tell him that. Those were feelings she didn't even want to admit to herself.

"Is that what you want, Marianna? Do you want to return to that place? To that life?"

"Oh, Dat"—tears prickled her eyes—"I don't know! I like it here. I think Montana is beautiful. But well, I always thought my life would go one way, and I don't know anything other than that. I don't know what to dream in its place."

"Well, I don't have an answer for you, except to say if you're leaving because of fear, that's the wrong choice. Why don't you come back until you know."

She stared at her father, letting his words soak in. "You mean . . . it's possible to have peace over a decision like this?"

Dat nodded. "It's a peace that comes even when you can't know the future. It's the peace that comes knowing that God is already there."

Marianna looked down at their joined hands, then back up into Dat's face. She'd never heard him talk this way before. Not to the men at church, not even to Mem. Certainly he'd never talked to her before of such things. Could it be . . .

Had her dat also found God in a new way here in this new place?

"Dat, it's not just Montana—the place. There's so much more."

"Tell me, Mari." He stroked his beard, his gaze intent on hers. That was all she needed. Something broke free inside and her words poured forth. She told him about praying aloud, and about God's answers. Told him how God had calmed Charlie and her own heart when she asked.

And though he didn't say much, she could tell. He understood.

As she talked, a certainty grew within her. All her questions, all her doubts . . . she'd been doing what Dat said, pushing them aside out of fear. But she needed to listen to them.

Needed even more to listen to the One who could answer them.

If she went back to Indiana now, that wouldn't happen. She'd go back to the old ways, back to praying in silence, to not talking about God as though He were a friend.

And she couldn't do that.

A jerk of motion started her from her thoughts. The train was stopping.

Dat straightened beside her. "This is where I'm getting off. You coming with me?"

Marianna didn't hesitate. She rose. "Yes."

He smiled at her resolute response. "But I have one question." She looked out at the platform, then back up at Dat. "How are we going to get home?"

Dat motioned her to follow, and when they got off the train she saw it. A small blue truck with a yellow camper. Trapper sat in the front seat, his head sticking out of the window.

And then she saw Ben's hand, waving her home.

Marianna listened as her dat talked to the baggage handler about unloading her things, and then she walked to the truck.

Halfway there Trapper leapt from the window of the driver's side door and darted to her.

"Trapper!" The dog reached her and jumped, his paws

muddying her skirt. His tail wagged at double speed and short yips both scolded and welcomed her.

"Don't worry, boy. I'm back."

She hunched down and grabbed him up in her arms. Hearing footsteps on the gravel, she brushed off her skirt and rose.

"He missed you." Ben's voice was gentle.

She dared to look into his face. "I can see that."

"He was sad . . . thinking he wouldn't see you again."

She tilted her head, eyeing him.

"Yes, well." She crossed her arms over her chest. "He doesn't need to worry about that now, does he? I'm here. I'm not going anywhere. At least not for a while."

"So . . ." Ben put his hands in his pockets. "You left the quilt for me. I—" He took a step closer. "I don't know what to say. It's beautiful, Marianna. You're—" he paused. "Uh, thank you."

"I should be thanking you. I wanted you to have it. You've done so much." She looked back and saw her father approaching. She turned back to Ben. "Out of all the things I found in Montana, the most important was God. I mean, I knew of Him before, but I now feel I'm on my way to knowing Him in ways I hadn't earlier. Ways I hadn't even known were possible."

"Ready to go?"

She turned to see that her dat held her two boxes in his arms. His face peeked around them.

"Here, let me help you with those." Ben hurried forward and grabbed the boxes, then carried them to the back of his truck.

"Your mem is going to be beside herself when she sees you walk through that door." Dat smiled.

"She doesn't know?"

Dat stroked his beard. "I didn't want to get her hopes up . . . in case you decided not to come." He placed an arm around her shoulders. "She loves you more than you can imagine, sweetheart."

Sweetheart . . . He'd never called her such before.

Marianna pressed her face into her father's shoulder. She nodded but didn't know how to respond.

"She considers you her miracle, you know. She held you more than the other babies. You were what kept her going after . . . after the loss of your sisters. You were her saving grace."

Marianna pulled back. "But I—" She blinked back tears. "I always thought I was a poor substitute . . . that whenever she looked at me, she remembered what she lost."

Dat pulled her back and turned her to see his face. "You thought that?" He lifted her chin with a curl of his finger so that their eyes met. "Just the opposite. She spent so much time with you as a baby—she favored you in so many ways—that people started talking. They said you received more attention than the boys, that it wasn't right. So she felt she had to make changes. Sometimes I thought she went too far, but one thing a good Amish woman never does is choose to love one child more than another."

Marianna felt a tear trail down her cheek. "I had no idea . . ." Could it be true? That her efforts to be the perfect daughter were not only in vain, but unnecessary. That she was loved—had always been loved—for the gift of who she was to her family. And that alone?

Marianna looked to Ben, and in his eyes she saw peace. He'd made mistakes—one that cost a man his life, and still he turned to God. She'd been the opposite. In trying to be perfect, she'd missed the joy of being loved for just who she was.

No, she never could replace her sisters, but that didn't mean she didn't have something to offer all on her own.

A smile touched her lips at the thought of walking in the front door and seeing her mother in the kitchen.

I'm loved . . . I'm loved. The phrase sang in her mind as she strode to the car. "C'mon, Trapper." She whistled to her dog. "It's time to go home."

Tramp Soup (Potato Soup)

(contributed by Diana Miller)

1 pound sausage
1 onion, finely diced
5 to 6 potatoes, peeled and cubed
2 stalks diced celery
Salt and pepper
1-1.5 quarts milk

Brown sausage with onion and celery. Drain. Add cubed potatoes and just enough water to cook potatoes until soft, not much. Add milk when potatoes are soft or until it is the consistency you would like. Sometimes I add cream to make it richer.

Serves about 6.

Fruit Tapioca

(contributed by Martha Artyomenko)

9 cups water
1 teaspoon salt
1 1/2 cups baby pearl tapioca (I let my tapioca soak in some of the
    water for at least a couple hours; it makes it cook faster.)
4 small boxes Jell-O (see note below)
1 cup sugar
Fruit—as much or as little as you want

Bring water and salt to a boil. Add tapioca. Cook until clear; keep stirring while it boils. Remove from heat and add Jell-O and sugar. Add fruit.

Notes:

This makes a lot. I would use orange Jell-O and add 2 #10 cans of mandarin oranges and some pineapple. (We were given lots of big cans of oranges and this was a favorite to do with them.) You can use strawberry Jell-O and add strawberries or any kind of fruit, really. It is great to stretch just a little fruit. You can add whipped cream or Cool Whip, if you like. My favorite was to use raspberry Jell-O and frozen raspberries. It you use 2 #10 cans of fruit or more, it serves about 30 people, or if you add less fruit, it can serve about 10.

Oatmeal Butter Crisps

(contributed by Martha Artyomenko)

2 cups oil
2 cups brown sugar
1 cup white sugar
2 teaspoons vanilla
2 teaspoons salt
2 teaspoons baking powder
2 teaspoons baking soda
4 eggs
3 1/2 cups flour
6 1/4 cups quick oatmeal (not instant)
1 cup raisins (You can substitute nuts, chocolate chips, coconut, craisins.)

Cream first 7 ingredients.

Add eggs, flour, and oatmeal.

Mix well. Add raisins.

Use cookie scoop to scoop onto trays and bake about 10 minutes at 350 degrees. They should look puffed up and not quite down. Let stand about 2 minutes before removing them from the tray.

This recipe makes a large batch of chewy oatmeal cookies.

Haystacks

(contributed by Martha Artyomenko)

2 pounds ground beef, browned
2 cans kidney beans (12 oz)
Some or all of the following:
>Grated cheese or cheese sauce (Sometimes this is made by thinning out melted Velveeta cheese with milk or using canned cheddar cheese soup thinned with milk.)
>Cooked rice
>Diced tomatoes
>Diced green peppers
>Shredded lettuce
>Tortilla chips
>Crushed saltine crackers
>Riced potatoes
>Garbanzo beans
>Salsa
>Sour cream

Brown ground beef, add beans. (Sometimes this is seasoned with taco seasonings or even made more like a chili.) Set out bowls of the ingredients you have chosen for your haystacks for your guests. Each person goes through the line piling their haystack with whatever toppings they like. Serves approximately 10 people.

Betty's Salad

(contributed by Martha Artyomenko)

1 head broccoli, finely chopped
1 head cauliflower, finely chopped
1 medium onion, finely chopped
2 cups grated cheddar cheese
1 package fried bacon cut in small pieces

Dressing:

3/4 cup sour cream
3/4 cup mayonnaise or salad dressing
1/2 cup sugar
Dash salt

Mix salad ingredients. Mix dressing ingredients. Toss together.

Notes:

Makes a big bowl, very typical for an Amish wedding salad. It's good but rich.

AUTHOR'S NOTE

Every great novel starts with a bit of fact. This story started with more than that.

A few years ago I was asked if I'd ever consider writing an Amish novel. The truth is, I hadn't. But the first seed of an idea was planted, and my mind started to feed and water it. That's how novels usually start.

Later that day I remembered that my daughter had a friend, Saretta, whose parents were raised Amish. They moved from an Amish community in Indiana to Montana, and that is how we met. I also remember my daughter telling me Ora Jay and Irene lost two daughters in a buggy accident.

Hmmm, I thought. *I'd love to hear their story. Maybe someday, if I see them again, I'll ask.*

The next day my daughter Leslie and I went out for some mom and daughter time. We went to a bookstore to browse and get coffee. As we looked over the bargain rack, guess who walked in . . . Saretta. We hadn't seen her for six months at least and there she was.

"Saretta," I told her. "I think I'm supposed to talk to your parents—hear their story."

"Sure, I'm sure they'd love to talk to you!"

Less than a week later Ora Jay and Irene sat in my living room. They told me about being Amish, about losing their daughters, about their move. They also talked about their faith. They shared what it meant to be Amish. They shared how their faith had grown after moving to Montana. They shared many ways God had changed their lives and their hearts. I listened amazed. Their story added more water—the Living Water—and sunshine to the seed of a novel planted in my heart.

After talking to Ora Jay and Irene, I met many other Amish women from the West Kootenai Community. I was honored as they shared their lives with me.

While this story is still a work of fiction, I've tried to be true to the lifestyle and faith of this Amish community. As you may know, each Amish community is different, depending on the place and rules of the church. While I may not have gotten everything right, I've tried hard to ensure my words reflect truth.

May this story—this faith journey—touch your heart as it has mine.

With care,
Tricia Goyer

P.S. By the way, for those of you who notice such things, the dialogue in this novel is intentionally incorrect to accurately represent the Amish manners of speech.

Teaser Chapter for Book 2

*A*aron looked at the borrowed suitcase realizing it was only half full. He'd put in a few changes of clothes. He'd put in an extra hat. He'd borrowed a book on cattle from Mr. Stoll, and under it all he'd tucked his sketchbook.

Turning to his dresser, Aaron picked up the last two things. A paper sack with a lunch Naomi had packed. Tears had filled her eyes as she'd handed it to him. She hadn't wished him a good trip. She hadn't begged him to stay. She'd come to him months ago in her desperation, hoping to find companionship. For a while he'd tried, for the same reason. But he knew better now. Lying was something he'd been raised to hate. And letting her think he felt about her the way he felt about Marianna . . .

That was a lie.

Which was why he was leaving. To find the truth.

He sighed as he set the lunch inside the suitcase. He knew that many in his parents' generation married for a home and family. His own mother said it was foolish for him to travel so far for love. Marriage did not take love, she'd insisted.

His younger sister called up the stairs. "Your driver's here!"

"*Ja, ja,*" Aaron yelled back.

He clenched the stack of letters he held, still unsure if he'd give them to her. There were fifteen letters. Nearly one for every week she'd been gone. He'd shared so much—his dreams, his hopes. He'd left nothing hidden.

Which was why he hadn't mailed them yet.

He had to go to Montana. He had to look into Marianna's face, peer into her eyes—her soul. Only then would he know if he'd be willing to hand over his heart.

Lifting his suitcase, he took one last look around the room he'd slept in since a babe. Then, determination straightening his back, he turned and walked out the door.